Hearts Wide Open

a novel

By
M. BLAIR MILNE

Copyright © 2010 M. Blair Milne
All rights reserved.

ISBN: 1449989349
ISBN-13: 9781449989347
Library of Congress Control Number: 2009914064

For my parents,
With love and gratitude

Acknowledgements

I'm thankful first and foremost to my wonderful friends and family. Your humor keeps me laughing, your wisdom keeps me grounded, and your love keeps me believing that I can do anything.

To my Mom, who was with me when I first heard the song that inspired me to write this novel, and whose prayers and encouragement have kept me going ever since.

And to my Dad; without your wisdom and guidance, I never would have been able to follow this dream.

I'm thankful beyond words for my big sister Meghan, as well as to all those friends who over the years have become like sisters.

I'm incredibly grateful to each and every member of my extended family who took the time to give me both their feedback and their encouragement.

Many thanks to Sherry Gnant and Karen Reiser for their time and effort in editing this novel.

And of course a big thank you to Get Talked About, for helping me create my website.

PROLOGUE

Now

Laura

Laura stood on her back porch with her eyes closed, willing the early October sun to feel on her skin the way it had felt when she was a child.

The crisp autumn air carried an excitement on its breeze that it seemed only children could feel—a cozy anticipation of the months to come that she had felt as a little girl and never since. She supposed it was similar to the way children could see a figure where their parents saw only a shadow; how they could read the expression on the face of a stranger long before they could read a sentence. Laura wondered now whether that was wide-eyed innocence, naïveté, or an innate ability to see things for what they really were, before the world closed in with its rules and restrictions around what was right and what was wrong, what was there and what was not. Maybe it was a combination of all three.

Either way, she decided, she would give anything to have it back. And so she stood, for most of the morning, struggling to once again hear the strains of Mozart that used to float behind every falling leaf, to feel the chilling breeze on her skin and taste not the bitter emptiness that surrounded her, but the warm comfort of hot cider and childhood.

The phone rang from inside the house, and she listened to a voice she didn't recognize as her own politely ask the caller to leave a message, that she or Steven would get back to them at their earliest convenience. "Laur…" Her sister's voice echoed throughout the empty house. "It's me. I know you won't answer. You're probably still not there, but I just needed to hear your voice on the machine. I stopped by yesterday, but no one answered. Of course you didn't. It's not like I expected you to." Laura could hear the sadness in Abby's voice. "But I didn't know what else to do. I know you're hurting. But you have to let us help you through it. This didn't just happen to you, Laur. We all lost a little bit of Faith after the accident. You have to let us help each other."

Do I? Laura whispered, listening to the silence that once again filled her empty house as she wondered about the word "Faith" and all that it implied.

Abby

Abby mindlessly watched her thumb skim the buttons of the phone in her hand. Her nails were immaculate and polished, and she squinted at them, closely inspecting what she thought might be a chip.

Tom looked up from the couch as he heard the dial tone pulsing from the mouthpiece; both of them realizing at the same time that she still hadn't hung up the phone.

"Did you try calling Laura again?" he asked gently, and then shook his head in frustration as she nodded yes.

"I need to, Tom." She was defensive, picking up on his obvious disapproval. "Even though I know she's not going to talk to me…I guess I just want to hear her voice on the machine." Tom's gaze softened, and he crossed the room to wrap his arms around her. And there, in the middle of a sun-filled kitchen, Abby wept in her boyfriend's arms for the third time that week.

"She'll heal," Tom said softly, kissing the top of her head. "We just need to give her time."

Abby shuddered, pulling the sleeve of her sweatshirt over her thumb and wiping at her eyes, sniffing loudly. Tom couldn't help but laugh, and she immediately prickled, anger welling up inside of her.

"What's so funny?" she demanded.

"Nothing." Tom's expression vanished, but she knew what he was thinking. Like her sister, Abby did everything with passion, and crying was no different. She knew she wasn't a pretty sight. Her green eyes red and puffy, skin splotched and tear stained, honey-colored hair stuck to her forehead, she almost laughed herself at the image she must be.

"Maybe we need to get out of here for a while, go do something. Just the two of us," Tom continued gingerly.

Abby nodded absentmindedly and gazed out the window at the clear blue sky of early October, her mind wandering back to Laura. This had always been their favorite kind of day, and she wondered if Laura could at least recognize how beautiful the world around her was today. She remembered lying on their backs under a similar orange and yellow ceiling, the autumn breeze dancing through the trees above them, where they lay counting the falling leaves.

Maybe she needed a change of scenery. Perhaps getting away with Tom *would* be a good idea, but as she turned to tell him so, the phone rang. Abby watched Tom's shoulders tense as Beth's name appeared on the caller ID.

"Yeah?" he answered. Abby could hear the other woman's muffled voice on the other end, and she strained to listen for her request as she heard Tom sigh. "Give me a few minutes. I'll be there." With that, he hung up, hesitating before he rose and grabbed his car keys from the counter, looking at Abby apologetically.

Suddenly angry, Abby threw herself out of her chair and across the room, stopping briefly to grab her coat from the front hall before hurrying outside, leaving Tom standing amidst the cyclone she left behind; the rush of cold air that followed her in dancing with the rush of emotions that followed her out, and the knowledge that the decision he'd just made would once again throw off the balance that he and Abby had been trying so hard to regain.

∽

Laura

Laura shoved her hands deeper into her pockets and shivered against the chill. A bitter cold had settled over Winnetka, and it fit inside the bitter emptiness that she felt with every breath, freezing her heart from the inside out. She shuffled her jean-clad legs back and forth, watching the blinking hand of the crosswalk she waited at, willing it to change faster. The sun was painting mosaics on the sidewalk with light and shadow, but she neither felt its heat nor noticed its beauty. Instead she looked around the quaint downtown, its charming storefronts decorated for the season, and thought of her mother. Like Laura, this had always been her favorite time of year, "the *real* start of the year," she'd said, as children went back to school and everyone found renewed energy in the change of seasons, welcoming the break from the heat and humidity of a Midwestern summer. And, of course, there was the promise of family gatherings as the holidays approached, the house warm and welcoming against the increasingly dismal elements. *She would have loved it today,* Laura thought, aiming her feet at any fallen leaf in her path, finding a quiet satisfaction in the slight crunch she heard as she stepped on them. The beautiful buildings that lined the west side of Green Bay Road were especially picturesque in the late afternoon light of October. Children laughed in the park across the street, and the telltale rumble of the Metra beyond that reminded her that life was continuing with or without her. She ducked into the corner Panera for a coffee, and then continued south on Green Bay. She had no destination in mind, and ten minutes later found herself strolling down Sheridan Road. Known locally as Lake Shore Drive, Sheridan was lined for miles with grand homes, each one unique and bigger than the last. What used to be summer homes of the fabulously wealthy were now single-family residences, the guest homes and garages built on a grander scale than most people hoped to live in during a lifetime.

She and Steven had struck gold when a friend who knew about their situation had offered to let them stay in her small guest cottage here while she pursued her career for a few years in London. She'd insisted they could pay her back when she returned, and so they had moved into a charming little home less than a mile from her parents, and just a short train ride from her older sister. She knew there were several families—her husband's included—that couldn't stomach more than an hour in such close proximity, but the Baxters had always been close. Growing up, divorce had been rare, but in such a small town where everyone knew everyone's business, it wasn't hard to tell who was happy together and who wasn't. John and Anne Baxter had been.

They had met in college. John had been playing a game of football with some friends on the quad when the ball sailed across the street and straight into the path of Anne and two girlfriends. Anne had picked up the football and thrown it back to John in a perfect spiral without a second thought, and he'd always said that *that* was the moment he'd known he would marry her. Marry they did, and spent the years of their lives raising Abby and Laura. Laura couldn't even remember seeing her parents fight. Her mother had stayed at home while her father worked, and memories of her childhood were simply idyllic. It had seemed that her mother was always playing Mozart, and his grand concertos had been the soundtrack for Laura's early life. The house had always been warm and fragrant, and both the smells of fresh baked goods and the sounds of classical music carried into the backyard where she and Abby spent every waking moment, lying on their backs and dreaming.

They'd found pictures and words spelled out in the leaves that danced above them the way that other children looked for animal shapes in the clouds. And in the winter, the naked twigs took on a life all their own against the background of the cold snow clouds that had gathered. But as a child, snow and cold meant something entirely different than they did as an adult. Where Laura now saw a longer, messier commute, she used to see a day off of school. Where she now saw hours of shoveling out her driveway, she had once seen elaborate forts and snow angels. She wondered when she had acquired the pessimism that could turn the mere idea of something beautiful into a sudden pain in the neck.

Looking up, she saw that she was approaching the very site of all those childhood memories. John and Anne's house stood proudly on the corner, its wrap-around porch friendly and welcoming. For the second time that day, Laura thought of her mother, wishing with all of her heart that she could have been there today, that she could have been here to help them all get through this. She would have known exactly what to say, what to do. As it was, her mother had been gone for nearly a year, and the windows of her beloved house were dark. With a closer look, Laura found her father's car gone, and recognizing the danger its absence meant, turned toward home with an urgency she had come to know well these last few months.

༄

John

John Baxter was a smart man.

He had always been smart, for as long as anyone could remember. His mother had bragged about him from infancy, as he was sure all mothers do. She'd told everyone who would listen about how he'd been potty trained well before his second birthday and about how he'd been speaking in full sentences while most of the kids his age had been fumbling around their first words. As a child he had possessed an innate curiosity that was constantly compelling him to discover new things. The small kitchen of his family's farmhouse was always covered with science experiments and other projects. He'd graduated valedictorian from his high school class—his parents' proud, beaming faces aglow from the bleachers where they'd sat and watched the first person in their family finish high school.

Numbers in particular had always come easily to him, and he breezed through math class after math class, majoring in accounting in college, and finally landing a job at one of the most prestigious accounting firms in Chicago.

He'd sailed through his years in the workforce with the same ease with which he did everything else, completing his work well ahead of time and leaving the office by five o'clock each day.

He was book smart, too, with the kind of photographic memory most people long for. To this day he could recite the periodic table from memory, something that he probably hadn't looked at in over forty years. Constantly reading in his spare time, he remembered the smallest of details—dates, names, circumstances.

He was street smart too, "more common sense in his pinky finger than the whole world put together," Anne used to say.

Yes, John Baxter was certainly a smart man.

Which is why, on a crisp October day, he knew beyond the shadow of a doubt that he shouldn't be here. Here on this earth—probably not. But in a much more specific sense, he knew that he shouldn't be *here*. He wasn't welcome here; that much had been clear since the day she'd been admitted. John was sure that even the nursing staff glared at him today as he passed, the depressing blue of hospital lights highlighting the disapproval in their faces.

Still, he continued down the hallway, gripping the handrail for balance. As he neared room 403, he slowed his pace, pausing outside the door to listen. The voice he heard inside belonged to his oldest daughter Abby, and as he listened, he could almost see her sitting at the bedside, one very still hand clasped between her two.

"I just don't know what to tell him," she was saying, and he realized he was listening his daughter disclose personal details to the one person she knew wouldn't repeat them. John began to back away, unwilling to eavesdrop on such a private monologue. But once again, curiosity had cemented his feet to the floor, and he realized he couldn't will himself to go.

"It's silly to be telling you this," Abby continued from inside the room. "Even if you could hear me, even if you could wake up, what could you possibly tell me? What do you know of this kind of problem?" She inquired, fully aware—John assumed—that no answer would come. "Still, I just like to talk to you. It makes me feel like you're still here..." Her voice trailed off, and he could hear the tears in her next words. "But what do I tell him, baby?" she repeated, and John pictured her forehead lowered onto the bed. "He loves me so much. And I know I love him, but I also know I just can't do this. No matter how hard I try to convince myself, it's just too much. There's not room in his life for both of us, at least not for me. Maybe I'm being selfish, but I want more than that."

There was a long pause, and again John considered walking away. But as he turned to go, Abby's voice cut through the silence.

"Is it petty of me to be talking about this, even *thinking* about it, while you're in here? I still feel guilty when I cry about it, knowing there are such worse things that could happen to me. I feel guilty when I laugh…I feel guilty for having any emotions unconnected to you, and what happened. And your mom… sweetie, you have to pull through, for her. I don't know if she…" Abby's voice broke once more, and this time John found it in him to turn and walk away before his daughter saw him there.

"Mr. Baxter?" John turned to see Nurse Harris studying him from the nurse's station across the hall and heard Abby's sharp, surprised gasp from inside the room. "Is there something I can help you with?" John shook his head, silently cursing her for calling his presence to his daughter's attention.

"No, I was just waiting to go in. Wanted to give my daughter some privacy," he rationalized as Abby appeared in the doorway, purse slung over her shoulder and jacket neatly in hand, clothes immaculately pressed and not a single strand of hair out of place.

"Hi," Abby gave him a tight smile, but he could see the coldness in her eyes. He smiled in return and, before he thought better of it, wrapped his daughter in a quick hug. She remained rigid, her hands limply patting his back twice, the way she would greet a mere acquaintance.

He wondered briefly why she didn't ask how much he had heard, but knew that his face betrayed his newly acquired knowledge.

"What was that about? Everything okay with Tom?" He skipped straight over the small talk.

"Everything's great," she said, her lie obvious to both of them, but each lacking the energy to press the issue any further than that. "Look, I've got to go. We'll see you soon, I'm sure." Then, for the slightest second, the coldness in her eyes melted away, and for the first time in a long while, John let himself hope. "You shouldn't be here," she said, touching his arm in the friendliest gesture she'd shown him in months. The friendliest gesture *anyone* had shown him in months.

"I know," he nodded through the tears that were springing to his eyes. "I just had to...I couldn't..." he trailed off, his throat swelling up.

She nodded, a sudden sympathy overtaking her and radiating from her eyes. With one last pat on his arm, she spun on her heel and left him staring after her in the cold hallway.

Tearing his gaze from his departing daughter, he turned to room 403, took a deep breath, and entered.

No matter how many times he set foot in this room, he never got used to it—never got used to the stale light streaming in through the small window, to the endless flowers, cards, and balloons lining the windowsill, the constant beeping of the machine that kept her alive, the buzz of its monitor, and more than anything, the way the vastness of the hospital bed made her body look almost infinitesimal. He sat down in the chair next to her bed and picked up her hand, curling his around it, pressing it to his tear-stained cheek and closing his eyes.

Words betrayed him, his usually vast vocabulary silenced under the crushing weight of his grief, of his guilt.

For a long time, he sat there in silence, until finally he opened his eyes, brushing her pale hair off of her forehead, a single tear falling onto her cheek. He wiped it away, her skin warm underneath his finger, and stroked the back of her tiny hand with his thumb, the coarse skin of his work-worn hands a glaring difference from the smooth skin of a child's.

"I'm so sorry, sweetheart," he choked out, toying with the wristband that encircled her arm, and as he read his granddaughter's name, he wondered now if it was there to identify her, or as one last instruction to everyone who came to sit by her bed.

Faith.

With one last squeeze to her hand, John rose and walked out of the hospital. He didn't make his usual stop, didn't even think twice—he just knew he had to get out of there. He moved quickly, ignoring the nurse who suddenly called his name as he pushed through the double doors into the bright October light, steering out of the parking lot mere seconds before she ran into it, waving her arms in a desperate attempt to get him to turn around.

༄

Steven

Steven McCord stirred the ice in his scotch and watched the phone ringing next to him. He'd decided as soon as he saw the name on the caller ID not to answer, but the green glow of the screen was mesmerizing in his slightly inebriated state. He wondered as he took a sip, when he'd switched from beer to scotch, knowing full well that it had been sometime in the five months since the accident, but struggling to remember making the conscious decision.

The phone finally stopped ringing, and he sighed in relief as the screen darkened and "Baxter, John" disappeared from view. He waited for his father-in-law's voice to come through the answering machine, but for once, nothing happened. Again, Steven wondered about the past months' recent changes, realizing that in the last few weeks John had finally accepted that no amount of voice mails would merit a returned call from his son-in-law, and so he had stopped leaving them altogether. But as was becoming common these days, he couldn't recall a certain day this had occurred. His days and weeks blurred together, aided considerably by the scotch, and he found that his last clear memory was of that fateful morning in May. The memory of it prompted him to pound what was left of the mahogany liquid in his glass and reach halfheartedly for the bottle to refill it.

Replacing the cap and pushing the significantly emptier bottle away, he thought again of John Baxter. To say that the two had gotten along wouldn't be entirely inaccurate, but to say that John disapproved of the choices he and Laura had made would have been the understatement of a lifetime.

Like John before him, Steven had met and instantly loved his wife in college. He remembered the first time he saw her on campus, crossing the bridge that had connected the mall to the union, and though to this day he could not name what it was, something about her had struck him motionless. He'd gone over it all in his mind—the confidence with which she moved, the kindness in her eyes, her slender waist, or the way her hair caught and reflected the sunlight like a prism. Though she could have easily been called beautiful, her petite figure and sweet voice gave her a girlishness that propelled her straight into the category of "cute," and he'd loved her all the more for it. Like an idiot, he'd stood there in the middle of that footbridge and watched her pass, staring in a less than subtle way that was foreign to him, but she'd just smiled as she passed and walked away without so much as turning around. He saw her around campus several times after that, but it wasn't until a year later when they'd finally had a class together that he'd worked up the nerve to talk to her. To his surprise, she later told him that she had noticed him as well and had been too shy to approach him herself, but was thrilled when he'd done it for her.

From that moment on they were inseparable, and within six months they had already talked about spending the rest of their lives together. If he had to, Steven could probably pinpoint that as the time when John Baxter had started to express concern over how quickly his daughter's relationship was progressing. His fatherly concern had turned to adamant disapproval when Laura got pregnant the summer going into her junior year, and had turned to bitter disagreement when they'd decided to raise the baby themselves. Though both were promising students, neither Steven nor Laura was majoring in something that would land them a great job right out of college. Steven was about to begin med school, with years of loans ahead of him, and Laura would be graduating with a degree in child psychology, something that she couldn't do much with until she'd completed a master's degree. As with Steven, her scholastic future promised a heap of debt, and neither of them had much money set-aside for the future. So Steven had grudgingly admitted, John Baxter had a point. What stable home environment could they possibly offer a child when they'd both be balancing work and school for at *least* the next four years? The schedule would be grueling and wouldn't allow for much family time, much less any time for just the two of them—to the objective eye, they it looked like they were setting themselves up for disaster. But they didn't care. They were in love, they were going to end up together anyway, and this was *their* baby. How could they ever hope to lead normal lives if they knew that out there somewhere was *their* child, being raised by someone else? So after very little thought, they both came to the conclusion that the only thing they could do was keep it.

Steven had held Laura's hand the entire way to her parents' house when they'd made the seven-hour drive from their school in Minnesota to tell them, but by the time they were within twenty-five miles of Winnetka, his palms had begun to sweat so badly that he'd had to let go. Laura had laughed and squeezed his leg, but he could see her own fingers trembling. Telling them that Laura was pregnant was going to be hard enough, but Steven knew the real fireworks would begin when they disclosed their plans for the future. Abortion had never been an option—both for Laura and Steven, and *definitely* not for her parents. But he knew that with "such promising futures for both of them," adoption would be the expected solution. And he'd been right.

As soon as the words were out of Laura's mouth, he'd expected to not be able to meet her parents' faces. On the contrary, he found himself unable to tear his eyes away. John sat in stunned silence for all of thirty seconds before rising and walking out of the room. Anne had immediately begun to cry. She cried the same way that Laura did—her face literally crumpled, feature-by-feature. First her lower lip began to quiver, and her physical effort to try to stop it made the rest of her face follow suit, until every inch of her was trembling in an effort not to well up. But her body eventually betrayed her, and the tears flowed unabashedly. She didn't even make an attempt to wipe them away, only stared first at Laura, then at Steven, and back to Laura again.

Steven had been the first to find his voice. "Mrs. Baxter, I—" but she had interrupted him.

"I didn't even know that the two of you were…Laura, I didn't know you had…" She trailed off, unable to say it, as if stating the fact out loud could make this moment any more awkward. That their daughter was not the girl they'd always considered her was not something Anne Baxter wanted to consider, much less justify by speaking out loud.

"Well," she said simply, pausing for a long time before repeating herself. "Well." She finally wiped at the tears on her face, composing herself as best she could. "What are you going to do?" she asked, her expression hopeful with renewed confidence that her daughter had made the right decision.

"We're going to keep it, Mom," Laura had said, in a voice calmer than Steven had ever heard it.

"I'll be damned if you'll keep it," John cut in, and Steven wondered when he had reappeared to stand in the doorway. He was about to say something when Laura surprised him with strength that, until then, he hadn't known she possessed.

"Yes, Daddy, we are." Before her father could interrupt, she continued quickly. "I know it's going to be hard. We've got a lot of struggles in front of us—school, work, loans, and a pretty crazy schedule for the next few years, even before the baby. But these are all things that we're aware of, and they don't change the fact that this is *our* child. We can do it. Somehow, we'll get through it, and we'll be okay."

Again, Laura's father had turned and left the room.

And he hadn't spoken to them for months afterward.

Laura had called and had written him letters explaining that this was not a reflection on him or on his parenting, that it wasn't his fault. It was no one's fault, really; it had simply been an irresponsible decision, and now she was going to take the responsible way out of it.

But John Baxter had wanted none of it. It wasn't until four months later, around Thanksgiving, that he finally began to come around. It may have had something to do with Steven and Laura's recent engagement, but even then his acceptance of it had seemed forced. It wasn't until Faith was born two months later that he played the part of loving grandfather. His pride made it hard for him to admit defeat, but Steven could see the love in the older man's eyes the very first time he'd laid eyes on his granddaughter. And from that moment on, it seemed there was no one who loved her more. John was constantly calling and stopping by just to be with her. As she grew, she became increasingly more like her grandmother, and when Anne died a week short of her granddaughter's third birthday, John gravitated to Faith in his grief.

Those early years had been hard for Steven and Laura, almost impossible. Both had struggled while Laura finished undergrad and Steven studied his way through med school, balancing school and work and hardly seeing each other, much less the baby.

When she graduated, Laura had taken a full-time job, putting grad school on hold until Steven had finished med school so they could always have a steady income coming in. Laura had worked long hours in order to bring in enough money for themselves and their daughter, and he had spent long hours learning his trade. When he had finished med school and began his residency at Northwestern Memorial, Laura had opted to put off grad school a little longer, wanting to stay at home until their daughter was situated in school. There in Winnetka, they'd slowly begun to rebuild from the ruins of what their relationship had become.

They had almost made it, too.

And then May happened. Now here he was, alone at the dining room table they'd picked out together as a wedding present. Drunk again, no amount of scotch capable of burning the sour taste that crept into his mouth whenever he saw his father-in-law's name appear on his caller ID.

And across town, John Baxter steered his Toyota frantically back toward the hospital and dialed Steven's number one last time, praying that he'd answer.

∽

PART I

Then

CHAPTER ONE

Laura

"Thanks for getting these." Laura gave Steven a quick kiss on the cheek before opening the jar of capers he'd brought her and adding it to the sauce she was preparing, smiling absentmindedly.

She and Steven had been dating since the previous summer, and maybe it was the warm spring weather that had finally returned to Minneapolis, or maybe it was Steven, but she knew she had never been happier. At times she even pinched herself to make sure that what she had with Steven wasn't a dream. They were happily in the midst of that phase of a relationship where they couldn't get enough of each other—all of her free time was wrapped up in him and vice versa. Phone calls from friends went unanswered and unreturned, and there were days when they never even stepped outside, but for now none of that mattered. She knew this stage had to end eventually, and she was in no rush to get there.

"Anything for you, mi amore," Steven replied to her thank-you with a smile, wrapping his arms around her waist from behind and kissing her neck.

"That sounds like a line from a cheesy movie," she laughed, shivering beneath his touch and shrugging him off of her. "Now leave me alone before I burn the place down."

Steven complied, but not before giving her a quick kiss on the cheek, winking as he did so.

"Where'd that come from, anyway?" she asked him.

"I don't know," he said, grabbing a handful of the pretzels she'd put out and shoving a few in his mouth before continuing, crunching loudly and spraying crumbs from his mouth as he spoke. "I've never said it before you."

"You realize that it just sets you up for failure, right?" She teased, spooning the sauce evenly onto a salmon filet, the mustard and olive oil sliding down its corrugated edges. "No one ever means stuff like that. Have you ever heard of anyone literally doing *anything* for the person they love?"

"As a matter of fact, I have," Steven argued with a grin. "Romeo and Juliet..." he paused, thinking, "Barbara Streisand, in that one movie."

"You're going to have to be a little more specific than that." Laura grinned over her shoulder, before turning her attention back to the sauce she was preparing. Whenever her tight budget allowed, she loved to cook for Steven, and tonight she was making him his favorite salmon.

"You know, that movie she was in with Robert Redford," Steven was continuing, and Laura scrunched her forehead, thinking.

"Out of Africa?"

"No, that was Meryl Streep," Steven said thoughtfully, the mind blank he was drawing visibly driving him crazy. *"The Way We Were!"* he suddenly shouted, startling Laura and causing her to send dried dill flying right over the corners of the bowl she was carefully measuring it into. "He did anything for her in that movie," he continued, unaware of the minor catastrophe he'd created.

"Okay, hold on a second!" Laura laughed, turning around and waving her wooden mixing spoon in the air for emphasis. "You can't even use those two examples in the same sentence! Romeo and Juliet, yes. I'll give you that. But *The Way We Were?* They broke up, and they learned to live with that. People do that every day! Now laying down your life for someone else, *that's* doing anything for someone. All I'm saying is that it doesn't happen anymore. It's the end of romance," she sighed, a faraway look tiptoeing into her eyes before she turned back to the salmon and put it in the oven.

"Since when is dying for someone romantic?" Steven laughed. "I mean, sure, it shows you love someone, but I can't imagine the person left behind feels much romance once it happens."

"Yes, but they'd know how much they were loved," Laura squinted as she turned the temperature dial from 350 to 400.

"You're impossible," Steven grinned.

"I get that a lot." She winked back at him.

"Hey, how did your Western Civ test go?" Steven asked

"It was fine." Laura made a face. "I'm just glad it's almost over—this is the last of my Gen Ed requirements. Next year I can actually start taking the classes I want to be taking. Do you realize that in a month, I'll be halfway done with college?" she shook her head.

"Well," Steven cut in, "not really. You still have grad school to think about after that, so really you're only a fourth of the way done.

"Fine," Laura threw a pretzel at him. "Do you realize that in a month I'll be halfway done with *undergrad*?"

"You're kidding!" Steven feigned surprise. "I had no idea…"

Laura made a face and stuck her tongue out at him.

"You're such a brat," Steven laughed, crossing the kitchen to grab her hand and twirl her in a circle before pulling her close. "But you're *my* brat, and I love you," he said, kissing the tip of her nose so lightly she wondered if she'd actually felt it. "And I would do anything for you. *Anything*," he repeated quickly, putting a finger to her lips before she had a chance to protest. "If it came down to it, I'd lay down my life for you—in a heartbeat. But at least for tonight, doing anything for you involves pouring you another glass of wine, taking you into the other room, and—"

"Okay, okay!" Laura playfully batted his hand away. "Don't get any ideas. I *just* put the salmon in." She maneuvered her way around him, wiping her hands on her jeans. "It won't be done for another half hour, and I still have to make the rice." She trailed off as Steven leaned down to kiss her neck, closing her eyes as the light scent of his cologne wafted into her nose. She opened them briefly to glance at her watch, but as his lips moved to hers, she found that she no longer cared. All that mattered was her, Steven, and this moment, so she let him lead her out of the kitchen, reaching behind her halfheartedly to turn off the oven as she went.

Later that night, they wandered back into the kitchen to find something to eat. After scraping the half-cooked salmon filets into the trash can, she threw together some peanut butter and jelly sandwiches, handing one to Steven before settling in on the couch next to him.

"Do you realize I wasted over twenty bucks on salmon we didn't even eat?" she questioned him, though in reality she didn't really care. It had been worth it.

"It was worth it," Steven repeated her own thoughts out loud, and she smiled at how well he knew her. "Plus, it will make some raccoon really happy tonight as he's rooting around the trash."

"Ew," she snuggled closer to him. "What do you want to watch?" she asked, flipping quickly through the channels.

"Well I can't see what's on if you're flipping through that fast," Steven laughed, grabbing for the remote. But Laura kept it away from him long enough to land on *The Notebook*.

"Here," she said, settling in. "This is perfect."

"No way," Steven argued, diving across the couch for the remote. "We're not watching *The Notebook*."

"Why not?" Laura made a face as he switched to the Twins game. "Ugh, is it baseball season already?" she groaned. "I know where I'll find you for the next six months!"

Steven laughed. "You can watch *The Notebook* on your laptop while I watch this. It's a compromise."

"No way!" Laura stood up and manually changed the channel.

"Are we really going to fight about this?" Steven asked with a smirk as he changed it back to baseball, and then threw his hands up in feigned innocence.

"Consider yourself lucky that *this* is the only thing we have to fight over!" Laura made her way back to the couch, draping her legs across his lap. "Plus, we need to fight about *something*, so we get to make up." She winked at him.

"Okay, you win." Steven wriggled out from under her legs long enough to change it back to the channel Laura wanted before pulling her close.

She sat there cuddled up to him with her head on his shoulder for most of the movie. His arm fell asleep five minutes into it, but he told her he didn't care—he wanted her close.

She closed her eyes as he carelessly played with her hair, talking right through the movie, their conversation punctuated with laughter and promises.

"What kind of a hole are you living in?" he asked at one point, and she burst out laughing.

"Yeah, it's not much, is it?" She looked around, surveying her small apartment. Its style wasn't old enough to be considered vintage, but *was* old enough to qualify as dingy. Dark brown shag carpeting covered all the floors but the kitchen and bathroom—where it was replaced by linoleum tile. The kitchen counters were a faded yellow, and combined with the dark cabinets, carpeting, and the fact that it was a basement apartment, the place had an overall feel akin to a cave. The total square footage was smaller than most living rooms. Still, Laura had done everything she could with it—decorating with bright pillows and blankets, and she always tried to have fresh flowers out.

"I'm trying to save money," she told him. "Between my tuition and living expenses, I don't have much leftover for rent."

"Your parents don't help you out?" he asked gently. Coming from anyone else, the question might have offended her. But from Steven, she didn't mind it in the least.

"They would if I ever really needed it—and they have the means to. But they told Abby and I from the beginning—once we leave the house we're on our own. They think it's good for us to learn how to budget and manage our own money. Plus, that gives them the chance to help out with the bigger stuff someday, like a down payment on a starter home, or my dream wedding…" she trailed off.

She didn't say it, but she was hoping that *someday* would be with Steven, and when he remained silent, she hoped he was thinking the same thing. She wondered if he'd be willing to go the distance with her, whatever happened down the road.

She must have asked this out loud, because suddenly he was answering her. They both fell asleep there on the couch, and some time in the night she woke, snuggling in closer to him and hanging onto the last words he had said to her before sleep, or had she dreamed it?

Anything for you, mi amore.

∽

Steven

"You're *what?*" Nearly two months later, Steven could hardly hear himself speak over the pounding of his heart, and he suspected his voice had been much louder than he'd intended.

"I'm pregnant," Laura repeated.

"How?" He jumped out of his chair and ran his hands through his hair, pacing in front of it before sitting back down, only to stand right up again.

"What do you mean, how?" Laura cried, suddenly angry. She looked up at him through teary eyes from her perch on the floor.

"Laur," he knelt in front of her and took her hands in his, wondering why he was finding it so difficult to think beyond himself right now. "I'm sorry. That came out wrong. It's just...*man*." Still holding her hands, he sank cross-legged to the ground and shook his head in disbelief. "I mean...*man*." he repeated.

"You sound like a frat boy." She offered him a tight smile, ruffling his hair with her fingers. "Very eloquent."

"Yeah, a frat boy who just knocked up the head cheerleader," he said wryly, and Laura laughed.

"That is like, *so* not funny," she did her best cheerleader impression.

"Man," Steven repeated, head still shaking and missing her attempt at humor completely before catching himself and looking at her sheepishly. "Sorry."

"So," Steven could see Laura choosing her words carefully as she began, and he wondered if she'd already made a decision. He didn't know how these things worked; did the woman make the decision, and the man didn't even get a say? Was it even appropriate to voice his opinion, when it was her body? What *was* his opinion, anyway? Before he'd had a chance to answer any of these questions, Laura did it for him.

"I don't feel right making a decision unless it's one we can make together. I know it's my body and all, but this is just as much yours as it is mine."

"Your" what? Steven thought. *Your baby? Your problem? Your mistake?* He kept these thoughts to himself and simply nodded in agreement. That part he said out loud. "I agree. And thanks, I think."

Laura smiled and squeezed his hand before she continued. "I don't think that abortion is an option for me," she said softly, her eyes trained on the floor in front of her as she tapped her feet anxiously, unwittingly. "For a long time I thought it would be the *only* option…I can't even imagine telling my parents. But when it comes down to it, I don't think I could go through with it. What would give me the power to take a life away from someone?"

Steven nodded. Eliminating that option scared him beyond belief, but he was surprised at the relief that swept through him when she eliminated it and knew that he agreed with her wholeheartedly.

"As for the other two," Laura continued, "I don't know. I just don't know. I know I'm—*we're*—not really in a place right now to raise a baby, right?"

Steven nodded his agreement and was about to vocalize it when Laura continued.

"But then I can't imagine giving it away to someone else. I just don't know..." she repeated, trailing off, her eyes filling with tears again, and Steven reached out to catch one.

"Hey," he soothed, pulling her into his arms as she collapsed into sobs. "Shhh, it's okay. It will be okay. We'll figure this out, and we'll do it together," he stroked her hair as she cried, looking beyond her head out the window as he wondered what they had gotten themselves into. He knew beyond a shadow of a doubt that he loved Laura, but he couldn't help but wonder what this would do to their future—to their relationship. His feelings for her would never change, of course, and in fact he felt the need to profess his commitment to her now, more than ever.

It wasn't his relationship with Laura that concerned him; it was his ability to be a good father. For starters, he hadn't even finished school yet. He'd always imagined that if he ever became a father, it would happen when he had settled into a career and could provide financially for his family.

That was really all he had to offer, anyway, because he wasn't sure he could *be* a good father.

His own father had been indifferent toward him growing up. Steven had never wanted for anything, and had slept in a warm bed in a warm house every night of his life, and was grateful for that. But as he watched his friends' fathers come to cheer them on at each and every sporting event, he couldn't ignore the empty seat where his own dad should be. He'd vowed at an early age that when he had children, he'd be different—he'd support them, be there for them. But as he breezed through high school and college and noticed more similarities between himself and his father, he wondered if he might just end up the same way. He wasn't even sure he had anything to give until he met Laura, and even now he was just beginning to realize how to be a good partner. Being a good parent was a whole new ballgame.

He knew he'd love their child, and he knew he loved Laura.

Still, he knew that in the course of an instant, they had suddenly stacked before themselves some incredible odds.

☙

Laura

It was all Laura could do not to laugh at the man kneeling in front of her. When Steven had gotten in the car mere minutes after she'd told him she was pregnant, he'd insisted that he was running out to get her some ice cream. Almost two hours later, he'd returned with a small velvet box.

Now here he was, box open in front of him, his high-school ring placed carefully inside of it.

"I mean it, Laura," he was saying. "Marry me. I love you. I want to spend the rest of my life with you."

Swallowing her smile, Laura reached out and tipped Steven's chin up so he was looking at her and not at her knees, where his eyes had been focused for the entirety of his proposal.

"Steven, I mean this in the best way possible…but you're kidding, right? First of all, I didn't even know you in high school. *Why* would I want your class ring to signify our engagement? But most importantly, Steven, would you be kneeling right here, right now, if I hadn't just told you I was pregnant?"

A sheepish look crept slowly across Steven's face, and he looked down again, defeated.

"Hey," she said, far more gently this time. "You know I love you, and I know you love me, and you've told me before that you want to spend the rest of your life with me. But *I* don't want to spend the rest of *my* life wondering if you only proposed to me because you got me pregnant."

Steven looked away. "I didn't—"

Laura interrupted him. "Look at me. If I hadn't told you a few hours ago that I was having your baby, would you have proposed just now?"

Steven shook his head slowly, wincing as he looked at her, probably sure she'd smack him.

But Laura just offered him a warm smile. "You'll know when it's right, and when it is, and you ask, I promise to say yes. But please not now, not like this. Okay?"

Steven nodded, a look of relief coming over his face.

"Now get that ugly thing away from me," Laura finished, laughing as she swatted the box from his hand and jumped off the couch into his arms, pinning him to the ground with a kiss.

Relaxing, she stretched out beside him, her head on his chest, and listened to the steady beat of his heart.

"Steven?"

"Mm hmm," came his response, distant as he absentmindedly played with her hair.

"I'm scared," she whispered.

Steven didn't answer, just pulled her closer, but she couldn't help but notice his heart begin to beat faster.

༄

Abby

"Steven did *what?*" Abby leaned across the table, eyes as wide as saucers, unsure as to whether or not she'd heard her sister correctly.

"He proposed," came Laura's answer, grinning behind her menu. Abby knew immediately that something was wrong—that wasn't the grin of a woman who'd just gotten engaged. There was something behind it, a secret hidden in the way the corners of her mouth turned down just so, despite her smile.

"Well? What did you say?" she asked, realizing as soon as the words were out that there was no ring on her sister's finger.

"I said no." Laura's answer was short and simple, and again Abby guessed at a deeper meaning behind it.

"Good!" The relief in her voice surprised her, and she wondered at it briefly before pushing it away. "You're only twenty-one, for crying out loud! Slow down, Steven! What, did he get you pregnant or something?" She laughed at her own statement, the very thought of her little sister pregnant a ludicrous one. But her laughter was met with an even stare from Laura, and she immediately silenced herself, amusement turned to complete and utter shock.

"Laura, you tell me right now," she addressed her sister seriously, "are you pregnant?" The tears that filled Laura's eyes were all the answer Abby needed, and in a second she was by her side, stroking her hair as she cried.

This was certainly not what she'd expected from this weekend. She had flown up to Minnesota, where Laura and Steven were going into their junior year of college, to help celebrate her sister's twenty-first birthday—to take her out for her first legal drinks. That certainly wouldn't be happening now. Laura had picked her up from the airport, and they'd gone straight to Annie's for their famous burgers and milkshakes, but as she looked at the food on the table, she found she didn't have much of an appetite. As she sat here holding her baby sister, who was carrying a baby of her own, she couldn't help but wonder what their parents would say about this.

"Whatever you decide to do, I'm here. For anything."

Laura nodded, her chin digging into Abby's shoulder, already wet from her tears.

Abby pulled away and took Laura's face in her hands, her eyes searching their identical counterpart. The two sisters looked so much alike that they were often mistaken for twins, but today Laura's eyes, which usually matched her older sister's perfectly, brimmed with emotions that Abby couldn't even comprehend.

"I'm fine, Abs. I am." Laura said, wiping at her eyes with her wrist. "It's just," she continued with a sniff, "a baby is supposed to bring somebody happiness. What kind of mother am I that all I can feel right now is anger at my own stupid decision, and worry about what my future will hold? I mean, I just called my own baby a stupid decision!" Laura dropped her head into her hands, shaking it slowly.

"So you're going to keep it?" Abby clarified. At Laura's muffled yes, she felt a shockwave run through her body. *I'm going to be an aunt. At twenty-two. My little sister is having a baby...*

She couldn't name the emotions that were running through her, but she knew she didn't like them. There was something in the way she was feeling that didn't sit right with her, but for Laura's sake, she put her hand on her sister's and said the only thing that she could think to say.

"It comes with the territory, honey. You may be scared now, and mad at yourself, mad at Steven, whatever it is…but when that baby comes, it *will* bring you joy, even if you can't see that through your pain right now."

Laura nodded again, still not lifting her head from her hands.

"How are you going to tell Mom and Dad?" Abby changed the subject ever so slightly, and suddenly Laura was shaking so hard the silverware began to clink together. "Hey," she tightened her grip on Laura's hand, shaking it from side to side on the table. "I didn't mean to make it worse. I just…" She trailed off as Laura looked up and she realized that her sister wasn't, in fact, crying harder.

She was laughing hysterically.

"Oh my God…" she finally gasped, catching her breath, "I'm sorry, but…" She was taken over by another fit of giggles, finally regaining enough composure to say, "Can you just *imagine* Dad's face when I tell him?" At this, Abby erupted into uncontrollable laughs as well. Not because it was particularly funny—in fact, it wasn't funny at all. It was just incredibly uncomfortable, and since they were kids, she and Laura had laughed at the most uncomfortable, inappropriate moments. Funerals, memorials, serious speeches delivered by their father at the dinner table—the sheer discomfort of it all was always enough to bring a bubble of laughter to the surface, popped immediately if they dared to make eye contact.

So they laughed, harder each time they looked at each other, until the whole restaurant had turned to look at them. This made them laugh even harder, and they doubled over the table, tears streaming from their eyes.

"Oh…" Laura was the first to regain her composure, and she wiped at her eyes as she caught her breath. "Thank you…I needed that."

Abby wiped the tears from her eyes as well, grinning at her sister. "Can I be there when you tell him?"

This threw the girls into another fit of laughter, but this time, Abby could see the fear grinning at her from behind her sister's smile.

As she sat on the plane a few days later waiting for it to take off, thoughts of her sister's changing life consumed her mind. She wasn't sure what to feel for Laura; it was hard to feel excitement for a situation that would bring so much struggle and hardship. On the other hand, there was a baby on the way, and it was hard to keep the twinge of anticipation and wonder out of her stomach. Yet even that emotion was laced with another one—that sinister emotion that crept into so many of her sisterly thoughts.

It may have been their proximity in age, or their similar life goals, or a million other factors, but whatever propelled it, there was a constant competition between Abby and Laura that tiptoed into the stillness of their whispered late-night conversations. It was their constant companion through years of milestones—that weight on her shoulders that kept the stifled sense of pride she felt every time she watched her sister do something magnificent from being the wholehearted emotion that it should have been.

As it was, Abby was the older sister and therefore did everything first. She was the first to get her driver's license, the first to go on a date, the first to graduate, the first to go off to college. She knew there was a part of Laura that resented that—that the fact that by the time she got around to something, it had become somewhat of a nonevent. And if she were honest with herself, Abby always felt a little bit smug when such a situation arose—for that one minute, *she* was the shining star in their parents' eyes—all eyes were on her. And though she hated to admit it, she'd always expected and looked forward to having the first grandchild—that first of a new generation that would always hold a special place in its grandparents' eyes for being so. Why the constant approval of her parents meant so much to her even now at twenty-two, she didn't understand, but that's the way it was.

Now she was faced with a situation she didn't know how to read. Initially, she knew, they'd be upset and disappointed with Laura, and she closed her eyes in almost physical pain as once again that smug, satisfied feeling threatened to surface. But once that baby was born, she knew they'd love it more than anything, and there was that tinge of jealousy again.

You're over-thinking this. Just chill. Everything will work out, she told herself, angry that she could not, even now, put her own selfishness aside and simply be there for her sister, better or worse. She and Laura were as close as sisters could be, best of friends, and she resented the fact that no matter what she did, she could never quite squelch this competition between them.

"Nervous flyer?" A soft voice startled her from her thoughts, and she opened her eyes, unaware that they'd been shut so tightly.

A pretty brunette smiled warmly next to her, waiting for an answer.

"Not usually," Abby exhaled, again unaware that she'd been holding her breath. *You really are a mess,* she told herself. "But I have a lot on my mind today."

"Ah, I see," the woman said. "I never used to be nervous on planes, but ever since I had a family, it seems I have more to lose." A shadow crossed the woman's face, and she wrung her hands nervously. Before Abby could inquire after the family she was talking about, a small hand gripped the side of the seat in front of her.

"Mommy?" came a small voice. "When are they going to take off?"

"Any minute now, Luke. Now turn around and make sure your seatbelt's on." She turned to Abby and smiled. "My sons, Luke and Ben. It's hard to travel just the three of us—one person always sits alone." The shadow that had lifted at the sight of her son settled in again, but Abby didn't feel right about inquiring.

Instead, she said, "They're cute—how old?"

Immediately the woman's face brightened, and she began to tell Abby all about the boys. But even as her seatmate chattered away beside her, Abby's mind wandered back to her own life.

She knew that her jealousy was rooted only in what was missing in her own life. There was a part of her that had been jealous, as she'd watched Laura meet and fall for Steven. It came back every time her sister talked about the man that she loved. And now Laura and Steven, though the timing was less than ideal and the pregnancy was unplanned, were nonetheless starting their family. Official or not, they were committing to a life together, and while Abby was beyond happy that her little sister had found someone, *she* wasn't even close to that. She didn't even have a boyfriend, and not only that, there hadn't even been anyone who had caught her eye in months. She was restless and anxious to get on with her life—and to do it *with* somebody. An ever-deepening loneliness had become her constant companion, finding its way into each moment of solitude.

She'd give anything to have what Steven and Laura had, and as the plane took off she recalled the woman's words.

Now that I have a family, it seems I have more to lose.

She'd risk it, she decided. She'd give anything to have a family, even if it meant the risk of losing it. It was all she'd ever wanted, all she and her sister had dreamed about since they were little. And while her sister's dreams were finally coming true, albeit in a different way than she had imagined, Abby wondered if hers would ever follow.

∽

Tom

Think about it.

Tom Reynolds tried to push the thought from his mind as he stepped out of the office, squinting against the bright sunlight. The air in Chicago was brisk for early June, and he straightened his overcoat on his shoulders before buttoning it and walking slowly toward nowhere. He had no destination in mind, at least not yet. In a few hours he'd be picking Beth up from the airport, but he had some thinking to do first. All day he'd been doing everything he could to keep from focusing on this, but with only a few hours left before he saw his wife, he couldn't put it off any longer.

Think about it, she'd said before taking the boys to her mother's in Minneapolis. He hadn't wanted to; it was the last thing he'd ever thought he'd have to consider. But then, the factors leading up to this situation had been the last things he'd ever thought he'd encounter. It had been three weeks since he'd found the letters, another two since he'd looked into the phone calls that had been placed over the last few months to a number he didn't recognize. It had been exactly eight days since he'd confronted her about it, seven since she'd left to give him some space. Space to *think about it*.

What was there to think about? She'd cheated on him—*been* cheating on him. With a man he *still* wasn't sure how she'd met. She'd cried when he stood before her with the phone bill in one hand and the letters in the other, all signed with the same closing thought: *Can't wait to see you again, Ryan.* Just the name grated on him now, and he found himself more aware of it than ever. The man behind the counter at Starbucks was a Ryan, and in the four months he'd been going to that location, he'd never once noticed. His dentist's assistant was a Ryan; the neighbor's dog walker was a Ryan. He even heard the name in *songs* now. In his high-school days, in another world, Tom had been a hopeless romantic and had truly believed that every time he heard the name of a girl he was in love with, it was a sign. He'd first noticed Beth, for example, in Spanish class, and for weeks before she agreed to go out with him, he'd began to hear her name everywhere. Believing wholeheartedly that it was a sign, that the universe was telling him to pursue her despite her (multiple) rejections, he'd persevered.

But it was situations like these that made that romance of his earlier life fade faster than the heat of a Midwestern summer. He knew now that it was not about signs; it was simply about a newfound awareness of the world around you and the people in it. *Like Ryan.*

He shuddered again, shivering despite the weight of his coat. Just the name alone was enough to conjure up images of the two of them, tangled together like the twisted branches of a weathered oak, like the braided chain of the necklace he'd bought Beth for their fifth wedding anniversary.

Think about it, she'd said through tear-filled eyes before closing the door behind her. She'd insisted that it was nothing—that it "had just happened." She said she was lonely—he was never home, and it was just her and the boys all day, and that Ryan had made her feel comfortable again, safe again, that it had been a moment of weakness and she hadn't known how to get out of it. *You're never around, Tom.* Once again, she had a way of making her indiscretions sound like they were *his* fault. She swore she'd stop the whole thing, call it off right then and there, that Ryan meant nothing to her. She asked if he could ever forgive her—that she'd do whatever it took.

I don't know, had been his answer.

She'd nodded sadly, tears of shame running in jagged lines from her eyes as if they too were sheepish and looking for a place to hide. *Think about it*, she'd told him, before telling him she'd take Ben and Luke to her mother's for the week so he could have some space from the situation.

That week had flown and dragged all at the same time. The hours he was awake he was consumed by images of the two of them, by the words he'd read in those letters. When he slept he dreamt of them. He'd found it hard to focus on much else. Could he forgive her? Could he ever look at her and *not* see her with Ryan? Could he trust her again? All of these questions tormented him, but there was a bigger question that was even harder to swallow, one that he'd been asking himself since he'd seen the first letter.

Was it even worth the effort?

If he were completely honest with himself, he'd have to admit that he *hadn't* been around that much, mostly because he didn't want to be. For his kids—yes, in a heartbeat. He'd walk through fire for Ben and Luke and never missed or turned down an opportunity to spend time with them. But he couldn't suppress the feeling that there was nothing there anymore between him and Beth, that he looked at her and felt indifference.

They'd dated through high school and college and had gotten married a year after graduation. Thinking about it now, he couldn't help but feel like they'd done it simply because it had seemed like the next step—because they'd gotten so comfortable with each other that neither of them had thought to question that this may not be right.

The thought had crossed his mind once, right after the honeymoon, when he'd realized that there was no passion in their marriage like there was supposed to be in that first year.

They'd done more talking than anything on the honeymoon, and when they returned to their everyday lives, they both were too tired for much of anything at the end of the workday. *Is this how it's supposed to be?* He'd asked himself as he watched friend after friend marry in a haze of infatuation and passionate romance. The romantic in him had yearned for that same connection with Beth—but no matter how he tried, it wouldn't come, and he wondered if they were missing a very important part of those early years together. Before he'd been able to bring it up with her, however, Ben had been conceived on an overnight trip they'd taken for their fifth anniversary, and any doubts had been silenced, at least temporarily, by the larger excitement of their first child. Those next two years—first the pregnancy and then the first year of Ben's life—had been enough to convince him that he'd made the right decision. He and Beth were as close as ever, bonded over this shared experience. But those old feelings had come back to haunt him as he lay awake one night, Beth asleep beside him, wondering why he felt nothing when she tucked herself in next to him, skin on skin. Why he felt nothing when her hand brushed his the next morning in church—no warmth, no excitement. The arrival of Luke less than a year later had again merely been a band-aid, and for months now he'd been asking himself those same old questions.

Hence this new question—*was it even worth the effort? Why do I even care that much?* He'd lost trust in her—he knew that, lost faith in her word—and he knew that's what hurt him the most. But why did he feel jealousy? That emotion he could only rationalize with the fact that it must be human nature to be jealous. Hadn't it been he, after all, who only months before actually *wished* that one night she would meet someone new and move on, so he didn't have to be the bad guy? Hadn't he almost *wished* that she'd look at him one night and announce that she was moving out? So why, now that it was all happening—unraveling—before him, did he care at all?

His answer came as he pulled a few dollars out of his wallet for a coffee and caught a glimpse of the family photo he carried in his wallet. Those two little boys—one on Beth's lap and one on his, both grinning at the world through eyes bright with optimism. *That's why*, he thought, and right then and there he knew. *Yes.* He had to find a way to forgive her, had to find a way to look at her and not see Ryan, had to find a way to trust her again. Those boys were counting on him. Ben and Luke knew nothing of the world but one father and one mother and one life as a family, and he'd be damned if he was going to let anyone take that away from them—most of all himself or Beth.

And later that day, as he stood at the baggage claim waiting for his family, he'd almost convinced himself that he'd made the right decision. The boys were the first to come into view, and they rounded the corner at full speed, flying into their father's arms. Beth walked a step or two behind them, cautiously meeting Tom's eyes as he straightened before her, finally taking her into his arms, all the answer she needed. Yet as she cried tears of joy into his shoulder, as she professed promise after promise to change, that old familiar feeling came back, his constant companion these past ten years of marriage. *Indifference.* And suddenly he felt trapped. Trapped in a passionless marriage, trapped in a *loveless* marriage, trapped in a faithless marriage—trapped.

Until suddenly he saw her.

A flash of hair the color of barley waving in a sunset, eyes the color of Christmas. She was standing at the baggage claim and looking around as if to orient herself—as if she'd been lost in thought—when she saw him. Something about the look in her eyes drew him in and made it impossible for him to breathe, all at once.

And there it was, an emotion he hadn't felt for years, an emotion he'd almost forgotten existed—hope. Hope that just *maybe*, there was still something more than mere complacency in store for him.

Yet as he looked back into Beth's remorseful face—although still all he saw was Ryan—as he looked down at his sons, grinning up at him with all the hope of the world, hope their father had long forgotten about, he remembered his earlier promise.

I'll do this for you, he thought, touching Luke's cheek as he took Beth's hand in his trembling one, heading for the doors, heading for a future he did not know how to predict.

And wondering, for the first time in his life, if there was a limit to the sacrifices you were willing to make for your children.

༄

Abby

Abby stared after the man as he walked out of the airport with the two small boys and the woman she'd sat next to on the plane, hoping though she knew she was wrong, that it was his sister and two nephews. She tried to still her pounding heart, wondering at the way she'd struggled to breathe the minute she'd seen him, the way his gaze had nearly paralyzed her.

She grasped the pillar she stood by as she waited for her luggage, straining to get one last glimpse of him as the doors closed behind him. She closed her eyes, turning away, oblivious to the fact that as those two little boys chatted away and the woman dug for her cell phone, he turned around, straining over his shoulder for one last glimpse of *her*.

Focusing on her breathing, she pulled her bag, neatly packed, off the conveyer before walking on shaky legs toward her car.

She called Laura to let her know she'd arrived back in Chicago safely, to thank her for hosting her, and to once again offer her support on the tough situation her sister had landed in.

But as she drove back toward the city, she found herself grinning from ear to ear, not only because of the man himself, but because of the sudden hope that her brief encounter had brought back to life in her.

∽

CHAPTER TWO

Laura

Laura looked around the cozy room and smiled.

She and Steven had made the seven-hour drive from Minneapolis to her parents' place to celebrate Thanksgiving with her family, and had made it there just before the biggest November snowstorm Illinois had seen in years hit, and hit hard.

Now, three hours later, the snow had finally subsided to a slow, steady pace, and it drifted past the windows on either side of the massive fieldstone fireplace, illuminated against the dark gray November sky. A roaring fire crackled from within the hearth, its smoky smell warming the room and giving it an old time feel. The wind rattled the windowpanes, but inside it was warm and cozy, and Laura wrapped herself in a hug as she shivered, imagining the chill beyond the walls.

Looking at the joyous faces around her, she wondered how she could be much happier. Steven stood talking with her father near the fireplace, his elbow resting on the mantle, beer in hand. The voices of her mother and Abby carried in from the kitchen, the sounds and smells of Thanksgiving dinner mixing with the smoke from the fire.

"You awake?" Steven asked softly, and Laura snapped to attention, unaware that she had closed her eyes.

"Just taking it all in," she nodded happily. As John went to get another beer for him and his future son-in-law, Steven plopped down beside her on the leather couch and put his hand on Laura's stomach, quickly kissing it before straightening and resting his head against the sofa.

"How are you feeling?" he asked. "How's the baby?"

"Good," she smiled, absentmindedly rubbing her belly where Steven's lips had just touched it. "She's been kicking a lot. I think she wants to be here with all of us instead of stuck inside."

Steven chuckled at the thought, rising as John reentered the room and handed him a beer.

"Laura, you're still okay on beverages?" her father asked, and she nodded.

"I am. I should probably go and see if there's anything I can help with in the kitchen." She excused herself, awkwardly pushing off the sofa with one hand as she braced her lower back with the other. She kissed them both on the cheek before leaving them to watch the game, and wandered toward the kitchen, running her hands over the familiar trappings of her childhood as she passed them. Her mother looked up in concern as she hobbled in, and Abby rushed to her side, guiding her to a chair off to the side.

"You would think I'm terminally ill, the way you two worry about me," Laura laughed, hesitating before settling into the seat her sister had ushered her toward. "I came to see if I could help."

Anne shook her head firmly. "You can help by sitting right there and keeping us company," and at that, Laura finally relaxed and sat down. "How's the game?" her mother asked, and Laura told her that she hadn't the slightest clue.

"I didn't even glance at the TV. They had it on mute, and to be honest, I'd forgotten it was even on."

"Is your father behaving himself in there?" she continued, and Laura nodded, knowing that her mother was referring to her father's feelings about Laura's pregnancy. He had been so angry that summer when they'd announced their plans that he hadn't spoken to his daughter, much less Steven, for several months afterward. Her letters had gone ignored and her calls unanswered, until finally one day out of the blue he had called and apologized. She knew that he was, most likely, still disappointed and wary of how things would work out, but though she hadn't pushed the issue, she knew her mother had played a large role in his sudden change of heart. *This is your daughter*, she would have said. *This is your daughter, and this is her life, and she's going to go about living it whether or not you're involved in it. Now, you can disagree all you want, and you can voice your opinion and offer your advice, but if you want to be a part of your daughter's—and granddaughter's—lives, you're at some point going to need to put aside your feelings and support her in whatever she chooses, even if it isn't what you would have chosen yourself. We've raised her the best we can, and now it's up to her to make her own decisions.*

That must have done it; John hadn't breathed a word of disapproval yet today. Though it still crept into his eyes when he looked at either her or Steven, she was finally able to once again see the love behind it and was perfectly content to spend the day in companionship with him and the rest of her family. And for his part, her father was not only making an effort to—but from the looks of it actually was—genuinely enjoying Steven's company. Five months had passed since Laura had discovered she was pregnant and told her parents, with Steven. She wondered if maybe time did heal all wounds.

"They seem to be getting along well," she reassured her mother. "I heard some political talk starting up as I left," and at that Anne smiled, familiar with her husband's love of talking politics.

"He's always been too smart for his own good," she was saying. "Things come so easily to him that it's hard for him to admit he could ever be wrong about anything. I hope Steven can hold his own!"

"Oh, he can," Laura smiled, leaning back in her chair to peek into the living room to see Steven laughing at something her father had said.

"Steven is such a formal name," Anne continued. "Why doesn't he go by Steve?"

"I'm not sure," Laura conceded. "His parents are pretty..." She trailed off, and Abby took a stab at the word she was looking for.

"Uptight?"

"Yeah," Laura continued. "Serious, uptight, formal, take your pick. His nanny practically raised him, and she just called him Champ. His grandfather called him Sport, I think, but to his parents and their high-class friends, he was always Steven." She put an extra emphasis on the name, trying to picture a young boy answering to that name, and the thought of it made her wrinkle her nose. Abby was chuckling to herself, and both Laura and Anne watched her expectantly.

"I just keep picturing," she began, laughing out loud now, "Steven as a little kid. But it's not the kid Steven—it's his head now, attached to a child's body, and he's one of those kids who wears a sweater vest and bow tie."

Laura had to laugh herself at this bobble-head description of her fiancé, leaning back again to make sure he was still holding his own against her father. She saw only the backs of their heads on the sofa, and she knew they must be engrossed in the game.

Steadying herself on the counter as she turned back, her new engagement ring sparkled from her left hand. Abby noticed her gaze and smiled, and though Laura could see a hint of some unnamed emotion in it, she ignored it as her sister addressed her. "Tell me again about the proposal, Laura," Abby asked, unaware that Laura had noticed the look on her face.

"The first one or the real one?" Anne winked at Laura. Steven's shotgun proposal was now a source of humor for her family, though he was mortified that she'd told them.

"Oh, it was perfect." She ignored her mom and looked at Abby. "It was last Saturday. We went for a walk around Lake Calhoun—one of those perfect Minnesota fall days. Nothing too elaborate or fancy, which was just fine by me—we were just standing underneath the most beautiful tree, and he asked. Seriously it was like a dream—these big yellow leaves were just floating to the ground, reflecting in the lake..." Laura trailed off, staring off into space.

"Oh, you're such a sap." Abby thrust a stack of napkins into Laura's arms, snapping her back to reality. "Make yourself useful," she added with a wink, and Laura willingly stood up and set about setting the table.

"When I get engaged," Abby was continuing, "I want over-the-top romance."

"What, like skywriting?" Laura teased with a smile. "You're so high maintenance."

"I am not high maintenance!" Abby looked hurt, as though she'd taken Laura's comment much more seriously than it had been intended. But before Laura could explain, Abby was continuing, "I just want the perfect engagement. That's all."

"Any idea when that will be?" Anne teased, and again Laura watched as that dark look came back to Abby's face.

"Abby, we're just joking around with you," she offered, trying to bring back the lighthearted mood from earlier, but her sister just shrugged, her lips pursed in a tight line.

Anne caught Laura's eye and shrugged, shaking her head as Abby carried the mashed potatoes to the table.

"Abby, can you go let the men know dinner is ready?" Anne called after her.

"Oh, Mom, I can do that." Laura was already rising.

"You'll do no such thing," her mother said firmly as Abby hurried back past her toward the living room.

Laura rolled her eyes. It had been flattering at first, knowing that her family was so concerned with her health and that of her baby. Now it was just annoying. She couldn't go anywhere without someone doting on her. "Geez, are you guys going to wheel me to the table?" she asked, but her mother just smiled.

"I just don't want you to overdo it," she said softly. "I remember how tired I was all the time when I was pregnant, and my back hurt so much. It would have been nice to rest for a change."

Laura's attitude immediately softened. Her mother was only trying to make things easier on her, she knew, and she smiled at her gratefully as John and Steven came into the room.

"All set?" Her father patted her firmly on the back as he always had. It was his way of hugging her. Her father was a loving man, and they never had to guess at his affection, but warmth had never defined him.

"Yep!" She took his outstretched hand, and he helped her out of her chair, ushering her into the dining room. The table was arranged beautifully—ivory placemats set off by the bright autumn leaves that Abby had sprinkled across them. Each place was set with a different colored napkin—red, yellow, orange, green, and brown—tied with a bright ribbon and set at the top of the placemat, next to the crystal water glasses that sparkled in the candlelight. Steaming china dishes held mashed potatoes, stuffing, rolls, cranberries, squash, yams, and more. John immediately set to carving the turkey, doling a generous helping on to each of their plates, which they held out to him before loading them with the other fixings. Laura could hardly wait to start eating and had a hard time sitting through John's thorough grace, just like she had when she was younger. She avoided looking at Abby, for she knew that her sister, like her, would have her eyes open and be looking around the room, and any eye contact would throw them into a fit of silent laughter. They loved the way their father's brow furrowed in concentration as he prayed, but it always struck them funny at times like these, as did almost anything else. As children, any time they'd had to be quiet had ironically seemed to yield the funniest things, and this would be no exception. Despite what she knew, she opened her eyes to glance at Abby, but instead of the giddy amusement she'd expected to find, her sister's eyes were listless and trained on the centerpiece. Laura waved to try to get her attention, but Abby's gaze remained unchanged.

As grace ended and everyone began to eat, Laura tried to maneuver her way closer to the table, but her seven-month belly made that nearly impossible. Steven watched her and burst into laughter. "She can't drive, either," he told the family as he stood up and helped push her a little bit closer.

"I can't help it. She's a big baby," Laura laughed. "I just want to be close enough to the table to put my elbows on it and make Mom mad."

Anne laughed. "There's nothing you can do to make me mad. You're giving me my first grandchild! You have a get out of jail free card for the next two months!"

Laura laughed, again trying to catch Abby's eye, but her sister was staring at her plate.

"What's wrong, Abs?" she asked finally.

"Huh?" Abby looked up, to the rest of the world simply distracted. But Laura could see the tears in her eyes.

"Are you okay?" She didn't want to embarrass Abby in front of everyone, but she could tell something was up.

"I'm fine!" Abby offered a bright smile and shoved a bite of turkey into her mouth for emphasis. "What are your plans after you have the baby?" she asked, mouth full.

"Abby," Anne shot her older daughter a warning look, and finally Laura was able to catch her sister's eye and laugh over their mother's pet peeve.

"Sorry, Mom," Abby said after swallowing her food.

"She hates it when we talk with our mouth full," Laura explained when she noticed Steven's look of confusion.

"I can't help it," Anne shrugged. "Old habits and such."

"Well," Laura began to answer Abby's question. "Since the baby's due about three weeks after the semester starts, I'm going to be taking the semester off." She looked nervously at her father before continuing quickly, "but we'll both be working, saving as much money as we can. And then next fall, I'll start courses at somewhere around here, actually. I've already applied for a transfer to Northwestern and Loyola, and I still want to look at DePaul and a few others. And Steven's been applying to some med schools in the area. We'll probably wait to move until he gets accepted, so he doesn't have to miss anything and fall behind, but once that happens, we'll be here.

"You're moving back down here? That's awesome!" Abby wore a look of excitement she could hardly contain. "Where are you going to live?"

John was shaking his head. "Are you two aware of how expensive it is to live here?" he asked, and Laura felt her shoulders sag a bit. "Not only to live here," he continued, "but to pay tuition to places like DePaul and Northwestern? I think you may be setting your sights a little high."

"You don't want us closer to you guys?" Laura felt her eyes well up with tears. Deep down she knew that's not what her father meant, but she'd been on an emotional roller coaster for most of her pregnancy.

"No," John amended. "It'd be great to have you around. I just don't think you guys understand how much it will cost you to pay rent at a place around here. Where are you planning on living?"

"Well," Laura sat up straighter as she began excitedly, "do you guys remember Carolyn Jeffers?" Abby nodded, but John and Anne looked lost.

"She was Laura's sorority sister, for the two months she actually stayed in a sorority," Abby explained with a wry smile.

"Oh yes, that's right," Anne nodded. "I remember the name."

"Well, she was a senior when I was a freshman, but we really hit it off, because she grew up just down the block," Laura began. "She went to private school in Maine for high school. Apparently she was a tough teenager," she laughed. "But she knew the older siblings of some of my friends from high school. Anyway, when she graduated she moved back here, and her parents basically gave her their house, because they moved to Florida but didn't want to get rid of it." Laura could see the looks of *where are you going with this* on her family's faces, so she cut to the point. "Well, Carolyn got offered a job over in London, and she leaves right after Christmas so she can be there for the New Year. And," she exchanged a private look with Steven before continuing, "she's going to let us stay there, in the guest cottage. For free! Can you believe it?" she cried, looking from face to face around the table, grinning from ear to ear.

Abby's jaw dropped to the table. "So let me get this straight," she said carefully. "You guys get to live in a house in Winnetka, for *free*?" Laura couldn't read her tone, but she detected a hint of jealousy.

"Basically," she continued. "We offered to pay her rent or something, but she said it wasn't an issue. Her family comes from old money, so the house has been paid off for a while, and she's been staying there for free anyways. I mean it's not like we're staying in the mansion—just in the guest cottage."

"Laura," Anne scolded softly. Her mother considered it incredibly rude and distasteful to discuss the financial affairs of others.

"What happened to my get out of jail free card?" Laura joked.

"Yeah, Mom, really. You're treating us like we're ten again," Abby added in a less than jovial tone.

"Abby, *what* is wrong tonight?" Anne sounded exasperated.

"Nothing," Abby looked away, and back at Laura. "Anyway, Laura, you were saying?"

"Well," Laura hesitated before continuing, looking between her sister and mother, "we'll pay for the upkeep and everything, of course, but she said *we'd* actually be doing *her* a favor by keeping an eye on her place while she's gone. It saves her from having to find—and pay—someone to come in and do it."

"Wow," John shook his head. "And how long is she planning on being there for?"

"Well, she signed a two-year contract," Laura stated, "but she said if she likes it, she'll consider staying there indefinitely. So in two years we'll basically have to move out or find a way to pay her for the place, if we want to stay."

"Sounds like an amazing deal," John said.

"Hear that, Steven?" Abby joked, suddenly seeming back to her old self. "You've got two years to make something of yourself."

"Actually," Laura looked anxiously between Steven and Abby, missing Steven's sudden frown, "*I'm* going to be working before Steven is."

At this, John looked up sharply from his plate. "You're what?"

"Well," Laura began in a rush, "Steven needs to get finish school and get on to his residency. The sooner he does that the better, and I can put off grad school for a while, as long as I have my undergrad completed. I can at least get *some* kind of job with an undergrad degree, and meanwhile I could start some grad school courses online."

She couldn't tell what her father thought of that idea, but before he could say anything, her mother cut in.

"Well," Anne smiled brightly, "it seems as though the two of you have this figured out." She cast a pointed look at her husband, letting him know that the subject was closed. "Now, let's start talking about Abby's graduation. That's coming up in May, you know."

Laura smiled at her mother, silently thanking her for changing the subject. She was always good at easing the tension in a room.

But as Abby began to chatter about ideas for her graduation party and plans for her own future, Laura caught a glimpse of a glance between her father and Steven. She wasn't sure what her father had been trying to convey, but as she reached for her fiancé's hand under the table and gave it a squeeze, she couldn't ignore the fact that it was clammy and trembling as he squeezed back.

∽

Steven

Steven put the car on cruise control and sat back with a sigh, glancing at Laura asleep beside him.

He was the one that needed sleep, he thought as he watched I-94 stretch out before him, a bright blue sky reflecting off yesterday's snow. Laura had slept like a baby the night before, or at least she'd said.

He, meanwhile, had lay awake in the guest room, twirling an imaginary ring around his finger—where soon there would actually *be* a ring. He'd felt a little ridiculous, sleeping alone in the guest room while his pregnant fiancée slept alone in her room. It was Baxter house rules—absolutely *no* sleeping in the same room as someone until you were married. He respected John and wanted to respect the rules of his household, but this seemed a little extreme. Laura was pregnant—the jig was up—there really wasn't much trouble the two of them could get into at that point, and John's insistence on them sleeping separately had seemed at this point like one last attempt to exert some semblance of control.

He liked John, but disagreed with him on many things, this one included. Still, he had never seen Laura as happy as he'd seen her around her family today, her love of the holidays and the closeness of her family combined.

He smiled, picturing her face lit up as it had been as they'd gone around the table naming what they were thankful for. There had been a warmth in his stomach when she'd announced that she was most thankful for him and for the little girl they were expecting later that winter. Looking around the table, he'd hoped then as he was hoping now that he could provide for her and their child what John had provided for his family. He'd promised her just a week ago that he would.

She had been right—he had just known when it was time to propose—and had done it, right there on the shores of Lake Calhoun. He didn't even have a ring picked out—they'd gone shopping for one together later that afternoon—but nevertheless he'd dropped to one knee and poured his heart out to her. He'd told her that he'd never love somebody the way he loved her, and that if she'd let him, he wanted to spend the rest of his life protecting her and trying to make her face light up the way it was lit up right then. She'd agreed on one condition—that he'd repeat those very words to their daughter on the day she was born.

A strange feeling had come over him this morning, however, as he watched John and Anne's easy banter at the breakfast table, the two of them still so obviously in love after so long. Usually watching their exchanges would have made him hopeful, but today it had seemed daunting—the combined tasks of providing for a family financially, taking care of a child, *and* committing to making his wife happy every day seemed like a lot to take on at once. There was a part of him that wished he could do it one step at a time, like others had the leisure of doing. Most couples got married first—and adjusted to that lifestyle and making each other happy within that marriage before moving on to trying to make a child happy as well. He, on the other hand, would be attempting all at once.

He knew he could do it, but under John's watchful gaze last night at dinner, he'd felt the pressure of providing for Laura and their baby like never before. Sitting there in that beautiful dining room, surrounded by beautiful things, and seeing how happy all of that made his fiancée—*that's* what he wanted to give her. And here on the road, he vowed that he would, whatever it took.

She stirred in the passenger seat, and he smiled as she opened her eyes and stretched.

"How long have I been out?"

"About an hour or two. You were snoring like a Tasmanian devil."

"I was not!" Laura cried, batting his shoulder playfully. Looking at her dainty hand, Steven wondered if she could even exert enough force to *actually* hit him.

"You call that a slap?" he taunted her, curious. "Really let me have it!"

Laughing, she smacked him harder.

"Wow, you really *are* weak," he smiled with a dare in is eyes.

"All right, that does it." She scrunched her face up and really pounded his shoulder, sending him swerving into the left lane. "Steven!" she cried, covering her eyes.

He laughed, steering the car easily back into the right lane. "God, you're cute." He watched her pull her hands from her face, surveying her surroundings to make sure she was safe. "So you can hit pretty hard. But man, you're such a girl with that form." He winked at her.

"Oh there's just no pleasing you, is there, Steven McCord?" She gave up, sitting back in her seat and crossing her arms over her impossibly large belly.

"How on earth is that a girl in there?" He changed the subject placing a hand on her stomach. "You're carrying that thing like a basketball."

"I know," she smiled. "I thought for sure we were having a boy."

"Me too," Steven agreed. "But I'm glad it's a girl. Aren't you?"

"Mm hmm," Laura nodded, smiling. "Very. It's what I wanted."

"Good. Me too." Steven checked his mirrors before moving to pass a semi.

"Hey, are you hungry?" Laura yawned, and then pointed to the radio clock. "It's almost dinner time."

"It's four fifteen!" Steven laughed.

"Yeah, but we ate an early lunch," she argued.

"We ate lunch at two." Steven looked at her like she was crazy.

"Fine, let me rephrase. Steven, your fiancée is starving, and eating for both herself and *your* child, so she would very much appreciate if you could pull into the nearest McDonalds."

"You got it," he chuckled. Minutes later he watched as she took a huge bite of a Big Mac. "I love that you're not afraid to eat real food," he said between bites of his own double cheeseburger.

"You call this real food?" She spit bits of lettuce as she spoke, her mouth full to the max.

"You know what I mean," Steven said, watching her fondly. "Junk food. Most girls order a garden salad on dates. But you know that a burger is *so* much sexier."

"I hope you're not implying that this is a date," she smiled at him, her cheeks swollen with food. "If these are the romantic dinners I have to look forward to, I'm getting out now."

Steven laughed along with her, but at her joke felt his fear of inadequacy come back.

For the second time that day, Steven vowed to himself that he'd give her everything she wanted and dreamed of. He owed that to her—he'd give her anything, do anything for her. After all, it's what he'd promised her.

༄

Tom

Tom looked across the table at Beth, who was at the moment focused on convincing Luke to try his green beans. Luke wanted no part in it and was sitting with his arms crossed, adamantly refusing.

"Luke," Tom said sternly, doing his best not to smirk at the expression on his youngest son's face as he shifted his gaze, "listen to your mother. You need to eat your green beans. Or you won't get dessert!"

"No!" Luke whined, looking on the verge of a breakdown.

"Okay," Tom said, reaching across the table with his fork and separating half of the hated vegetable from the rest. "I'll make you a deal. Just eat this half, okay?" As he spoke, he forked one up and began to make airplane noises, spinning the vegetable toward Luke's mouth, which at the last minute, opened miraculously. Tom's antics not only convinced his son to eat *more* than half his green beans, but also had him laughing by the end of the meal. It wasn't until after he'd placed an enormous frosted sugar cookie onto each of his kids (nearly) clean plates that he looked at Beth, only to find her glaring at him with a look that told him, very clearly, *I could just kill you.*

"What?" he asked with a shrug, oblivious to anything he could have done wrong. She shot him another look, this time one that said *We'll talk later,* and he sighed, clearing the table and starting to load the dishwasher.

He got the boys into a bath, listening to Beth's voice carry from the kitchen, where she was on the phone with one of her girlfriends, he presumed, complaining about him. He lingered longer than usual putting them to bed, knowing that there was a lecture coming from Beth but still unable to comprehend why.

She'd always been one to get angry over the little things, but lately she'd begun to get angry over things that weren't even justified in his opinion. He looked at her the wrong way, or he said the wrong thing to the kids, or he was wearing those shoes she hated. He couldn't do anything right.

And if he was honest with himself, neither could she. He'd spent more time than not frustrated with her for no reason in particular, and on more than one occasion had caught himself wondering if he'd made a mistake deciding to stay.

It was one thing to stay in a home that could be happy in if you were doing it for your children—but a home where you were doing nothing but fight—that made things all the worse for the kids, and he'd again been contemplating leaving for most of the six months he'd been back.

The thought was weighing heavy on his mind as he waited in the kitchen while Beth took her turn kissing the boys good night. He heard her coming down the stairs, and he focused on his hands, wrapped around his cup of steaming decaf.

"Thanks for pouring *me* some." She suddenly appeared in front of him, and he fought not to role his eyes at the sarcasm in her tone, the sarcasm that had dominated their conversations for longer than he cared to remember.

"Sorry," he mumbled, rising to get her a mug, but she was already to the cupboard and he slumped back into his chair. "So how did I piss you off this time?"

Beth sighed and sat down, running a hand through her short hair. "You just undermine my authority every time you do that," she said soberly, and he knew she must be talking about the green bean incident. Who would have thought, in the early years of their marriage, that there would be an *incident* involving green beans, of all things? Beth continued, "I'd been trying to get him to eat those, *all* of them, the whole meal, and suddenly you swoop in with your funny airplane noises, Mr. Funny Dad, and tell him he only has to eat *half* of them, and I become the bad cop again."

"The bad cop?" Steven tried to keep his voice down. "Come on, Beth! I was just trying to help you out. You seemed stressed, and let's face it—it wasn't going anywhere. He would have sat at the table all night and not eaten a bite of those!"

"So now you're questioning my parenting skills?" Beth shot back.

"What? Who said anything about parenting skills?" Tom felt his anger rising, pushing his chair back loudly and pacing the kitchen, vigorously rubbing his eyes in his frustration before finally focusing them on her. "Look, Beth," he started, searching for the courage to say what needed to be said. "This isn't working. I think we both know that. I tried to do this for the kids, after you told me..." He trailed off, knowing he didn't need to elaborate. "I thought I could do that, but if I were honest with myself, I think we both know this has nothing to do with Ryan. This has been a long time coming, and we both know it."

He waited for Beth's eruption of anger. Somehow, even when both parties knew it was wrong, the one who finally spoke up and brought the problem to the table turned into the bad guy, and he didn't doubt that his case would be an exception. But Beth surprised him, when he could finally meet her eyes. There was a glint of understanding in them, and she was nodding.

"I know," she said, reaching for his hand. "We've been trying too hard to make this work out...thinking that it's best for the kids. But *anything* has to be better for them than this. I won't raise kids in a house of fighting parents. I just won't do it." Tom nodded his agreement, and for a moment they just sat there, mulling in silence over all that had been lost between them—all that had never really been there to begin with—all the things they would change if they could, and all the things they wouldn't. The thoughts kept Tom awake that night as he tossed and turned on the couch, wondering how he would even go about the task of searching for an apartment. It would be better, he thought, to get one downtown. It was farther from the kids, true, but he worked downtown, and with a custody agreement he was sure would fall into Beth's favor, he'd be commuting to work more regularly than he'd be seeing his children, and it just made sense to him. Beth would probably be furious, and again he wondered about what he'd have done differently.

He loved Beth, and always would; she was a good woman. But he admitted to himself now what he had known all along—that he'd never really been *in* love with her; they'd been wrong for each other from the start. He loved Ben and Luke more than anything in the world, and he wouldn't trade them for anything. If this situation was the only way they could have come to be a part of his life, then he wouldn't change a thing about it. It meant having his two sons. Still, there was a part of him that wished somehow he could have had both—that he could have had Ben and Luke but at the same time not wasted these years of his life in an unhappy marriage.

And as sleep finally found him, somewhere from the dark corners of his mind where he kept only his most cherished memories, an image fleeted across his mind of a woman with eyes the color of Christmas. And in that moment just between reality and dreams, he let himself hope that somewhere in his future, he just might be able to find what he'd been looking for all along.

∽

Abby

Abby sighed as she sealed yet another resume into yet another envelope, holding it in her hands an extra second for luck before adding it to the pile that was accumulating on her desk.

She sat back and rubbed her eyes, glancing at the clock, blinking a red 3:00 a.m., and she knew she should get to bed. Usually she was meticulous about getting eight hours of sleep, but lately she'd been staying up later and later in order to focus on her job search. She'd be graduating in May, and in her final semester of her final year of college, her courses had really picked up, and she was loaded with work. It was the opposite of what she had expected—she'd always figured as she neared the end of her college career, there wouldn't be much left to do. Boy had she been wrong. Still, she wanted to start the interview process and find a job as quickly as possible. She'd always done everything by the book, and she desperately wanted to land a job straight out of college.

She envied those who were relaxed enough to take a year off after graduation to backpack through Europe.

There was a part of her that felt smug about it—her parents were also very by the book, and she knew how proud they'd be if she could pull this off. *Maybe more proud of me than they are of Laura*, she thought, and then immediately tried to push the thought away.

Standing up, she stretched deeply before crossing the short distance from her desk to her bed and falling into it. She'd just begun to doze when she heard her apartment door open. She didn't have to listen very hard to hear her roommates—clearly they'd brought whomever they'd met at the bar that night home with them. Within minutes, she heard the music start in the living room, and loud voices carry through her thin bedroom wall. Her door opened a crack, and Meredith stuck her head in.

"Abby?" she whispered, exaggeratedly loud.

"Hey, Mere. When did you get home?" she asked as though she didn't already know.

"Just now," Meredith came in and sat on the end of her bed. "Did we wake you?"

"No, I was up" Abby pushed herself up in bed and gestured toward the stack of envelopes on her desk. "Did you have fun?"

"Totally. I hope you don't mind we met a group of guys who wanted to come back and party here. What are you doing in bed on a Friday night, anyway? You should have come out with us!"

"Technically it's Saturday morning," Abby reminded her. "And I had some stuff to do."

"Well, come out into the living room. You don't even have to change out of your pajamas."

Abby shook her head. "I'm exhausted, Mere. I think I'm just going to go to bed."

"Oh you're such a grandma," Meredith sighed, rising slowly.

"I prefer to think of myself as an 'old soul,'" Abby grinned.

"Come on, you're only young once. You're never going to meet anyone if you stay in your room all the time," Meredith called out as she shut the door behind her.

Abby flopped back down onto her pillow and sighed. Meredith was right; she was never going to get anywhere if she didn't put herself out there, but the truth was she hated the bar scene. She'd never been a big drinker, and the whole ordeal was just ridiculous to her. Given the choice, she'd much rather stay in and watch a movie or cook dinner. Her parents and teachers had always told her she was just mature for her age, and that in a few years others would catch up. But she wondered if Meredith was right—if maybe she'd be seventy before they did. With a sigh, she threw back her covers and got out of bed, swinging her door open and heading for the living room.

"Hey!" Abby's other roommate elbowed Meredith. "Look who decided to join us!" Abby smiled and hugged them both, and then let them introduce her to the group of guys they'd brought home.

They seemed nice enough—one was actually pretty cute, and she slowly began to enjoy herself, even joining in a game of flip cup they'd set up on their island. Still, she found herself dreaming of her graduation, a few months away, and of starting her "real life." She'd had just about enough of the college scene, and was more than ready for a change.

CHAPTER THREE

Laura

Her daughter's birth, Laura discovered, was nothing like what she had prepared for. She'd been to the Lamaze classes, read all the books, spent months preparing the nursery, practicing lullabies and making her birthing arrangements. Aside from that, she'd also spent the better part of her teens as a nanny, so when her water broke very early on a cold January morning, she'd felt completely prepared and in control.

What she wasn't expecting, however, was the overwhelming feeling that was born mere seconds after her daughter. The daunting responsibility that would be hers for at least the next eighteen years suddenly became real when she heard her daughter's first cry. A love deeper than anything she'd experienced or expected overwhelmed her the minute she laid eyes on the squirming, purple bundle that the doctor handed her with a smile. An impatience she'd always possessed, but never to this magnitude, took over as she waited for the nurse to bring her baby back after cleaning her off and wrapping her in a soft pink blanket.

What surprised her the most was the sheer tininess of her daughter. Her head fit easily into the palm of her hand; her fingers barely closed around Laura's pinky. Her little eyes squinted blearily up at her from a swollen red face, and despite the resemblance Laura felt all newborns bore to Winston Churchill, she was sure she'd never seen anything quite so beautiful. One look at Steven's face was all she needed to know they'd made the right decision in having, and keeping, their daughter. She could hardly speak past the lump in her throat, so she simply sat there, beaming at her daughter and fiancé, feeling blessed beyond measure.

"What's her name?" Anne asked minutes later with a smile as she kissed her new granddaughter's forehead, cradling her lovingly in her arms despite her flailing attempts at movement. For now, the band encircling her tiny wrist simply read "Baby Girl McCord."

"Faith," Laura said with conviction. She didn't elaborate on their reasons; the meaning the name held for her and Steven was something that she felt was private, for only them—and someday their daughter—to know. Anne, for her part, didn't ask for more—just smiled and repeated the name in a soft whisper.

"Where's Daddy?" Laura tore her eyes away from her baby to scan the room. "And Abby?" Laura's family had flown up to Minneapolis a few days earlier—it was important to them to be there for the birth, and Laura's doctor had assured them it would be soon. With both Abby and Laura on winter break from school, the timing was convenient. When Steven had called the hotel that morning with the news, Anne had answered and promised to be there within minutes. Laura hadn't thought to inquire at the time after her father and sister, just assumed they'd be with her.

"Abby's got that interview down in Chicago that she had to fly back for, but I left a message on her cell phone. She's going to be crushed when she finds out she missed it—we all thought she'd be fine if she just went down for the day and came back up. But she flies back in this afternoon, so she'll be here. And your father is…" Anne didn't get a chance to finish as John rushed through the door, his face a mix of worry and excitement. All worry vanished as he looked around the room of happy faces and focused on the baby in Anne's arms.

"John, meet your granddaughter," Anne beamed, handing Faith, who was still squirming and fussing, to her husband.

Immediately upon landing in John's arms, Faith went still, staring up at his weathered face with unblinking focus.

"Incredible," Laura whispered as she watched her daughter, who had been moving since the minute the umbilical cord was cut, calm and drift off to sleep in her grandfather's arms. John seemed equally enthralled, and Anne leaned close to Laura's ear.

"I haven't seen him look at anyone like that since the days you and Abby were born," she said softly.

She was right; there was a peace and a joy on her father's face that Laura had never seen. Finally he looked up with a grin that split his face in two, tears in his eyes. "She's beautiful," he said in a voice brimming with emotion. Handing her back to Laura, he proceeded to pat Steven firmly on the back, seemingly unaware of the force with which he was doing so. Laura caught Steven's eye and winked as he winced in pain, but the smile never left his face. "You did well," John kept repeating, shaking his head in disbelief.

As Anne had predicted, Abby arrived as soon as she possibly could and was every bit the proud aunt as she cradled her new niece. Steven's parents were next, immaculately dressed, and as usual, on their way to a function. They hadn't even been in Minneapolis specifically for the birth of their first grandchild, but for a charity ball. They were dressed in their evening attire when they stopped in to "say hi," and they didn't stay long. While there, in their usual fashion, they kept a bit of distance—obviously pleased with the arrival of their granddaughter but without the warmth and emotion that Laura would have expected to accompany it.

Had she been paying attention, Laura would have seen the flash of disappointment in Steven's eyes as they said their good-byes and hurried out of the room, but as it was, she was too enraptured with the miracle in her arms to notice.

And Steven, for his part, pushed the emotion to the furthest corners of his mind where, at least for the time being, he could forget it existed.

༄

John

In over half a century on this earth, John Baxter had never experienced a feeling like the one that overwhelmed him now.

All of the joy that had been present at the birth of his own children was there now, but without that overwhelming sense of responsibility and pressure to taint it; he guessed that what he was feeling was pure, unadulterated joy.

All the hope of the future was, at the moment, wrapped in his arms in a soft pink blanket, and he couldn't tear his eyes away from her. He tried to picture her thirty years from now—heading a meeting, giving a presentation, holding her own child, changing the world—but struggled to see beyond the tiny face that stared back at him.

A sudden loneliness struck him as he realized he might not be here to see that—another difference between this and the birth of his own children—but even that couldn't dampen the overwhelming feeling of life that had consumed him.

Laura was asleep; the exhaustion of labor had finally caught up to her. Steven, Anne, and Abby had gone to the cafeteria for something to eat, so it was just John and Faith who sat awake in the warm light of dusk.

Hospital rooms had a tendency to take on a different feel depending on your reason for being there, and this one was no different. Everything felt warm and cozy. The soft evening light filtered in through the window behind the couch on which he sat, giving the room a golden glow and causing Faith to squirm in its glare. With his free arm, he positioned his hand over her face to block the sun from her eyes, and just as suddenly she stopped squirming. The dry weathered skin of his hand was a stark contrast to the smooth skin of her face, and a feeling of disbelief grasped him as he realized just how *new* she was. She hadn't even been on this earth for a day, yet she had a grasp on his heart that no one before her had ever accomplished.

"Faith," he smiled down at her, watching her eyes dart back and forth in their sockets as she took in his face. "You're probably pretty confused right now, huh? This world is a lot bigger than the one you've been in. Kind of scary, huh?"

She simply looked at him through impossibly big eyes.

"Yeah," he continued to coo, "it's scary. But you never have to worry. I won't let anything happen to you." He bent to softly kiss her tiny nose, and then positioned his body between her and the light coming in the window so he could free up his hand. She gripped his pinky with impressive force, and he smiled. "You're a strong one, I can tell. Pretty soon you won't even need my protection. You'll be beating up kids on the playground before you know it," he smiled at the fierceness he saw in her eyes. "But I'm going to protect you just the same, because you're my little girl. Yes, you are, yes, you are." He gave her an Eskimo kiss, rubbing his nose back and forth against hers.

"Were you like this with me when I was little?" A soft voice cut into his private moment, and he looked up a little sheepishly to see Laura smiling at him from across the room.

"Hey, you're awake." He rose to walk toward her and grudgingly relinquished his granddaughter into her arms. Laura just smiled sleepily and kissed her daughter on the forehead.

"Where is everyone?" she asked.

"They went to grab a bite. Do you want something? I can probably still catch them." He started toward the door, but Laura shook her head.

"I'm fine, thanks, Dad."

Unsure of what to do, John went back to the couch and sat down a bit awkwardly.

"Seriously," Laura continued, looking at him, "were you like that when we were little?"

Her question held no animosity or jealousy, but still he knew what she was getting at. He hadn't been the picture of warmth raising his own daughters. He'd loved them wholeheartedly and always took the time to let them know, but the hugs and kisses usually came from Anne.

When Laura was little, she'd bring her homework into his office in the evening and sit cross-legged on the floor as he worked, content to pass the time in companionable silence. At night he'd give each of his daughters a kiss goodnight, but this was usually the extent of his displays of affection. He couldn't understand why, with his granddaughter, it was suddenly different, but still he felt he owed Laura some sort of explanation.

"I wasn't the warmest Dad, was I?" he said apologetically and was about to continue when Laura laughed.

"Oh Daddy, you were the best," she said sincerely, and he felt his throat constrict with emotion. "We never had to guess at how much you loved us. I never felt uncared for, not for a minute. I'm just happy to see you like this with Faith. I can't explain how much it means to me, especially considering..." She trailed off and didn't have to finish for John to know what she was thinking about.

"I'm so sorry, Laur." He rose and walked to her bedside, placing his hand over hers. "You raise your kids, and you have these dreams and plans for them—a specific path you picture them walking. When that changes suddenly, it's hard." He swallowed the lump in his throat before continuing. "It's hard to see how their new path will bring the happiness you want for them. But now I see." Again he trailed off, unsure of how to finish that sentence, and so he decided to simply finish it there. "Now I see," he repeated, gazing with adoration at his new granddaughter, and trying to no avail to remember what life had been like before she'd entered it.

Tom

Tom shoved his hands deeper in his pockets and hunched his shoulders against the wind as he walked along upper Wacker Drive. Light shone from the windows of the buildings that towered over him, and he stopped to take in their splendor. Story after story of glass, steel, and stone lined either side of the river, all different and glorious in their architecture. He couldn't begin to comprehend the kind of mind that could conjure up those images and then turn around and create them. Just like that.

All men are gods, he'd read somewhere, a lifetime ago.

He'd liked that, the thought that man could create anything, do anything. But walking amongst these creations today, he felt none of his former awe.

He reached his hand into his briefcase, brushing his fingers against his newly signed divorce papers. Shaking his head, he started moving again, walking west, away from Michigan Avenue, away from the dinner he'd been dreading all day.

He tried to think of other things—of work, of Ben and Luke—but the overwhelming feeling of failure that he felt was what he kept coming back to.

He'd moved out of the house and into a small apartment on Huron Street. Its white walls made it feel impersonal and almost institutional, but at the time, anything had felt more welcoming than his house.

Well, Beth's house now.

The animosity between the two had been growing since their decision to separate—much due in part to Beth. He didn't want to place blame, but the woman changed her mind at the rate of an Olympic hurdler. One day she was fine with their decision to divorce—friendly even, asking about work and his new life downtown. The next thing he knew, she was in tears, lamenting her life in the suburbs with the kids, while he had "the time of his life" in the city.

Right, he'd thought. *The time of my life.* If anything, his life had become all the more complicated. Now, his time with his own children came with a forty-five-minute commute attached to either end of it. Add that to his long work hours and he'd barely had a minute for himself these last few months. Now that he took the time to think about it—he'd had *no* time for himself.

But this obvious imbalance did nothing to counter the effect of his overwhelming sense of guilt. It plagued him from the moment he woke up to that welcome moment when sleep finally found him. He felt it every time Beth called in tears, her words slurring ever so slightly, a result of drinks that she'd never felt the need for in the past. He knew his children were in no real danger—she'd never allow herself to slip—but still, those nights that she called crying, he felt less for her than he did for his two boys, upstairs in bed. He wondered at the toll all of this was taking on them—and as a result probably overcompensated, spending every spare minute with them that he could. Which, as a result, only confused Beth more, at times mistaking his time at the house for an attempt to reconcile with her. Which was exactly what had prompted her to burst into tears this evening when he'd presented her with the divorce papers—tangible proof that their marriage was over.

He had decided it would be best to do it at a neutral location, on neither of their "home turf." It was a decision he'd come to regret in the short span of an hour. Her tears had come and gone throughout the night, disappearing for a blessed span of minutes before reappearing with more drinks.

Now, walking home, some of Beth's cutting remarks haunted him. He knew they were little more than her anger and her hurt talking, but still he knew they'd stay with him forever. And again, he wondered why, when both parties had come to a decision together, it was the one who finalized it who became the bad guy.

Yet underneath these thoughts—behind the feelings of failure, peeking out from underneath those feelings of inadequacy and guilt—there were thoughts of someone else entirely.

He'd seen her today when she'd come into the office for an interview, and he couldn't shake feeling like he'd known her from somewhere. She wheeled a small black suitcase behind her—she must have flown in for it—and something about the addition of that small piece of luggage made her all the more familiar.

Tom had noticed her from the minute she entered the office—hair the color of honey, eyes the color of Christmas. And the thing he couldn't comprehend was that he knew those thoughts had come to him before—those descriptions had scrolled their lovely words across his mind already—but he couldn't place her. All he knew, though, was that from the moment he saw her, he didn't want to stop looking. Something about her had captured his attention within seconds, and he couldn't seem to tear his eyes away.

When she'd finally approached his desk for an introduction, he'd looked into her eyes and forgotten everything. He could hardly breathe. The voice of the office's administrative assistant, dutifully making introductions, had become nothing but blurred background noise. All he could see was the gentle curve of her face, the light in her eyes that seemed to double as soon as they'd focused on his. The way her smile just about split her face in two, the melodic sound of her voice.

And perhaps this was why his guilt overwhelmed him now, because during his entire dinner with Beth, a woman he'd at one time pledged his life and love to—a woman who at least deserved his attention tonight as all of that came to an end—all he'd been able to think about had been a woman named Abby Baxter.

༄

CHAPTER FOUR

Abby

"Anyone who knows my fian—*wife*," Steven corrected himself midsentence, shaking his head happily as though he still couldn't believe that he'd married Laura mere hours ago, "knows as well as I do that you can't spend five minutes with her and *not* fall in love with her. The light in her eyes, her sincerity, the kindness in her smile—these are all things I fell in love with immediately. It was only as I got to know her better that I learned, and loved, what was behind them. That light in her eyes is her constant stream of energy, love, determination, drive: her utter excitement for life and all the possibilities it holds. And that kindness in her smile...that kindness is the most genuine I've ever known. I've never met someone so generous, so sweet, so loving..." He stopped for a moment, his voice quivering with an onslaught of emotion and his eyes brimming with tears.

As Steven fought to regain control of his emotions, Abby stole a glance at the other men in the room and almost laughed. She could read the look on their faces as though they had spoken the words out loud. *Nice, you sap. Ruin it for the rest of us. As a direct result of this impromptu speech of yours, my wife is going to start asking me why I don't say nice things like this to her.*

"I don't know if it's unconventional for the groom to give a speech," Steven was continuing, gesturing to his four-month-old daughter who was asleep in the arms of his bride, "but we've certainly been pretty unconventional up to this point." His comment brought a ripple of laughter from the guests, but Abby thought she saw tension in the way the corner of her father's mouth rose into a smile. She looked at Laura to see if she'd noticed, but her sister's eyes were trained adoringly on Steven and seemed unaffected. "Laura," he continued, turning to her. "Knowing you...knowing I get to wake up next to you for the rest of my life...well, it just makes me want to live that much longer."

With that simple statement and a trembling hand, he set down the microphone and kissed his new wife on the forehead. Laura's eyes were dancing, her face aglow with happiness, and as she picked up the microphone to utter a response to Steven, Abby looked around the room. Her sister had picked a beautiful venue for her wedding reception—floor-to-ceiling windows lining the far wall, which overlooked the lake, chandeliers dripping with crystals suspended from vaulted ceilings. Tea lanterns surrounded periwinkle hydrangeas in the middle of each table, the napkins adorned with antique lace. Each guest's name was encased in a vintage silver frame, the shiny surfaces reflecting the candlelight and casting it in the most flattering way upon all the faces in the crowd. A dance floor stood ready and waiting in the corner, an orchestra of musicians ready to play the big-band music her sister had requested. The only word that came to mind to sum up the ambiance was *exquisite*, and she felt ashamed for the flash of jealousy that overcame her.

She was happy for her sister in every way. She'd found someone to love, who loved her; she had a beautiful baby girl, and now a beautiful wedding. It was everything she'd ever dreamed for her little sister, but no matter how she spun it, she still struggled to look past the fact that it was also everything she'd ever dreamed for *herself*.

She hadn't brought a date—telling everyone it was because she'd be too busy with her maid of honor duties, but she figured they all knew the real reason behind it—she didn't have one to bring. Pushing her own feelings aside, she watched as Steven led Laura onto the dance floor for their first dance as husband and wife.

Laura's gown floated behind her as he twirled her around, her train bustled in the back. With a smile, Abby recalled shopping for that very dress with her sister.

Laura had flown in from Minneapolis the previous November, two days before Steven would be driving down to join them for Thanksgiving before driving both of them back up, to do her dress shopping in Chicago and scope out wedding locations. He'd only proposed a few days before, but as was consistent with her personality, she'd wanted to get started right away. She'd arrived in typical Laura fashion, two suitcases and a purse the size of a hockey bag, all for a long weekend. Abby hadn't seen her since her visit to Minneapolis nearly five months before, when Laura had told her of her pregnancy, and was waiting anxiously by the baggage claim for her. When she finally appeared, Abby almost didn't recognize her. Her sister *would* be the only woman in the world who actually looked thinner during her pregnancy, her face lean and absolutely glowing, toned arms expertly navigating her bags through the crowds.

"What on *earth* have you been doing?" Abby had cried. "You look fantastic!"

"Yoga!" Laura practically shouted, literally bursting with happiness.

There was that familiar pang of jealousy. Abby shoved it back where it came from and flashed her sister a grin. "Well, it's certainly working! You've never looked better, lady!"

"Thanks," came Laura's response, and all of a sudden, she was in tears.

"What the...Laura? What's wrong?" Abby's concern was immediate, and she ushered her sister over toward the doors where they could have a little privacy.

"Nothing!" Laura choked out. "It's the hormones. I've been all over the place!"

Abby had laughed as Laura pulled herself together, her face once again animated.

"Who in the world decides to go wedding-dress shopping when they're seven months pregnant?" Abby had inquired the next morning as she twirled from side to side and admired the veil she had draped over her head. Their mother was wandering around the shop, after giving Abby strict instructions to call her over the minute Laura came out of the dressing room.

"I do!" Laura called happily from the dressing room.

"Yeah, but you really can't try anything on! I mean your waist is going to go back to being disgustingly tiny by the time you walk down the aisle." Even as she said it, she knew Laura's waist, even seven months pregnant, was about the same circumference as most women's were normally. You couldn't even tell she was pregnant from behind or from the front—only when looking at her from the side could you tell that her sister was carrying a child. She gazed at her own waist in the mirror—slender, but nothing like Laura's. Her sister had certainly gotten the good genes.

"I wouldn't have any other time to do it!" Laura protested. "Plus, I think I just found my dress!"

"You did?" Abby was suddenly interested, tearing her eyes away from her own reflection. "Isn't that the first one you've tried on?"

"Yeah, but this is it!" Laura said with confidence, pushing aside the dressing room curtain and appearing in front of Abby.

Abby literally had to bite her tongue to keep from laughing out loud. Her sister stood before her wearing a circus tent. It was a beautiful, *ivory* circus tent, dripping with beads and lace, but it was a circus tent nonetheless. "Well, my first question was going to be how you got into it without my help, but that answers it for me. Laura! Are you serious? That thing is about fourteen times too big for you!"

None of the defensiveness she'd expected to see in Laura's eyes appeared, and for the second time that weekend she wondered if maybe this pregnancy thing wasn't such a bad idea after all.

"It's one of a kind," Laura justified. "A vintage gown, the only one they have. I can have it altered."

"Who did it belong to, Mama Cass?" Abby cried. "I mean it's huge!"

"I'm getting it," Laura shot back.

There was the defensive sister she knew and loved.

"Fine, your call. But I'm not cancelling your bachelorette party the week before your wedding to take you emergency last-minute dress shopping because this one turned out to be a bust."

As Anne and Laura paid for the dress that day, Abby had watched from the doorway, shaking her head and wondering if her sister knew what she was doing. But watching Laura on the dance floor today, her beloved dress tailored to a perfect fit, she felt nothing but a sense of awe at the way her sister seemed to have an innate ability to see the extraordinary in the mundane, to see the promise in something that no one else could.

It was as if she could see the outcome *before* she made the decision.

"Can I have this dance?" Her father's voice pulled her from her reverie, and she smiled, accepting his outstretched hand.

"Absolutely!" Abby's floor length satin gown swirled around her legs as John led her onto the dance floor. All the bridesmaids wore the same black strapless dress and had carried a small bouquet of tea roses down the aisle.

"It's a beautiful wedding, isn't it?" John mused, and Abby nodded, resting her chin on her father's shoulder.

"She did a good job." She let her eyes rest on her mother, who sat at the head table holding Faith, her face aglow with pride as she talked to a group of women who were admiring the baby.

"How are you doing?" John asked, and Abby pulled back to look at him.

"I'm fine, Daddy. Why?"

"Well, you know. It's got to be a little difficult to watch your sister go through all of this. I know that a good marriage and a good family has always been a dream for both of you girls, and to watch Laura get all of that in a year..." Abby's eyes had filled with tears, and John trailed off when he noticed them.

"Abby, I—"

"No, Dad," she cut him off. "I'm not crying because I'm sad—it's just so sweet of you to think of that. Yeah, it's a little hard. I mean, it would be easier if I were dancing tonight with a serious boyfriend." She flashed him a wry smile, and her father laughed.

"If you think for a minute, Abby, that all of this isn't in store for you, well, then you're wrong. Somewhere out there is a guy who will be the *luckiest* guy in the world the day he finds you."

"Oh, Dad," Abby wiped a tear from her cheek before resting it on his shoulder. "Thank you."

"That's not lip service. It's the truth," John said, back to his gruff self. "But listen to me, I know it seems like your sister is living out the life you've always wanted, and sure, in a way she is. But those two have quite the road to travel. It's all uphill from here, and it's not going to be easy. I hope you understand that, and that you can put this competitive side behind you. Because she's going to need you every step of the way," he concluded.

"I know," Abby nodded. "I'm trying, Dad. Just human nature, I think. Sister stuff."

"Well," John cleared his throat, out of things to say. "It's a beautiful wedding."

"Yes, it is," Abby repeated, and let her father twirl her around the dance floor.

∽

Steven

Steven lay awake and watched his new wife sleeping beside him. Her hair fell across her forehead and over her nose, and it puffed out with every breath. He smiled as he gingerly pushed it out of her face and tucked it behind her ear. She stirred at his touch, reaching up to cover his hand with hers.

"Laur?" he whispered, but realized, when she didn't answer that she had done so in her sleep.

With a sigh, he closed his eyes and drew her closer to him, the heat of her body warming him to the core. He opened one eye to glance at the crib they had set up against the far wall—the crib where Faith slept peacefully, and suddenly felt a tightening in his chest that caused him to sit up and gasp for air.

"Babe? What is it?" Laura groaned, propping herself up on her elbows before dropping her head back onto the pillow in her weariness.

Steven gasped, struggling for breath. "Sorry to wake you, just a bad dream," he lied, watching as she drifted back to sleep. As soon a her breathing was steady again, he eased himself out of bed and walked over to Faith's crib, peering inside to where she was sleeping peacefully. His pounding heart slowed a little to see her safe, but as he looked around the room, it picked up again. He'd never had an anxiety attack before, but he assumed he was in the throes of one now and tried to focus on the normalcy of the room around him.

Laura's bouquet sat amidst many other party favors on the hotel dresser; her veil hung over the bathroom door. She had changed out of her dress at the reception and sent it home with her mother to take to the dry cleaners before heading off with Steven and Faith for the weekend getaway that would pass as their honeymoon.

They'd arrived at the lakeside lodge an hour ago, and after getting Faith to sleep in her traveling crib, had toasted their new life with champagne the hotel had provided. The champagne glasses sat empty on the bedside table amidst scattered flowers from his boutonniere.

These mementos from such a happy night combined with his wife and baby daughter asleep a few steps away should have filled him with joy, yet here he was, struggling for breath.

He knew he loved both Laura and Faith more than anything he'd ever loved, but couldn't help but wonder, as he paced the room restlessly, if he could give them what they needed. His life suddenly held ten times the responsibility than it had just a year ago, and the abruptness of the change left the room spinning around him.

He thought of his own parents—their presence at his wedding tonight the first time he'd seen them since the birth of his daughter four months before. What kind of example had his own father set for him? Wrapped up in his work and hardly ever home, Steven had lived in fear, since the day he found out Laura was pregnant, that he would be the same kind of father, that kind of husband.

"No," he said out loud as he walked back to Faith's crib now. "I love them too much. I won't let it happen."

"Let what happen?" Damn, his wife was a light sleeper. "Steven? What are you doing? Is Faith okay?" A look of panic crossed Laura's sleepy face as she saw him standing near the crib in the middle of the night, and she hurriedly began to get out of bed.

"Everything's fine." He quickly sat down, urging her back under the covers before joining her there and pulling her into his arms. "Just thinking," he said, kissing the back of her head.

"About what?" she yawned, relaxing in his embrace.

"Tonight. How much I love you."

"I love you too," she slurred as sleep found her again, but Steven remained awake, listening to the steady breath of the woman in his arms, straining to hear his daughter breathing nearby—and as he felt the tightening return to his chest, wondered how he could keep this up for a lifetime.

༄

Laura

"How'd it go?" Laura cradled the phone on one shoulder a few days later, balancing Faith in her other arm while simultaneously trying to get her to take the bottle she held in front of her mouth, only half listening to her sister's response.

"Good, I think," Abby was saying. "I had no idea this process would take so long!" She'd just had her third interview with an agency she desperately wanted to work for.

"Well, I've heard it's pretty standard to go through several interviews for those kind of firms," Laura sympathized, sighing with relief as Faith began to eat, finally relaxing and giving her full attention to her sister. "How long has it been now?"

"Since just before Faith was born," Abby groaned, "so I don't know, four months? This has to be the longest interview process ever!"

"Yeah, I'm not looking forward to that day," Laura said, for once glad that she had a few years of college ahead of her. Abby had been job searching for almost half a year with no luck. She'd graduated earlier that month and had just moved into an apartment in Lincoln Park. Rent was expensive, and Laura knew she was anxious to start paying the bills.

"Was this your third interview with them?" she inquired. As Abby began to talk about how her first interview had been simply informational, since they'd had no job openings at the time, Laura turned on the TV, stopping on the Ellen DeGeneres show and laughing to herself as two members of the audience ran blindfolded across the stage, both in pursuit of the same object.

"Are you listening to me?" Laura could hear the annoyance in Abby's question.

"Yeah." She grimaced and quickly pressed the mute button. "You were talking about meeting with the team you'd be working with, and how they each have samples of the product you'd be representing on their desks."

"Right," Abby continued. "It's cool. It really makes you want to get involved with the product you're advertising. And they have big bowls at the reception desk full of the brand of gum they represent—it's free, so all the employees grab some on their way back from lunch."

"I like that." Laura shifted Faith's weight in her arms. At a little over four months old, she was already more than twice the weight she had been when she was born. "I like that they really get behind their brands. Is that required when they sign on with a company?"

"I don't know, maybe," Abby said thoughtfully. "I guess I should probably find out."

At that, Laura chuckled. "Yeah, probably. So when do you hear about the job?"

"Hopefully by next week. They really seemed to like me, and I know the interviews themselves went well. Now it's just a matter of how much experience they're looking for—I only had one internship through college, and that was the summer going into junior year."

Laura could hear in her sister's voice how badly she wanted this job. "You'll get it," she assured her. "I have a feeling about it."

"Thanks," Abby sighed, and Laura waited, listening to what sounded like drawers slamming on the other end of the line.

"Well, the honeymoon was great, in case you were wondering," she offered when Abby didn't say anything.

"Great," her sister sounded uninterested.

"The hotel had a daycare service, so Steven and I got to go out for nice dinners all three nights," she continued. "There was one place in particular that was amazing—you'll have to get your next boyfriend to take you there. The food was—"

"I'm glad you guys had a good time," Abby cut her off.

"What's your deal?" Laura asked, bristling. After all the times she had listened to Abby talk about one heartache or another, the fact that she couldn't talk about her *honeymoon* with her sister made her mad.

"Nothing," Abby said. "I'm just sick of hearing about it."

"After all the times I've let you talk and talk after a breakup, you can't let me talk about my honeymoon?" Laura tried to keep her voice down for the sake of her daughter, who was dozing in her arms while slowly finishing her bottle.

"No, you can talk all you want about it. I just don't think you're being very sensitive!" Abby shot back.

"What are you talking about?" Laura cried.

"Look," came Abby's hurried response. "I know you're in love, and you guys have this great life, and I couldn't be happier for you, really. I mean that. But Laur, I'm not even *close* to that. I don't even have a boyfriend, much less someone I'd consider settling down with. So I just wish you'd keep that in mind every time you call me to gush about how perfect your life is."

"My life is *not* perfect!" Laura shouted, startling Faith. "Do you know how hard this is? Steven and I barely see each other already, and we've been married all of a week. And it's just going to get harder before it gets easier. We're both working on crazy-busy schedules, money's tight, and we have a baby to worry about! Don't tell me my life is perfect!"

"That's not what I meant and you know it," Abby sighed. "I know it's not perfect, but you have a daughter and a husband—people to love and who love you, and you guys can get through it together. That's all I'm talking about."

"You have people that love you, too," Laura said, unwilling to let this go. "Me, Mom, and Dad," she paused, and Abby took full advantage.

"That's not the same. You know what I mean! You were single just a few years go. It sucks! I don't have a last call of the night, or someone to bring to family functions…" Now Abby trailed off, and Laura shook her head.

"I'll be your last call of the night," she offered. On some level she understood and wanted to comfort her sister, but she thought Abby was being ridiculous.

"I know," Abby sounded defeated, frustrated, and Laura softened.

"I know though, Abby. It's not the same."

"No," Abby choked back a sob, and Laura sat up, startled.

"Hey, Abs…why is this such a big deal to you?"

"I don't know," Abby began, clearly crying. "I'm just lonely. Everything feels unsettled—I don't have a job, all my friends kind of dispersed after graduation, I'm in a new apartment in a new part of the city…I'm just in transition, and it sucks."

"Well, I'm unsettled too," Laura argued, thinking of all the uncertainty her and Steven's future held.

"Yeah, but you just committed to someone for a lifetime," Abby seemed hell bent on feeling sorry for herself. "You have someone to be unsettled with, which isn't nearly as lonely."

"Yeah, I guess you have a point," Laura relented. "Sorry, Abby, I'll try not to talk so much about Steven and I."

"No, that's not what I—" Abby began, and then sighed loudly. "Never mind, you don't get it."

"What don't I get?" Laura started to argue, and then thought better of it. "You know what—let's just change the subject."

"You know what, Laur, I actually have to go. I'll call you tomorrow." Abby barely gave Laura time to say good-bye before hanging up, and she flung the phone down in frustration.

"Your aunt has trouble seeing past her own nose," she said to Faith, and then immediately regretted it. Maybe Abby was right, and she needed to be a little more sensitive. Still, as she looked down at the child in her arms, she reminded herself that she had bigger things to focus on.

∽

CHAPTER FIVE

Abby

"I want to apologize," Abby put down her glass of champagne, "for the way I've been acting the last few months." She looked around the table at her parents, sister, and brother-in-law. The group had gathered for a night of celebration. Laura and Steven had both been accepted into their programs of choice at local schools and began classes in a few weeks. And as for Abby, she had *finally* gotten the job she'd been after, and started in a few days. Faith, now almost seven months old, was at home with a babysitter, and the five adults now sat with champagne in front of them, toasting each other's recent successes. Abby's toast, however, was turning into more of an apology.

"I've been pretty selfish," she continued, "and it wasn't fair to take it out on you all. I think the larger issues at stake were my own insecurities—worries over finding a job, worries over finding an apartment, worries over finding anyone who will ever love me the way you guys love each other." She motioned first at her parents and then at Steven and Laura. "But dwelling on that has kept me from being as happy for you as I should have been, and I'm sorry. I'm taking some time to focus on myself, and I think I'm at a better place. Or I will be."

Awkwardly, she put her champagne back on the table.

"I feel like we're at an AA meeting or something." Steven broke the tension, and Abby burst out laughing.

"Hello, my name is Abby, and I'm a worry-holic."

"Hi, Abby," the table said, in unison, which made everyone laugh. Steven winked at Abby, and she smiled back, enjoying the easy banter between herself and her brother-in-law. She'd always hoped to get along with whomever Laura chose to marry and was glad she got along so well with Steven.

"Well, I for one could *not* be more proud of my big sister." Laura raised her glass. "Taking the conventional route, doing everything by the book, and doing it *really well*," she smiled and toasted Abby.

"Here-here!" John cried, raising his own glass.

"And to two *wonderful* parents," Anne added, gesturing toward Laura and Steven. "You two are raising a beautiful daughter, and we're both proud of the way you're taking on each new challenge."

Abby watched Laura blush, and they all took a sip.

"All right, this is getting pretty cheesy," she laughed. "Congratulations everyone. Now let's move on. What I want to know is what Faith is going to be for her first Halloween!"

"That's still over a month away!" John chuckled.

"Yes, but knowing Laura, she's had the costume picked out since before Faith was born," Anne laughed, and Laura nodded.

"It's true. I have."

"That's news to me!" Steven protested. "How did I not know about this?"

"Sorry, babe, I picked up the costume a few months ago and just forgot to show you, I guess. But wait until you see it."

"Well? What is it?" Abby asked, curious.

"It's a surprise!" Laura beamed. "You'll see it on Halloween."

While Abby and Anne protested, John held up his hands.

"Whatever she goes as, she'll be the cutest trick-or-treater there is," he smiled. Abby could see the love and warmth in her father's eyes, and one look at Laura's face told her she'd seen it too.

"Wait until you see her, Dad," she was saying, as if it had been months since John had seen Faith instead of mere days. "She's starting to fumble around words."

"Not *words*," Steven cut her off loudly, a little confrontationally.

"Well, *sounds*," Laura continued, shooting her husband a look that Abby couldn't read. "She—" Laura looked thoughtful, and then put her head in her hands. "I *completely* forgot what I was going to say."

"That happens a lot these days," Steven kidded, but again Abby heard a hint of confrontation.

"Well, I'm always *tired*," Laura shot back. "I don't get a whole lot of time to sleep, if you haven't noticed."

"Oh, I've noticed," Steven said under his breath before changing the subject. "The Bears look like they'll have a good season, huh, John?"

As the men began to talk sports, Laura stood and excused herself to go to the bathroom. Abby quickly followed suit.

"What was that about?" she asked as the door swung shut behind them.

"What?" Laura seemed oblivious to the tension as she fluffed her hair in the mirror before letting herself into the second to last stall.

"That thing between you and Steven. Did you have a fight or something?"

"Oh, no, not really," Laura called through the metal partition. "We're just both pretty stressed and tired. Yesterday he got home after working all day, and I literally handed him Faith on my way out the door so I could get to the restaurant."

Abby nodded, listening as she carefully applied lip-gloss in the mirror, waiting for her sister to emerge.

"I'm so ready to be done there," Laura was continuing. "I mean, I'll miss the tips, but I won't miss the hours."

For the time being, Laura had been waitressing at a local restaurant while Steven worked construction, something he'd done throughout high school, much to his parents' dismay. He was up and out the door by 5:00 a.m., leaving her with Faith all day. When he got home at four thirty, Laura was on her way out to the restaurant, where she worked until one o'clock in the morning, getting home well after both Faith and Steven had gone to bed. Even weekends were busy, both of them working Saturdays and sometimes Sundays to get some extra money.

"We just need some time together, and with our new schedules this fall, I think things will get better." Laura joined Abby at the sink and began to wash her hands.

"What are your new schedules?" Abby leaned close to the mirror to inspect a mascara smudge.

"I'll be in school all day while Steven works, then he's going to try and schedule whatever courses he can at night, so when I'm not working, he'll be at school. That way one of us is always home with Faith."

"So if you're in school all day and working at night, when are you going to see Faith?" Abby questioned.

"Well, I was able to figure it out so most of my courses are online. So I can spend Monday's and Tuesdays at home with Faith, and Wednesday's she'll be in daycare."

"What about Thursdays and Fridays?"

"Mom and Dad are going to watch Faith for us. That way we only have to pay for day care once a week."

"How is that any better than the schedule you have now?"

"Well, we saved enough over the summer that neither of us have to work weekends anymore, so at least we'll have Saturdays and Sundays together now."

"Yeah, that's really a treat," Abby said dryly. "Geez, Laur, I didn't realize just how crazy your schedule would be. Can I help at all?"

"You're a great big sister." Laura gave Abby a squeeze as they walked back out into the restaurant. "But we've got it covered. Maybe you can just try to get Steven to smile. He's been a sourpuss all week." She winked at Abby.

"I can't make any promises," Abby laughed, "but I'll try."

"I thought you'd fallen in," Steven said as Laura sat back down beside him, and Abby wanted to kick him. He'd tried to pass it off as a joke, but Abby could see Laura's face fall a little as he said it.

"She did fall in." She looked directly at him. "You should be impressed at how quickly she dried off."

Steven gave her a funny look before picking up his fork and taking a bite of his chicken, turning to Laura to ask her something Abby couldn't hear.

"Laura said you're going to watch Faith for her a few days a week this fall," she addressed her mother.

"We're excited about that," Anne beamed, glancing at John before looking back to Abby. "It will fun to be a more constant part of her life, and get to see her more often."

"Mom, you guys see her once a week as it is," Abby reminded her. "You're already a huge part of her life."

"Well, you know what I mean," Anne laughed, and Abby nodded.

"I'm jealous," she said through a bite of halibut before catching her mom's warning glance. "Sorry," she said, tempted to stick out her food-filled tongue and teach her mother a lesson. Instead she kept her tongue in her mouth and looked back to Steven and Laura, who were laughing over something private.

Maybe it's not so bad after all, Abby thought as she watched him give her sister a quick kiss on the cheek before returning to his dinner. They seemed happy at the moment. Laura was probably right; they were just at their limit right now, and things would calm down soon.

༄

Laura

The next night Laura tried to raise her voice over Faith's wails as she attempted to answer her husband's question. "She's fine," she was saying, "I think she may just be constipated. She's been fussy all day and hasn't pooped yet." As soon as the words were out of her mouth, she stopped in her tracks. *Did I just say that?* she thought, cradling the phone on one shoulder and her squirming, screaming daughter on the opposite hip. *Sexy. Probably just what Steven called to hear.* To his credit, Steven seemed legitimately concerned about their daughter's digestive issues, and did his part to offer some advice, but what did he know about it? What did either of them know, for that matter? Faith wouldn't even turn one for another few months; technically this was still foreign territory.

On the other hand, it was this kind of conversation that had begun to dominate their time together, whether in person or on the phone, which gave the illusion that they'd been parents far longer than they actually had. Laura longed for the days of intelligent conversation—even talk of politics, which would have usually bored her, would be a welcome break right now. Last night she'd actually caught herself speaking to Steven in the same baby voice she used when she spoke to Faith.

It didn't help that they were running on the busiest schedule in the world. Between the stress of their individual lives and the strain of seeing each other so infrequently, perhaps they'd simply given up on trying to catch up on each other's lives and simply talk about the one thing they had in common these days—Faith.

Which was where they'd wound up on the phone today, discussing their daughter's pooping habits over a bad connection as her cries carried over both of their voices.

"Hey, B, I'm going to go. I'll see you in a few hours." Steven was clearly frustrated, and it wasn't until Laura hung up the phone that she realized neither of them had said "I love you." It was becoming less and less frequent, and she wondered if they were simply comfortable enough in their love that they didn't need to verify it verbally, or if there was a larger issue at stake here. She tried to focus on him calling her B, a shortened version of "babe" that was his term of endearment for her, but even that didn't offer much consolation. Lately he hadn't seemed interested in talking on the phone for any longer than it took to cover the basics, and he'd been staying away from the house for longer intervals. Though she knew she could trust him, she wondered why he so often stayed away—choosing to study at the library when he could do it at home, or taking on all the extra hours of work that he could.

Laura glanced at her reflection in the front hall mirror as she walked around the house, Faith still in her arms, trying to calm her down. Her hair was greasy and matted to her head in the ponytail she'd put it in—yesterday. She did a mental calculation of the last time she'd showered and decided after ten seconds that if it took this long to figure out, it had been too long. Her T-shirt was stained, her jeans ripped, and as she looked down, she realized her toenails were a disaster. *When was the last time I've had a pedicure? When was the last time I've even **cut** my toenails?* The latter of the thoughts came to her upon closer inspection of her toes, and she wondered how on earth Steven woke up in the morning *not* bleeding from the ankles down. *Gross, Laura,* she scolded herself and made a mental note to put a little effort into her appearance—as soon as she got Faith down for a nap.

But the child was still crying, too young to tell Laura what was wrong but old enough to know exactly what crying would do for her.

"*What* can I do for you, darling?" Laura asked through gritted teeth, looking into her daughter's face. Her nose and mouth were chapped from the morning of crying, her eyes red and swollen, forehead crumpled in her discontent. "Are you hungry? Do you want a some sweet potatoes?" She reached to open the fridge, but this only seemed to make her daughter angrier as she struggled in Laura's grasp, her cries intensifying. *As if I'm supposed to know that this is exactly what you **don't** want!* She thought, unaware of whether or not she'd actually muttered the words out loud. "How about *Baby Einstein*? Should we watch some *Baby Einstein*?" She tried, but again, as she reached for the remote, Faith only seemed to get more upset. "All right, then, you know what?" Laura cried, at the end of her rope. "You're going to take a nap." She marched toward Faith's nursery, fighting her daughter every step of the way. She plopped her down in the middle of her crib, the side guards up and locked in position, and handed her that ratty blanket she loved so much before plopping a kiss on her tear-stained forehead and walking out of the room. Faith's screams only seemed to get louder the farther she walked from her bedroom, and she stopped in the hallway to massage her throbbing temples before picking up the phone and dialing a number she'd already dialed twice this morning.

"Hi, Dolores," she said wearily as the nurse at the pediatrician's office answered. Dolores didn't even have to say anything to know where she wanted to be transferred, and within seconds she was on the phone with her daughter's doctor, asking him if he was *sure* that she shouldn't bring her in, and what was she supposed to do for constipation? Was it rub her stomach first counterclockwise once, and then clockwise three times, or was it clockwise first and then counterclockwise? And from whose perspective—hers or Faith's? He patiently fielded her questions—again—and as she hung up, she wondered how many phone calls he must get like this per day. *Poor man*, she thought, and then immediately replaced it with *poor **me***, listening to her daughter wailing from the other room. Pulling an egg timer out of the drawer next to the oven, Laura set it for ten minutes. If Faith hadn't quieted down by then, she was going back in there and taking her to the doctor, no matter *what* he'd just told her.

It was her proximity to the oven that reminded her that she hadn't even *thought* about dinner.

Damn, she checked her watch. The number that stared back at her told her two things: It was far too late for Faith to be starting her nap—she'd be terrible for Steven tonight and he had to study, and it was far too late to do anything about dinner. Steven would be home in a half hour, and she still had to get ready for work. *Grab dinner on your way home, forgot to get it started. Sorry,* she texted Steven as she surveyed the empty freezer. She made a mental note to make sure and get groceries tomorrow, wracking her brain to try to conjure up the other mental note she'd *just* made, to no avail.

I'm losing my mind, she thought as her phone vibrated on the counter. She flipped it open to find Steven's curt response: *K*. Steven was a man of few words, that was for sure, but lately he'd started speaking to her strictly in letters and acronyms. *Where are you* had become *WAU*, and although some of them could be romantic, like those little messages he sent her that simply said *MU, LU* (miss you, love you), she found herself wishing he'd take the time to actually spell them out. Or better yet, call her and *say* them like everyone else seemed to manage. But not only did she not complain, she found herself doing the same right back to him, seduced by how quickly you could pound out an e-mail if you didn't actually have to spell any words. Time was of an essence these days, and so like so many other aspects of her life, communication with Steven had become little more than short, informative quips.

Her phone vibrated again, and she flipped it open to see that Steven had elaborated his response—quickly adding on that acronym that made her heart melt every time.

AFUMA. *Anything for you, mi amore.*

With a grin, she flipped her phone shut and listened for Faith, who had, miraculously, reduced her noise to a slight whimper. Laura pictured her in there—fighting sleep to the death, thumb in mouth. She smiled at the image, thinking *this day just might get better* as she ran up the stairs two at a time, baby monitor clipped to her jeans, to get ready for work.

John

The minute Steven answered the door John could see the relief on the younger man's face. The lasagna in John's arms was probably the only dinner his son-in-law had even had time to think of all day, and he had eyed it hungrily the whole way to the kitchen.

Faith, who looked like she had just woken up, broke into a huge grin from where she sat in her baby bouncer.

"Hi, Princess!" he grinned right back at her and, after setting the casserole dish on the counter, took her face in his hands and planted a kiss on her forehead. Pulling away, he marveled again at just how much she was starting to look like Anne. Straightening, he turned to Steven, who was already lifting the tin foil off the lasagna and pulling two plates out of the cupboard, as well as a jar of baby food.

"Thank you, you made my night. I was just standing here rifling through the fridge and trying to find something. Laura told me to grab dinner on the way home, but I completely forgot until I was pulling in the driveway."

John simply nodded and patted the younger man on the back as he dished a steaming scoop of lasagna onto both of their plates. Both of them laughed as Steven attempted to spoon-feed Faith from the jar of baby food. Most of it ended up on her face, the rest on the floor, with a very small amount actually making it to her mouth, and Steven's smile turned to a grimace as he rose to get a rag. "Laura's going to kill me," he announced, surveying the mess. There was food all over the floor, and Faith had even managed to fling some onto the living room carpet.

John frowned. "I'm sure she'll understand—Faith's just a baby yet!" He gestured to the little girl, happily gumming her food.

Shaking his head, Steven began to wipe up the table. "Usually, yeah, she would. But God…" He trailed off, staring off into space before continuing the task at hand. "Lately she's been pretty stressed out," he finished.

"It's a difficult age, huh?" John motioned to Faith once again.

"Yeah, but it's more than just Faith. It's been a rough year on both of us. We just don't see each other much at all, and she works so late, then has to get up early with the baby…it's just tough. On her especially, but it takes its toll."

John didn't pry further, but he could see in the sag of Steven's shoulders that he wasn't exaggerating.

On the drive home, he couldn't get the image of how he'd left Steven out of his mind. John had stayed to help put Faith to bed and then cleaned the kitchen while Steven began his studies. Yet after he'd snuck into Faith's room to blow her one more kiss good night, he'd reentered the living room to see his son-in-law sitting with his head in his hands, books sprawled in front of him, stress and exhaustion personified. *They're young and strong and in love,* he kept telling himself, but as he hung his keys on the key rack, he wondered just how much love allowed you to tolerate before other factors had to be weighed.

There was an anxious message waiting on his machine from Abby; after more than six months of interviews, she'd finally gotten hired at an advertising agency downtown and started work tomorrow. She'd wanted this job so badly, and the agency had wanted her; they'd just needed to wait for a spot to open up. It had, and he hadn't seen Abby so excited about anything in a long time. The message stated very clearly that she'd be going to bed at eight thirty, and that he shouldn't call her back if he got home later than that, because she wanted to get a good night's sleep. John smiled at his eldest daughter's specifications. She'd always been that way. He could hear the excitement in her voice, and as the message ended, he checked the clock. It was 9:05, too late to call her back.

"I left the message from Abby on the machine for you," Anne said as she walked in from the living room and gave him a kiss on the cheek. "I called her back when I got home from knitting. She really sounds excited."

"Good," John smiled, pouring himself a glass of water. "She really needed this job. I can't believe what a tough road it's been."

"Well, the economy hasn't been great. Some agencies actually went out of business," Anne reminded him, and he nodded.

"Yeah, but still. I'm just happy she got in."

"Me too," Anne agreed. "How were Faith and Steven?"

"They loved your lasagna," he told her, and she smiled with satisfaction. If there was one thing his wife loved, it was cooking for people, and he was especially glad she had done it tonight. "He really seemed stressed out," John continued.

"It's a tough schedule they're keeping," she agreed.

"He seemed exhausted," he continued, and Anne laughed.

"They'll be fine, John." She patted his hand. "No one said this would be easy. They knew what they were getting themselves into. Their eyes were wide open."

"Well, their hearts are wide open too, and that's what concerns me," he said. "That opens them up to a lot of potential hurt."

"It also opens them up to everything life has to offer. I'd have it no other way," Anne said firmly. "That's the best kind of love there is." Suddenly she grimaced, rubbing her stomach slowly.

"Are you okay?" he asked, even as he felt his brow furrowing in concern.

"Fine," she nodded, reaching for the bottle of Tums she'd recently been keeping by the sink. "I can't kick these stomachaches. I think I must be developing a food allergy or intolerance to something we've been eating. Jeannie said she struggled with stomachaches for a year and a half before she finally was diagnosed as Lactose intolerant."

"You should get it checked out," he told her softly, and she nodded, reaching out to squeeze his hand when she noticed his concern, comforting him even while she was in pain. That was Anne.

John studied his wife, clasping his hand around hers as she moved to pull it away. She was used to this kind of moment by this point in their marriage. John's adoration of her just seemed to grow as the years went on, and often he'd find himself just watching her as she went about her daily routine, wondering how he'd gotten so lucky. "You know," he told her now, "you're a great woman. And a great mom."

"Oh! Speaking of moms," Anne cut in, "Abby wants to plan a surprise belated Mother's Day brunch for Laura, since we couldn't pull something together in May. She's thinking next Sunday. I told her we'd be there."

"Sounds good." John pushed his worries about Steven and Laura aside and smiled at the thoughtfulness of his oldest daughter. That was another thing he loved about Abby. No matter what, above all else, she'd always looked out for her little sister.

She needs it now more than ever, he thought as he rinsed his glass and put it in the sink, watching the water disappear and willing Abby to somehow hear him.

༄

Abby

Abby rolled over in bed, throwing the covers off in frustration as she glanced at the nine thirteen blinking at her from the bedside clock. Almost an hour later than she'd wanted to be asleep, but she was more awake now than she had been when she'd gone to bed.

As usual, she couldn't seem to turn her mind off, though she couldn't quite figure out why. She'd called her sister that morning and had never heard Laura quite so stressed. She wanted to call back and offer to somehow help—to offer to babysit Faith this weekend so she and Steven could have some time to themselves, but she knew that Laura was at work tonight, so talking to her would be out of the question until morning, and she tried to put it out of her mind.

She'd carefully set out and pressed her outfit for the next day, and had read over her new duties until she knew them forward and backward. She'd studied up on the agency's client list and knew just about everything she could know about the industry she was getting into the next day. All of this preparation had taken almost all day, and she had gone to bed confident and feeling like there was literally nothing more she could do to prepare.

But here she was, nearly an hour later, tossing and turning, thinking about everything and nothing all at once. She was wildly uncomfortable—too hot underneath her covers but too cold without them, and finally threw them off, got out of bed, and grabbed a book. She knew she wouldn't be getting any sleep tonight.

Though as she settled into the overstuffed chair in the corner, Abby knew that it wasn't her temperature, or Laura, or even work that was keeping her awake.

It was him.

She'd first met him when she'd been walking through the office the afternoon Faith was born—her first interview—while the administrative assistant had shown her around the office and introduced her to the employees.

They'd reached the final desk, and Abby had been introduced to an account supervisor named Tom Reynolds. And though she couldn't place him, she knew she'd known him before. Or seen him before. She'd known it as soon as her eyes had locked into his—eyes the color of mocha that she somehow felt she'd gotten lost in before, just as she was getting lost in them now. He'd flashed her a smile laced with a recognition that lit up his own face, and she vaguely remembered seeing it before, though again, she couldn't place it.

But more surprising than his familiarity was the feeling that coursed through her veins the minute she touched his hand. He'd reached out to shake hers, and the minute their skin touched she'd shivered. She'd felt it all the way up her spine—the way she did when she came inside from a cold winter night and standing by the fire, felt that first wave of heat begin to warm her from the core.

She'd pushed the feelings aside during the long months of her interview process there, but now as she readied herself for her first day of work, knowing that she'd see him again tomorrow, she felt the warmth once again creep up.

She knew that tomorrow, under the fluorescent lights of the small office, she'd feel it again. There beneath his warm, familiar gaze, she'd let herself begin to thaw.

∽

CHAPTER SIX

John

John stood up slowly, his knees cracking as he did so.

"This body's not what it used to be," he grunted, looking at Faith as she watched him from her blanket on the floor. "You don't know a thing about that yet though, do you?" he asked her as he watched her easily place her big toe in her mouth. "Enjoy that while it lasts," he said dryly, more to himself than to her as he limped into the kitchen to pour himself a glass of water.

"I'll tell you," he called to Anne as she came in through the back door, "my body just doesn't bounce back like it used to. Can't spend ten minutes on the floor with that child without stiff knees for a week." He kissed her cheek as she walked by, and his lips came away salty.

"What's wrong?" he asked, following her back out into the living room where Faith was. "Have you been crying?"

"Nothing's wrong," she smiled as she lifted her granddaughter into her arms for a kiss.

"How was the doctor?" He stood baffled, studying her, trying to read her expression.

"It was fine," she replied, but he saw her eyes get misty as she put Faith back onto her blanket.

"Anne," he pushed, but she turned and smiled brightly at him.

"I'll tell you all about it, John. I just want to run up and take a quick shower first. You know how those waiting rooms are—just *breeding* grounds for germs." She squeezed his arm as she passed him on her way to the stairs, pausing and standing there a beat longer than usual before moving on. "Why don't you make us some tea, and we can catch up when I'm done."

He watched her walk away, bewildered.

"You women are a mystery to me," he said to Faith, shaking his head bending to scoop her into his arms and heading for the kitchen. "How about some peas and carrots," he checked his watch. "It's just about lunchtime—your mom says you love those vegetables."

Faith made a noise that sounded less like she was trying to speak and more like she was trying to gargle mouthwash, but he went with it. "Good! That's right, say *vegetables*."

Again she gargled, and he shrugged as he put her in her high chair and took the tiny jar from the refrigerator. "You women are a mystery to me," he repeated, twisting the cap off and grabbing a small spoon. "You expect us to be mind readers—well we're not. You come home and don't answer our questions—then get mad at us, saying we never ask or don't care about your feelings." He spooned an orange heap into Faith's open mouth, and she smiled, sending carrots oozing out the sides.

"You're unconcerned with all of this, aren't you?" He watched his granddaughter's smiling face. "Good, that's just the way it should be. Don't listen to me, just your old grandpa, grumbling away." He paused, spoon in midair, as he heard the water start from Anne's shower upstairs. Faith made a noise and grabbed for the spoon, snapping him back to attention. "Sorry, baby." He spooned another bite into her mouth before rising to put on a pot of hot water. He heard Anne fumbling around in the upstairs bathroom, taking longer than usual to get into the shower. He knew she couldn't possibly be upset over what happened at the doctor; for years she'd gotten one clean bill of health after another, and they lived a very healthy and active lifestyle. It had just been a routine checkup, to check for food allergies, even though her stomachaches had subsided recently. *Better safe than sorry,* she'd said as she left that morning.

And he knew if something was wrong with one of the girls, she would have been far more upset than she had been, so he knew whatever she told him wouldn't be that serious. Still, it plagued his thoughts for the next few minutes until he finally heard the water turn off.

"Hey, pretty lady," a few minutes later Anne was in the kitchen. Sitting down next to Faith, she took over feeding her while John pulled two mugs out of the cupboard. Her dark hair was still wet, and she'd slipped into a pair of khakis and a sweater despite the heat of the late September day. As it had so often since their marriage, his heart skipped a beat when her dark brown eyes found his.

"How did your morning with Faith go?" She looked up at him as she spooned another bite of vegetables into their granddaughter's mouth.

"It went fine," he said impatiently. "What I *want* to know is what's wrong!" He was frustrated with the lack of information she was giving him. She was usually an open book—that she was hiding something worried him.

After looking at Faith for a long minute, Anne looked at him with a level gaze. Her eyes were filled with tears, and immediately John felt the room start to spin around him. He grasped the counter for balance, holding her stare.

"Oh God," he breathed, knowing now that something was wrong. "Tell me what it is."

Anne drew in a shaky breath. "It's cancer, John."

And suddenly the room went black.

༺༻

Steven

"Mom said you had quite a fall." Steven watched his wife lean over the table to inspect the bandage on her father's head. She and Abby had been clucking over him like mother hens all evening, and he could see the John had had about enough.

"I'm fine," he said gruffly. "Just a dizzy spell." Steven watched his father-in-law exchange a private glance with Anne and raised his eyebrows in surprise. There was something they weren't telling them.

"Okay, so what's this dinner all about?" Abby asked the very question that had been on his mind. "We just saw each other a few weeks ago for dinner. Twice in a month? We're not that lucky...you two are up to something." She pointed to her mother over her water glass as she took a sip, and Anne stood up a little too quickly.

"There are the rolls," she said before the timer had even gone off, and this time Steven caught Laura's eye, who looked just as confused as he did.

"Mom," she called, "come back in here! What's going on? You guys are acting funny." She looked between the kitchen door and her father, who was fidgeting with his napkin, staring at his lap. "Daddy," Laura warned, and when John looked up, Steven felt himself suck in his breath.

He'd never seen John Baxter cry, and to see it now was unnerving. "Daddy," Laura said again, pleading now.

"Guys," John addressed the table, Anne coming to stand behind him with her hands on his shoulders. "Mom got some news from the doctor yesterday."

This time Steven heard Laura gasp. Usually John referred to the girls' mother as "Anne"—calling her "Mom" only when he thought they needed the comfort of that word.

"They found a mass," Anne started to say, but Steven had tuned her out. He only had eyes for his wife as he watched her bite her lip, trying to stop the tears that had welled in her eyes from falling. Her hand was trembling, and he impulsively covered it with his own, aware that at his touch, her tears began to fall freely. He glanced at Abby, who looked so much like her sister when wrapped up in this emotion that he swore he was looking at Laura.

Anne was smiling bravely as she continued. "It's not something they can remove, but they're hopeful that with both chemo and radiation, we can beat it."

Steven winced at the word "we." People felt the need to use "we" when they had big news or needed support, and he'd never understood it; *we're* pregnant, *we're* going to beat this thing. To him it was a pronoun of denial in situations like this, and hearing Anne say it now gave him a glimpse of the severity of the situation.

He wasn't quite sure how to act or what to do as Laura and Abby stood and joined their parents in a group hug. He was sure he'd never been in a situation quite like it. While he of course knew the Baxters well and had come to love them as an extension of his own family, he'd known them for less than three years and was still unsure of how to show his affection or support. His own parents rarely showed any to begin with; to be a part of such a close-knit clan was foreign to him, and as the foursome pulled apart and Laura sat down again next to him, wiping her eyes, all he could think to do was drape his arm around her shoulder and pull her close.

"It's going to be all right." He kissed her on the temple, realizing that he'd said those words louder than he'd intended them.

"Thank you, Steven," Anne smiled warmly at him. "Now, no more talk of this. I will keep you all posted on a regular basis, but as for this dinner, I've already gone and put a damper on enough of this. Please eat, everyone, and *please* someone change the subject."

Steven almost laughed at the absurdity of her request—asking her daughters to eat when he was sure they'd both just lost their appetites, but to their credit they picked up their forks and began to. He did the same, wracking his brain for a new conversation topic.

"We think Faith's starting to cut teeth," he offered, and Laura smiled gratefully at him, though he saw a look of pain cross Anne's face, and he regretted his choice of words. His statement had probably served only to remind her of the possibility that she'd miss out on Faith's life, and he was sorry he'd brought it up. Still, that's the way the conversation began to unfold, and chatter returned to as normal as it would get that evening.

Yet later that night he walked into the bathroom to find Laura sitting against the wall, her knees pulled up to her chest and her face wet with tears.

"Hey," he soothed, sinking to the ground beside her. "She'll be fine. You know she will. Your mom is strong and healthy, and if anyone can beat it, she can."

"What if she doesn't?" Laura looked up at him through impossibly big eyes. "What if she dies, Steven?"

"She's not going to die."

"Don't *say* that!" Immediately he knew he had said the wrong thing, but again he didn't know what comfort to offer her. "What if she *does* die?" Laura pulled away and wiped at her face with both palms. "I just don't see how I could ever live without her." She collapsed into another fit of sobs, and Steven pulled her close. He had absolutely no idea what to say to her, if anything. He had no words of wisdom, no words of comfort—though he tried, nothing came to him. Yet before he could open his mouth anyway, Faith began to wail from the nursery.

"I'll get her," he said quickly, rationalizing that Laura was in no state to try to take care of their baby.

"Hey, Faith, it's okay," he called as he rapidly covered the distance between their room and hers. "Shh." He scooped her into his arms from where she'd been flailing in her crib. She was dry and had just eaten, so he figured she must be teething and in pain.

"What can we do for you?" he asked. His mother told him often how she'd simply rubbed vodka on his gums, and that had helped—but he wasn't anxious to go down that road.

"Hey, Laura?" he called, "Where's the baby Tylenol?"

There was no answer from the upstairs bathroom, just the muffled sound of sobs, so he plodded down the stairs, Faith still screaming in his arms, on a quest to find it himself.

"Hey, it's okay," he tried to sooth her, but it seemed to only make it worse. "How much do I give her?" he started to call upstairs as he pulled the bottle from the medicine cabinet, but realized she probably wouldn't hear him. Juggling Faith in one arm, he turned the bottle over in his hand to read the dosage instructions, loosening his grip just long enough for his daughter to bat it out of his hands in her angry attempts to free herself from his arms.

Ten minutes later, medicine finally administered, he began to pace the back hall as Faith continued to cry for what felt like hours. "How long until this kicks in?" he muttered to himself as he bounced Faith up and down, which only made her angrier.

And there he paced for most of the night, Faith crying in his arms and Laura crying upstairs, feeling like he was failing them both, and wondering if maybe he should start crying as well.

∽

CHAPTER SEVEN

Steven

"Da!" Faith cried with enthusiasm, hurdling herself into Steven's arms.

"Did you hear that?" He grinned up at Laura. "She said 'dad'!"

To Laura's credit, she agreed wholeheartedly before settling onto the floor next to them. He knew she hadn't *actually* said *dad*, but he was willing to take what he could get. Just her proximity to the word warmed his heart, and as he snuggled her closer, he breathed in the scent of her.

Faith was dressed in pink footie pajamas, the bottoms bulky over her diaper. Her skin was still warm from her bath, and the baby shampoo Laura had used on her wafted into his nose from where her head rested on his shoulder, soft curls cascading across her forehead.

"Faith," he took a closer look at her. "Give me your Nuk," he scolded gently, holding his hand out for her.

She shook her head fiercely, pulling away from him.

"Faith," he continued more firmly. "You know the rule, no Nuk unless you're going to bed. Do you want to go to bed now?"

She balked, clearly weighing her options.

"Give Daddy the Nuk, unless you want to go to bed now."

After a brief hesitation, she thrust the Nuk in his outstretched hand before smiling widely at him, her nose and eyes scrunched in the enthusiasm of it.

"Thank you, sweetheart," he grinned right back and gave her a kiss on the nose, sending her into a fit of giggles.

"Does Daddy's beard tickle?" he asked, running a hand over his stubble. Shaving was one of the many things he hadn't gotten around to today. Faith followed suit, her tiny hand rubbing the texture of his face. "Does that feel funny?" he asked her again, and again she began to laugh.

"Oh to be entertained that easily," Laura said dreamily from beside him, her head resting against the sofa behind her and her eyes closed.

"I don't know," he began. "I think you'd be surprised at just how entertaining this can be." He moved to rub his chin against her neck, and she laughed, shoulders tensing.

"That tickles." She moved away from him, but he just moved closer.

"Stop!" she laughed, pushing his face away halfheartedly. "You're such a goof!" This only made Steven more intent on tickling her and was laughing himself when he heard her yell.

"Stop it, Steven! That just hurts now." She pulled away, a scowl on her face.

"Sorry," he said as he quickly sat back up, aware that Faith was watching them with an expression he couldn't read. She seemed to be deciding whether to be happy or sad—laughing had turned to yelling, and she wasn't sure what to make of it.

"It's okay, Faith," he said, pulling her into his arms again. "We were just goofing around."

"Sorry," Laura said softly, straightening as she rubbed her neck. "I shouldn't have yelled. I'm just tired."

"I know." Steven kissed her cheek before returning his attention to Faith. "It's okay."

He knew she had a lot on her plate, between her mother's illness, school, her demanding job, and raising Faith. Still, her rebuke had made him angry. He'd just been trying to make her laugh.

"Hey." She turned his face toward her. "I'm sorry. Don't pout."

After deciding for a brief instant, he kissed her quickly. "Okay, I won't," he smiled, tousling her hair. "What do you want to read, Faith?" He turned back to his daughter. "It's almost bedtime, which means we get to read a book. Why don't you go pick one out?" Steven stood up and scooped Faith into his arms. "I'll read with her tonight," he told Laura. "I know you've got some homework to finish up." Laura thanked him with a kiss on the cheek before heading for the computer. It was February, and Laura was a month into the semester, her courses in full swing. Faith had turned one the month before and was now constantly on the go. The combination left her with little time or energy for much else, and he knew she'd be grateful for a chance to focus on studying.

"I'll come in and say good night when you're done," she said, giving Faith a big hug.

Steven's courses had lately been keeping him away from the house for even longer than usual, so he was glad for this one-on-one time with his daughter.

"Isth!" Faith attempted to say "this," pointing to her *Baby Colors* book and holding out her hand expectantly. Laughing, Steven gave her the Nuk and settled down beside her. She snuggled up to him, her head resting on his chest, and as he began to read, he was sure it didn't get any better than this.

Two books later, Faith had fallen asleep, her tiny fist balled up around her blanket. Gently he'd lifted her into her crib and turned off the light, watching as her firefly night-light turned on and cast a soft purple glow across the floor. Quietly, he made his way back downstairs, where Laura was at the computer.

"Can I get you anything? Some tea?" He bent to give her a kiss, surprised to find that she was crying. "Hey," he asked gently, "what's wrong? Is it your mom?" He was immediately concerned, knowing that in the five months since Anne had discovered her cancer, the news hadn't been great.

"Nothing, I'm fine," Laura said briskly.

"Are you sure? Because you don't seem fine."

"I'm *fine*," she repeated.

"All right," Steven put up his hands. "Just trying to help."

"I don't *need* your help, Steven. I've done pretty well on my own so far." She turned to face him, accusational.

"What are you talking about, *on your own?*" he asked, offended.

"I mean you're never around," she spat.

"I'm around as much as I can be, Laura! And it's not like I'm out gallivanting! I'm attempting pretty much the busiest class load ever, so I can graduate as soon as possible, get on with things, and provide for you and Faith!"

"Faith needs you *around* more than she needs anything else." Laura seemed intent on arguing.

"Oh, I'm sorry," Steven retorted. "Who was just in there reading to her? I thought for sure that was me."

"Reading to her at the end of the night isn't enough, Steven," Laura said. "I'm here all day with her, then I go to work while you come home and put her to bed. That seems a little unbalanced."

"That's the schedule we agreed on, Laura." Steven tried to keep his voice down. "Look," he took a deep breath. "What is this really about? Were you set on picking a fight tonight?"

"No." Laura dropped her head into her hands. "Look, I'm sorry. I'm just stressed."

"Well, we're *both* stressed, Laur." Steven shook his head. "You can't go ruin a perfectly good night by picking a fight just because you're *stressed*."

"Oh, so I ruined tonight?" Laura was defensive again.

"All right, I'm walking away," Steven said, heading for the kitchen. "I'm going to make some coffee—do you want any?"

Laura didn't answer, and Steven shook his head, grumbling to himself as he pulled the coffee filters out of the cupboard.

"Maybe do that a little louder, so Faith wakes up." Laura was suddenly behind him.

"You know, could you do me a favor," Steven turned to face her, "and give me a little warning when you're PMS-ing, so I at least know to stay away from the house for a few days?"

"That's nice, Steven, really it is. Stay away a little *longer*."

"Oh, because you're so fun to come home to?" He was angry now. "You think I enjoy coming home to this every night, after working hard all day?"

"What do you think *I'm* doing all day?" Laura's eyes were blazing. "You think raising a daughter is easy? Like I just sit here and watch movies?"

"You say that as though *I'm not raising a daughter with you*," Steven seethed.

"Well, it doesn't really feel like you are!"

Steven put his hands on the counter, breathing deeply and counting to ten. When he looked up, Laura was crying.

"Laura," he sighed, frustrated that this seemed to happen every time they talked. "Look, what do you want from me?"

"I'm sorry." She dropped her head onto the counter, arms folded beneath it. "I just don't know how to deal with all of this. Mom's sick, and you're never around." She looked up sharply at her own words. "I'm sorry. I mean, you're right. It's what we agreed on, and you're not doing anything wrong…it's just so much harder than I thought it would be."

"It's no walk in the park," Steven agreed. "But isn't it worth it?" He motioned toward the upstairs, where their daughter was asleep.

"Of course it is, every second." Laura sighed. "I don't know… is there a limit to how much a person can take? If there is, I'm at mine."

"I know." Steven moved beside her and pulled her into his arms. "But you have to cut me some slack here. I'm trying as hard as I can. This is a lot for me to take on too, you know. I didn't ask for all of this at once, either. Three years ago I was single, and just a kid myself - now I have a baby, a wife, a mother-in-law who's battling an illness…sometimes it just seems like too much."

"You don't think it feels that way for me, too?" Laura was defensive.

"No, hey," he tried to smooth things over. "I was agreeing with you—yeah it's tough. I'm just saying that we need to help each other—this isn't any harder or easier on one of us than it is on the other."

"Oh, you don't think so? Last I checked, it wasn't *your* mother who was dying," she spat out, bursting into fresh tears.

"Okay, I'm just not going to talk." Steven shook his head in frustration and simply held his wife, thinking that if there *was* a limit to how much a person could take, he just might be over his.

∽

Abby

"A toast to our newest team member," Abby watched as her boss Dave Kissel raised his glass and addressed the table. "Abby," he focused his attention on her, "we're thrilled to have you joining us, and excited to get to know you better over the coming months. I apologize that it's taken us so long to pull this happy hour together, but I think I speak for everyone when I say we've all enjoyed working with you so far, and we look forward to more to come." Abby smiled as she thanked him. She liked Dave immensely; he was the kind of boss everyone hoped for, and she could tell he would be a joy to work with.

Also around the table were the other direct members of her team—all assigned to the same account—as well as a few others from different accounts at the agency, including Tom Reynolds.

He sat a ways down the table talking to a few other men, yet every time she looked up, it seemed she caught him looking at her. She studied him now, a rare moment where he was otherwise occupied, trying to decide what it was that drew her to him. He was definitely handsome, but not necessarily the type of man she'd usually go for. His dark hair and dark eyes gave him a brooding and mysterious look, or at least they would have had he not been smiling *all* the time. That's probably what did it, she thought. His face absolutely lit up when he smiled, his eyes turning into half-moons that she just wanted to get lost in and laugh with. In her first few months at the office, she'd learned enough about him to want to get to know him better. In meetings where others stressed about menial details and deadlines, Tom took on each problem with a perspective she'd never known before, letting things roll easily off his shoulders. "In the grand scheme of things, does it *really* matter?" she'd overheard him asking someone, and she'd laughed to herself, thinking that as an employee in the midst of her first few months of her first real job and desperately trying to make a good impression, *everything* mattered. Yet she knew even as he said it that working hard was important to him as well; he always seemed to be the first to arrive and the last to leave the office, except twice a week when he left at three, for a reason she hadn't yet learned. Perhaps this is what intrigued her about him—he seemed to be a walking contradiction. She'd always liked a challenge, and wouldn't have been surprised to learn this was behind her interest in Tom Reynolds, but still she knew it was something *else*.

"Earth to Abby." Nicole, a junior copywriter she'd had lunch with a few times, waved her hand in front of Abby's face, snapping her from her reverie. She hadn't realized she'd been staring at Tom this whole time, and when she blinked back into focus and saw his eyes focused on hers, she felt a deep blush begin in her neck.

"Sorry, just zoning out." She turned her attention to Nicole. "What's up?"

Nicole gestured at the waiter standing expectantly beside their table, and she cleared her throat.

"Oh, sorry." She looked down at her empty glass. "I'll take a whiskey on the rocks, please," she ordered, only to be met with a chorus of comments from the table around her.

"Now that's my kind of drink." Tom grinned at her, and she blushed again as she tried to remember if he'd said it was his kind of *drink* or his kind of *girl*. Why it mattered at all she didn't know, but she liked the warmth she felt under Tom's gaze.

"If she's having one, I'll take one too," he told the waiter, and his order was followed by five more from others around the table.

"You started a trend," Nicole laughed. "Strong drink for an office happy hour."

"I'm a very no muss, no fuss kind of girl," Abby said loudly, hoping Tom would hear but not understanding why. As the conversation continued further down the table, he slid down the booth so he was sitting directly across from Abby and Nicole.

"Cheers," he toasted them, and they laughed as they clinked empty glasses. "So how are you liking it so far, Abby?" he asked her, and she grinned at him across the table.

"If this is work," she gestured at the party going on around her, "then I love it."

Tom laughed and shook his head. "Yeah, it's all fun and games until the week before a deadline," he mused. "And its you creatives," he focused on Nicole, "that really make it tough on us."

"Us?" Nicole feigned disgust. "Whatever! You come at us with ridiculous client requests, and we're just supposed to be creative on the spot? It takes time and effort to come up with the good stuff," she smiled.

"I'll believe it when I walk onto a creative floor that doesn't have hula hoops hanging from the walls and foosball tables that are always in use." He winked at Abby, and she smiled back. She still wasn't sure enough of what to make of the office politics to join in the banter, but she liked the easy way people laughed with each other here. The environment was laid back and relaxed, and she found herself actually excited to get out of bed in the morning. She said just that, and Tom laughed.

"That will pass, trust me. Where are you living?" He raised his eyebrows and thanked the waiter as he delivered the next round of drinks, taking a sip of his before focusing on Abby.

"I'm in Lincoln Park." She wiped the condensation from her glass. "Right by the lake."

"Yeah, that's a beautiful area. I lived there for a few years." Tom's smile was seriously contagious, and Abby smiled herself, for no apparent reason.

"Where do you live now?" she asked him.

"Schaumberg," he began to reply, and then caught himself. "I mean," he shook his head quickly. "Illinois Ave. Sorry, I just moved, getting used to the new address."

Abby glanced quickly at his hand, looking for a ring and wondering why she hadn't done it before. She couldn't picture a single man living in the suburbs. But his hands were bare, and she didn't feel like pressing the issue further.

"Right downtown," she said. "That must make the commute to work nice and easy!"

"Definitely," he said as a look she couldn't read flickered quickly across his face.

At the other end of the table, someone stood up with an announcement, and though Abby couldn't make out what he was saying, she was glad for the distraction. She was usually great in situations like this one—she could have struck up a conversation with a wet rag. But somehow Tom had gotten under her skin, and being around him made her nervous and self-conscious, unsure of quite what to say. But one smile from him and all of that melted away, and she relaxed into an easy banter back and forth. They shared a similar sense of humor and, by the end of happy hour, had each other laughing so hard that whiskey was coming out of their noses.

"Oh, that burns." Tom was laughing as he blew his nose in a cocktail napkin. "I never knew laughing could be so painful."

Abby focused on breathing, so she could swallow the sip of her drink she'd been threatening to spit out. "Ah," she breathed once she was out of the danger zone.

People were starting to file out, and Abby checked her watch.

"Yikes!" she cried. "I had no idea it was so late." She rose and reached for her wallet.

"No, you're fine." Tom reached out to stop her, his hand resting on hers. "They'll expense it," he was continuing, but Abby couldn't hear over the blood pounding in her ears. She could literally see her pulse quicken under his touch, and hoped he wasn't paying that much attention to her wrist in the darkened room. She stole a cautious glance at him, only to find the very same expression on his face that must be plastered on hers.

"Sorry." He pulled his hand away quickly, flexing it before shoving it awkwardly in his pocket. "How are you getting home?"

"I can take her," Nicole said quickly, shooting Abby a look that clearly said *be careful*.

Abby said her good-byes before following Nicole out of the pub. "What was *that* all about?" she asked Abby as she hailed a cab and ushered her in.

"What was what all about?" Abby asked, fumbling through her purse to make sure she had her cell phone and wallet.

"You flirting, the *whole* time, with Tom Reynolds."

"I was not flirting!" Abby shouted defensively, zipping her purse back up and turning to look at Nicole. "We were just having a conversation."

"Oh please, you were *so* flirting."

"Well, even if I was, what's the harm in that? We get along well."

"Yeah, but I don't think you want to get involved in that."

"Is there an office policy against it?" Abby asked suddenly, wondering why she hadn't thought to ask sooner.

"No, not at all," Nicole said. "Actually, Matt and Angela have been dating for a few years now."

"Have they?" Abby had seen them together but never bothered to ask.

"Yeah, apparently he's going to propose in Mexico in a few weeks."

"Well then, what's the problem?" Abby could care less about Matt and Angela—what she wanted to know was why her flirting with Tom Reynolds was such an issue.

"He just got divorced a few months ago," Nicole explained.

"Oh." Abby put the pieces together—his slip up about where he lived, his odd schedule. "Does he have kids?" she asked, figuring that might explain why he left at three o'clock two days a week.

"Yeah, two boys," Nicole confirmed.

"Well, it doesn't matter anyway, because nothing's going to happen," Abby told her. "I don't even think I was flirting with him. We just get along well," she justified.

"Whatever you say," Nicole laughed and shook her head. "Just take it easy—you're way too young, with way too much going for you, to get mixed up with someone with that kind of baggage."

Abby laughed and shook her head. "I'm not getting 'mixed up' with anyone, I assure you."

"Good, don't you settle!" Nicole said. "Call me tomorrow," she added as Abby jumped out of the cab at her stop.

"Don't you want cab fare?" she asked as the cab began to pull away.

"You can buy me lunch next week!" Nicole called as she waved out the window, leaving Abby alone on the sidewalk with only the thoughts that were spinning inside her head.

John

"How are you feeling?" John asked his wife as she settled back onto the couch next to him. The combination of chemo and radiation had been making her sick lately, and she'd just come back from the bathroom for the fifth time that night.

"Ugh," was all she said before dropping her head wearily onto his shoulder. "This is killing me," she said, just an old expression before she thought better of it. "Sorry," she added.

"Don't say things like that," John murmured as he stroked the hair back from her face. He gently squeezed her shoulder, recognizing the sweater he'd gotten her the Christmas before Abby had gone to college. It had been their last Christmas as a family before a child went off to school, and though Abby would be home for Christmas each year following, they all had known it wouldn't be quite the same. Anne had insisted they make an ordeal of it, and that particular Christmas had been even more special than any before it. Anne had spent the weeks leading up to it sewing a quilt for Abby, covered in pictures. Abby's baby picture, pictures of the two of them together, Abby and John dancing at a wedding when Abby was a little girl, standing on John's feet, the four of them as a family. Their daughter had been thrilled to open it, and a year later, Laura had been thrilled to open one of her own, the Christmas before *her* high school graduation. Having the two girls so close in age had been a blessing and a curse—Abby and Laura were inseparable, but because they were so similar, also very competitive. But Anne always seemed to know just what to say to smooth things out, to make everything okay. The sudden knowledge that she might be here much longer to do that left him short of breath.

"How could we ever live without you?" John asked her quietly.

"You could, and you will," came Anne's response.

John jerked his head up. "Don't *talk* like that," he told her again, but Anne stopped him.

"John, let me talk about this. We can't ignore it and pretend it isn't there, thinking that will make it better. I have cancer, John, and right now, it's winning. We have to talk about what will happen. Please."

John swallowed the lump in his throat and nodded, studying the intensity of her expression, memorizing it.

"You know where I want to be buried," Anne said quietly, and John nodded. They'd picked out their plots together, one next to the other, a few years ago, never dreaming they'd need to use them so soon. "I think everything's in order…" She trailed off, staring into the distance. "I don't regret anything, about our life together." She turned to face him, her brown eyes glistening. "You've been an amazing husband, John, more than any woman could have asked for. I couldn't have loved anyone more."

"Anne," he looked at her desperately.

"No, let me finish. I want to say these things to you while I'm still able to say them. Right now I feel like I have a sharp mind in a failing body, but I'm sure the mind isn't far behind."

John nodded silently, taking her other hand, facing her in the same way he had on their wedding day so many years ago.

"We've raised such fantastic daughters, and now there's Faith…I just can't imagine a life more blessed with happiness."

Until this, John wanted to say. Instead he said, "Neither can I, sweetheart." He reached out to touch her cheek, wiping a tear away as he did so. "Are you giving up?" he asked, afraid of the answer but needing to know.

"No," Anne shook her head. "I think life might be giving up on *me*," she added as she flew off the couch and back toward the bathroom.

∽

CHAPTER EIGHT

Laura

"Faith, give the pencil to Mama," Laura repeated, for the hundredth time that morning. And again, she wondered if her daughter had gone temporarily deaf as she watched her daughter toddle the other way, pencil in hand. *That's it,* she muttered, stomping off in the direction Faith had gone, overtaking her in just a few steps. She grabbed the pencil in the gentlest movement she could muster through her frustration, and promptly put it back in the drawer where Faith had found it. She waited for the onslaught of tears, and sure enough, Faith began to scream so loudly that Laura was sure her neighbors would send the police over in a few short minutes. She crossed the room and scooped up her daughter, tragic tears running down her face, lost in a sob so gripping that Laura wondered if she would recover her breath.

"It's okay, honey," she soothed, wondering if she was doing this right. If you take something away from a kid as punishment, are you supposed to comfort them when they start to cry about it? Or is that part of the punishment? "You need to listen to Mama," she continued. "You can't run with pencils in your hand. That's dangerous. You could poke your eye out." *When did*

I turn into my mother? She asked herself, not for the first time that week.

Faith's tears were subsiding, and she was taking gasping breaths. "Shh," Laura repeated. "It's ok."

"Nana," Faith squeaked in a hopelessly pathetic voice.

"You want a banana?" Laura asked, backing away from her daughter's face to look in her red-rimmed eyes. Faith nodded, bringing a small fist to her eye and rubbing it. *Just about naptime,* Laura thought as she reached for the yellow fruit. "Say please," she said, peeling away the skin and holding it just of Faith's reach.

"Peas!" Faith said enthusiastically, and Laura couldn't help but smile as she placed the banana in her daughter's eagerly outstretched hands. She knew Faith would gum the banana, at best, and that most of it would probably go to waste, but she didn't care, as long as it distracted her from that pencil.

Laura glanced out the window at the gloomy sky, the gray clouds so low it looked like they would touch the tops of the trees, their leaves gone and the wet branches nearly black against the dark background. She loved storms, especially on a day like today when she had nowhere to go. She had the night off from the restaurant and was looking forward to spending some quality time with Steven. The two of them had hardly seen each other in the last few months, and tonight all Laura wanted to do was be next to him. She knew she'd been impossible lately, stretched to her limit and taking it all out on Steven, and longed for just one night of normalcy between them.

She heard the first crack of thunder a few minutes later as she put Faith down for her nap. Tucking her daughter in, Laura kissed the top of her head, surprised at what little resistance this nap was being met with. "Keep your eyes closed," she cooed as she tiptoed out of the room, leaving the door open just a crack.

She went back downstairs and clicked the monitor on, listening to Faith tossing and turning in her bed before it finally went silent. With a sigh, Laura sunk onto the couch and closed her eyes. She knew she should be using this time to get something done—laundry, dishes, whatever that was—but she just needed a few minutes to relax.

It wasn't until she let herself do so that she realized she hadn't heard from Steven all day. *Weird*, she thought—he usually called midmorning to check in. Grabbing the phone off the end table she tried his cell, but after three rings was directed to his voice mail. She waited as the recording she hated instructed her that to leave a voice message, she could please press one or just wait or the tone. When she was finished recording, Laura could hang up or press one for more options. *I really don't need instructions on this,* she thought impatiently, diving into her message a little too enthusiastically when she finally heard the tone.

"Hey! It's me. Laura. Not that there'd be any other 'me'… Anyhow, just wondering why you didn't check in on your break. Is everything okay? I haven't heard from you this morning, just calling to check in. Did I say that? Anyhow, give me a call back when you get this."

She hit the talk button angrily with her forefinger and dropped the phone onto the couch beside her, checking a few times to make sure the ringer was on. She didn't want to miss his return call.

Thinking about it now, she wondered about the last time they'd actually sat down and caught up.

She flipped on the TV for distraction, dragging a laundry basket into the living room to get some folding done as she did so. When she was done with that, she cleaned the kitchen, twice, then dusted the living room, and started her preparations for dinner that night.

The realization that Steven still hadn't gotten back to her sat there on her shoulder, whispering in her ear every time she let herself be silent. And so, for the rest of the afternoon, Laura busied herself with anything she could, ignoring the obvious with all her might.

༒

Tom

Tom glanced up from his desk and again found himself looking at Abby. She leaned over her desk, engrossed in something, her nose inches from her computer screen and her brow furrowing in concentration. Tom couldn't help but smile as he watched her work, oblivious to the fact that anyone as looking at her, least of all him.

The truth was he couldn't *stop* watching Abby. He caught himself looking for her as soon as he entered the office, and almost resented the soft crush of disappointment when he arrived only to find she was out for the day. The days he wasn't close to her dragged longer than any other, and he even found himself considering going to bed earlier that night in order to put less time between him and the time he would see her again.

Watching her now, he studied her features, trying to understand what it was about her that captivated him this way. She was beautiful, to be sure, but in kind of a plain way. Unlike the other girls around the office who wore a lot of make-up and flaunted their beauty in an obvious way, Abby's came from elsewhere. She wore her honey-colored hair long and straight, her hazel eyes bright and clear. *It's those eyes,* he thought. If ever eyes had been able to convey emotion, hers could times ten. Sometimes when she was happy, he swore that her eyes themselves were laughing, and the one time he'd seen her angry, he'd thought for sure fire was going to come straight out of the heat he saw inside of them. She wore her heart on her sleeve, but even if she didn't, her eyes could betray her true feelings in a heartbeat, and he realized now that *that* was probably what kept her so often on his mind. For years he had seen woman after woman morph herself into exactly what she thought a man wanted her to be. Here was someone who was *genuine*, and not afraid to tell him exactly what she thought as she was thinking it.

They'd been talking more and more frequently for a few months now, and he found himself looking forward to their conversations—excited for the first time in a long while to get out of bed in the morning and get into the office.

"Don't you have anything better to be looking at, Reynolds?" she called to him now, endearing him with her flirty use of his last name. Startled, he laughed nervously and looked away, unaware that he had still been staring. *Say something,* he told himself as the seconds passed. She was still watching him, waiting, and no words came to mind. *Say **anything**,* he willed himself, feeling his face grow a deeper shade of red by the second.

"Uh, probably...sorry," he stammered.

Probably?

He wondered if the fact that he had been staring in the first place was enough to negate the unwitting insult he had just thrown at her. Willing himself to sheepishly meet her gaze, he was surprised to see the smile in her eyes. He shivered as he looked away, amazed how she seemed to know exactly what he was thinking without so much as a word from him. *Get a grip, Tom*, he told himself, throwing all of his energy into finishing the brief he was working on. It was a brief he should have finished hours ago, but he couldn't gain control over his mind. He'd taken Abby out on their first date the night before, and since the moment he'd dropped her off at her door, had been consumed with thoughts of her. The knowing smile they'd exchanged as she walked in the office door that morning had made his knees go week, and he'd been thinking of her nonstop ever since. He tried to focus, but couldn't help but notice that when Abby Baxter walked out of that office at five o'clock, despite the colleagues that were still at their desks finishing up for the day, he felt as though he was suddenly alone in it.

His thoughts of her were interrupted by the ringing of his phone, and he glanced at the caller ID. He didn't have to look at the caller ID to know who was calling.

"Yeah?" he answered, trying his best to zone out the voice on the other end. "What happened?" he asked for clarification, suddenly sitting up straighter. "Is he okay? Well, who was watching him?"

He listened to what he soon realized was not an emergency at all, and finally asked her, "Well, if he's okay, then what's the big deal? How is this my fault?" He added at her accusation.

With a sigh of frustration, he checked his watch. "Yeah, I'll be there. I *said*, I'll be there." With that, he hung up the phone, ending his conversation with the one person who probably had the power to forever keep him from Abby.

༄

Abby

Abby walked slowly out of the office, careful to avoid the puddles, in no hurry to return to her apartment. Her roommate from college, Meredith, had recently moved to Chicago and had subsequently moved in with Abby until she could find her own place, and this weekend she had houseguests. Their presence made Abby a little uncomfortable. Anyone who knew her could attest to her being a neat freak. Just yesterday she'd cleaned the apartment from top to bottom, spending hours scrubbing the floors with wood polish, sprinkling deodorizing powder on the area rugs before vacuuming, Windex-ing every possible surface.

This morning when she'd left, the place was immaculate, sparkling from floor to ceiling, and she suspected that between her less-than-neat roommate and the guests she was entertaining, all of her hard work had been for naught, and was in no hurry to witness it firsthand.

Plus, she had some thinking to do.

Lately she couldn't seem to stop thinking about Tom. She loved the way that his hair fell across his forehead, those bright brown eyes watching her from underneath the kind of eyelashes that women dreamed about having themselves. But she was smart enough to know that there was something there beyond physical attraction.

Since that first happy hour, they'd bonded over a shared hatred of the weekly reports they'd been asked to start filling out, and had been talking more and more frequently as the weeks had gone on.

He teased her incessantly for the way she organized her desk and her (even she had to admit) ridiculously specific morning routine. She cringed every time she walked past his desk, messy stacks of paper littering the surface with no clear definition between them, between what was what. But she couldn't help but notice that she found it endearing and found herself more and more intrigued by him every day. Just today they'd gone to lunch with a group of coworkers and, as usual, had gravitated toward each other.

And last night they'd gone on a date. It hadn't started that way; over the past months they'd found that they had two things in common—both loved history, and neither had been to the Chicago History Museum. He'd suggested they go, and they had—but the museum had turned to dinner, and dinner had turned to drinks, and it had been almost midnight by the time she'd gotten home. She thought back to the moment she'd seen him waiting outside for her. The rain had been coming down in sheets, and she'd hurried from the bus toward the entrance, her umbrella no match for the Chicago wind, which kept turning it inside out. He'd been standing there with an umbrella, facing the other direction, and when he'd turned to face her, her heart had stopped. His eyes were arresting and held her gaze for just long enough for her to know that he was interested, before his face had broken into a huge grin.

"Hey," was all he had said.

"Hey, Reynolds," she'd smiled back at him as he swung open the door for her. They'd stood in the lobby, shaking out their umbrellas before looking at each other and laughing, realizing that they'd both ended up soaking wet anyway.

"So much for these," he'd said, and she'd nodded.

"At least it's warm in here."

As they'd strolled the museum, Abby had been fascinated by the dioramas of the great Chicago Fire and the White City that had been constructed for the Columbian Exposition. Tom seemed to know everything about it and filled her in on small details about the event. She was mesmerized, and they stood in front of one display for nearly an hour as he talked animatedly about Daniel Burnham and what he had done for the city of Chicago. Later, they'd sat on the replica of an original El car and talked about what they'd like to see if they went back in time.

"I'd like to see Colonial America," Abby had breathed, closing her eyes and imagining it. "Wouldn't it be exciting? To be surrounded by that kind of ambition—that sense everyone must have had of a fresh start?"

"I can only imagine," Tom said, and Abby had thought she heard a hint of longing in his voice, so she opened her eyes and looked at him.

"If *you* could get a fresh start, or do one thing over, in your life, what would it be?"

"I don't know," Tom said immediately, making it clear to Abby that he had been thinking along the same lines. "As much as I feel like I've wasted the last several years of my life in a marriage that didn't go anywhere, it was those years that brought me Ben and Luke, and I wouldn't trade those boys for anything."

Abby had nodded. "Tell me about them," she said. "I can tell from the picture on your desk that one of them looks exactly like you. The other one must look more like Beth?"

Tom shook his head. "Yes, I mean, no. Yes, Luke looks exactly like me. Ben looks just like my mother. Neither looks much like Beth. But man, are they good kids. Ben's sensitive—pretty artsy. I think he'll be a musician. Luke can't carry a tune in a bucket, but he's getting really athletic. They're so different in that regard, but so alike in others."

Abby grinned. "Sounds a lot like me and my sister."

"Yeah?" Tom raised his eyebrows, and Abby had nodded.

"Do they fight?" she'd asked, but Tom had just shrugged.

"Over little things, brother stuff. But this divorce has bonded them together, I think. I don't know…I worry about what it will do to them."

Abby hadn't known what to say to that, and instead she'd just found herself reaching for his hand as he'd continued.

As she thought back on their date now, she appreciated the way he'd opened up to her about his kids. She liked him; that much was for sure. But she knew those kids weighed on his mind heavier than anything else, a fact that kept her from even letting herself *think* about falling in love with him.

She'd always played things so safe, done everything by the book, and now she felt herself falling for a man who was once divorced, with two kids. She knew it was selfish, but she wanted to go through all of that with someone for the first time. When she walked down the aisle toward the man who would become her husband, she wanted it to be the first time he'd looked up and seen his bride coming toward him. She wanted that moment when their first child cried to be one they could share together for the first time. And then there was the age difference to consider—no, she *couldn't* date Tom, she just *couldn't*. But something told her that even with her firm resolve, logic would be no match for the way she was beginning to feel about him.

Abby was so lost in thought that she didn't even notice the puddle before her until she was ankle deep in it. She swore under her breath, the cold and murky water seeping through her stocking and into her shoe. Steadying herself on a lamppost, she bent her leg at the knee and removed her shoe, unsuccessfully shaking what moisture she could from it, finally giving up and pushing her foot back into its soggy insoles. Again she swore, taking a few jagged steps toward the curb and raising a hand to hail a cab.

She was still adjusting her shoe when she heard the horn and looked up fully expecting to see a taxi pulling to the side of the road. What she saw instead made her catch her breath. Her sister's husband pulled to the side of the road, rolling down his window as he did so.

"Can I give you a lift home?" he asked, flashing her a bright grin.

"Sure," she accepted cautiously, the question she wanted to ask him burning at the back of her throat. *What on earth are you doing all the way down here at this hour?* Steven usually worked during the day. Abby desperately wanted to know what he was doing downtown, but she decided to stay silent as she slid into the seat beside him and offered a quick hug before he pulled away from the sidewalk.

"I'm on my way back from a lecture," he offered, a little too eagerly. "Don't ask why they sent us all the way to the downtown campus, but it's a nice change of pace from the suburbs."

I'll bet, Abby bit her tongue.

"Didn't you have to work today?"

"I took the day off - it was an important lecture that I really didn't want to miss. And the guest speaker was only available for the afternoon classes - so it was now or never."

Steven offered the information with the enthusiasm of someone trying talk his way into - or out of - something, and Abby wondered if this is how he'd pitched it to Laura - if he'd told her at all.

Steven passed the rest of the drive in relative silence, every so often asking her about her work, or her love life, or what her plans for the weekend were. As she listened to him, she wondered if it was still foreign to him to belong to such a close-knit family, his discomfort in making small talk with his sister-in-law apparent. She felt a pang of sympathy toward him and smiled warmly as she stepped out of the car and thanked him for the ride.

Still, as she watched him drive away, she couldn't help but wonder if he'd been telling her the truth about his whereabouts.

∽

Steven

"Where have you been all day?" Laura's angry voice was so loud that Steven had to pull his cell away from his ear, propping his elbow on the center console of his SUV and holding the phone a few inches from his ear in disinterest. He could hear Faith crying in the background, and for a moment felt a twinge of guilt that he pushed away as quickly as it had come. *I wasn't doing anything wrong*, he justified to himself, careful not to say the words out loud.

"I thought I told you, we had that lecture downtown today. I had my phone on silent." It was the truth, after all. He left out the attractive med student he'd sat next to, running out for a quick lunch together between lectures. He didn't add that he'd checked his phone and seen her missed call at lunch, but just hadn't felt like dealing with it. She would have paged him if it was an emergency, and as for now, he just didn't have the energy.

"Hello?" There was silence on the other line, and he wondered if she'd hung up on him.

"I'm here," came Laura's response, quiet when compared with what sounded like a fire engine siren in the background. "I muted it for you. Faith was screaming so loud." Again, Steven felt a stab of guilt, induced by his wife's thoughtfulness, but again told himself that he hadn't done anything wrong. "What time will you be home?" Her tone of voice held a meaning he had become familiar with. She was going to act as though she wasn't mad anymore; at least, she was going to drop the subject. But he knew as well as any man that it didn't mean she wouldn't exude coldness for the rest of the night until he apologized or offered a more detailed explanation. That didn't mean that the space between them in bed tonight wouldn't be cold, her back turned on him the minute they lay down, silent tears on her cheek that she wouldn't think he heard.

"Probably a half hour or so. Look, B...I'm sorry I missed your call. It's just been a crazy day. I barely got a chance to eat, much less check my phone." A little white lie for the sake of smoothing things over never hurt anyone, right? It's not as though he had done anything wrong, just a harmless little lunch. But once again, his guilt crept back as he heard the tension ease from her voice, her desire to trust him outweighing her suspicions. Or at least, he figured, overpowering them for the moment. They'd be back.

"It's fine. I'm sorry for being crabby. It's just been a hell of a day over here." Faith was still crying in the background.

"Is she okay? What does she want?" he asked, his tone far more accusing than he meant it.

"She *wants* her father," Laura snapped, defensive. "She's been asking for you all afternoon." Her toned softened, and she added, "and the thunder woke her up from her nap, so she's tired and cranky. Just like me," she added so softly that he wondered if he'd imagined it.

"Do you want me to pick up dinner on the way home?" he asked, hoping his offer would lift her spirits.

"Thanks," she replied unenthusiastically, "but I've got a pot of spaghetti on." Faith's cries intensified. "Look, I've got to go. I'll see you when you get here."

"Bye," Steven started, but she had already hung up.

He sighed, tossing his phone into the cup holder next to him and running a hand through his hair. He hated that their relationship had gotten to this point. Somehow they had lost control, and now the energy required to fix the problems between them was energy neither of them had, and thus their relationship slipped farther and farther through the cracks.

John and Anne tried to help with Faith when they could, but with Anne's progressing illness, she often lacked the energy for it. Abby took the train up a lot on weekends to help out, never missing the opportunity to point out how strange it was that she, the older sister, was taking the train up from her downtown apartment to spend the day in the suburbs watching her *younger* sister's kid. *"Life's funny that way,"* Laura would remark, but sometimes Steven could see in her eyes a flash of regret of the life that could have been hers. But then Faith would come into the room, and that look would disappear, replaced by a look more loving than he imagined possible. That little girl had them both wrapped around their fingers.

But it was on days like today that he wondered if they'd even be together right now if not for Faith, or on the contrary, if it was actually parenthood that was driving them apart. Their busy schedules had meant very little time for each other. At first it was gradual, they'd go a day without talking and catch up quickly over breakfast before they both ran their separate ways. But by now, they'd missed so much of each other's lives that catching up seemed almost impossible, so they hardly tried. Any date night they got these days consisted of talking about Faith, followed by long periods of silence or small talk, one of them commenting on the décor of the restaurant, the other agreeing that yes, it was very nice.

As much as he hated to admit it, Steven felt himself growing to resent the turn his life had taken. Just a handful of years ago, he'd been young and vibrant and full of energy and interesting knowledge. Now his social circle was confined mostly to the boyfriends or husbands of Laura's friends or other fathers in their neighborhood. He heard himself make the very remarks he'd heard his own parents make. "It's a good thing they're so cute when they sleep," he'd say as he watched the neighborhood terror sleep in his mother's arms. Or he'd catch himself saying things like "Man, to have that much energy" as he watched his daughter and her friends toddle through the backyard.

Immediately he'd catch himself wistfully recalling that he *did* have that kind of energy not very long ago. But now he just felt tired and trapped. He loved Faith more than words could describe and wouldn't have traded her for anything, but sometimes in the darkest depths of the night, he'd lie awake and catch himself wishing that he had enjoyed his single life more while it had lasted. Or that he had waited longer before having children, or that he and Laura hadn't gotten married so quickly. But they were useless desires; he couldn't go back and change things now. Nor did he know if he wanted to—he really didn't know if there was one thing he could peg his unhappiness on—he liked his job, he loved his daughter, and he loved his wife.

It was at lunch today with a woman who was by far the prettiest in his class that he had finally realized what had died between him and Laura. Her obvious flirtation with him was flattering, to be sure, and it pained him a little to admit that he hadn't tried to stop it—that he'd hid his left hand from her as best as possible to keep his marriage from becoming a topic of conversation. But it was her questions and her keen interest in *him* that was intoxicating. Their conversation was not in the least bit mundane; it was witty and flirty and exciting, no old baggage bubbling to the surface because there was none. Beyond that, she was interested in what he had to say. If he thought about it, he couldn't remember the last time Laura had asked him about what he was doing in school. There were so many nights he came home on an absolute high, thrilled about something new that he'd gotten to do, and intent on telling his wife all about it. But when he walked in the door she was either upset or asleep, and he'd squelch the urge to talk about it. Today there'd been a woman across the table from him who had been leaning forward on her elbows, intent on not missing *any* of what he was telling her about. And the best part of it was, since she was studying the same thing - she understood it, and had stories of her own to share.

He shook his head now, dismissing the image from his mind of her white smile and glossy lips as she'd laughed at his jokes. *It was just a lunch. Laura's got nothing to worry about,* he told himself.

But the realization that struck Steven as he pulled into his driveway minutes later sent a fear through him that he'd never expected. No matter how he rationalized it to Laura, he realized that even *he* was unconvinced.

CHAPTER NINE

John

John still couldn't get used to the sight of a hospital bed in the middle of his living room. It seemed so invasive, as if the cancer hadn't already taken up enough of their lives; here it was next to his couch. The bed seemed institutional and impersonal—all wrong for the warmth of this house.

But what he really couldn't get used to was the sight of his wife lying in it. He'd summed up his biggest fear the day before, by mistake. He'd walked into the living room to see her sitting up—an increasingly rare occasion. He'd gingerly cupped her face in his hands as he gave her a kiss, pulling back to look at her face and ask how his "lovely wife" was feeling. Yet emotion had gotten the best of him, and he'd fumbled his words, calling her instead "my wovely life." He'd realized, however, that he hadn't necessarily been wrong after all. Except for the fact that *wovely* wasn't a word, Anne *was* his life. His every happiness had been wrapped up in her for more than thirty years, and here he was faced with the knowledge that they might not have thirty more *days* together. The fear of what was inevitable sat in his stomach like a hangover he couldn't sleep off—an ache and fatigue that made getting out of bed feel impossible. He walked around with an uneasiness and discomfort following closely like shadows; sleep was his only refuge.

Death was a strange thing when it announced its plans to visit. You expected it, knew it was coming, but still hoped beyond hope that it would get tied up somewhere on the road to your door and forget all about its plans.

Watching Anne as she slept today, he felt himself hope all over again. Rest was good, he told himself. Each minute she slept, he was sure she was gaining strength to beat this thing.

Logic did him no good; he would continue to hope until the very end. With a sigh, he put down the soup and crackers he'd brought in for her. He'd expected her to be awake, but he knew he should have known better. Lately she'd done hardly anything but sleep, and despite his hopeful thoughts just moments before, he knew it wasn't the good sign he tried to convince himself it was.

After quickly kissing his wife's forehead while she slept, John turned and lackadaisically made his way back to the kitchen to fix his own lunch. His appetite was gone, but he knew he had to eat. Facing the fridge, however, he found nothing that appealed to him and was considering skipping the meal all together when he heard someone come in the back door.

There was Abby, a white bag in one hand and a drink tray in the other.

"I figured you wouldn't feel like eating." She gave him a quick kiss on the cheek. "So I decided to bring all your favorites and *make* you eat."

He watched as she laid the food out on the table, overwhelmed with gratitude at her thoughtfulness. She'd brought him a cheeseburger, curly fries, and a chocolate milkshake. It was a meal he hardly allowed himself, only on *very* special occasions.

And in the midst of terrifying ones.

Smelling the food now, he had to admit he *was* hungry, and slowly he sat down at the table. "Thank you," was all he could manage.

Abby didn't answer, just peered through the door into the living room. "How's Mom?" she asked, less a question than a statement of concern.

"The same," he answered anyway, aware of the tears in her eyes when she turned back around to face him. Quickly, he tried to change the subject. "Your eyes look really green today," he commented, leaving out the fact that they reminded him so much of her mother's it hurt him to see them. "That color really brings them out," he gestured to her sweater. "I like the hunter green. It's classy."

"Thank you, Daddy, but hunter green," she tugged at the bottom of her sweater, looking confused. "This is navy blue." Her expression changed from one of confusion to one of concern as she quickly crossed the kitchen and sat down across from him. "Are you okay, Dad?"

"Of course I am." John took a big bite of his cheeseburger, trying his best not to let her see him squinting at her sweater. He could swear it was dark green. "This is good," he smiled at her and tried to change the subject. He could worry about his eyes later. "Thank you for getting it," he added as he took another bite.

"No problem," Abby was reaching into the bag for her own chicken sandwich, and the two ate in companionable silence.

"Laura hasn't been out here much," John said finally.

"She doesn't like seeing Mom like this." Abby was quick to defend her sister.

"Well, she doesn't have much of a choice. If she wants to see her mother before she dies, she's going to have to see her like this."

John immediately regretted his words as he watched Abby's face crumple across from him, her earlier tears returning. "I'm sorry," he said quickly. "That sounded harsher than I meant. It's just that," suddenly he had to fight for control of his emotions, the lump in his throat threatening to turn to tears. For a long while he sat, concentrating on swallowing, before trying to continue. "She doesn't," again the lump in his throat made it impossible to speak, but this time there was no stopping the tears. "She doesn't have much time left," he choked out. His lip was quivering so hard that he had to bite it, the effort of trying to keep from breaking down causing his whole face to shake. He wanted to be strong for Abby though, who was freely crying now, so he put on the bravest face he could. "I think it's time to say our good-byes." The admission of what he'd been denying for so long finally caught up to him, and his hand flew to his mouth in an attempt to keep the sobs back.

But they came anyway, and in a second Abby was across the table and in his arms, where they held each other—tears streaming down their cheeks for the woman they loved so deeply but could not save, their salty taste betraying their worst fears and breaking their hearts.

Abby

Abby stared blankly at her computer the next day, unable to motivate herself to work but at the same time unable to make herself leave. Her boss had made it clear that she could take whatever time she needed to deal with "her situation," as he'd put it, but she felt a loyalty to her work that she couldn't explain.

She knew, though, that she was in no state to be here—and in no state to be around people. She felt tears welling up in her eyes and grabbed her purse for a quick run to Starbucks.

"Going on a Starbucks run?" Tom called as she breezed past his desk, unaware of her situation.

"Yeah." She barely slowed down—in fact she sped up, breaking into a jog and jabbing the down arrow forcefully, waiting impatiently for the elevator to arrive.

"Abby, wait!" Tom called, and she could hear him hurrying through the kitchen and toward her.

Hurry up, she willed the elevator, pressing the button again and again and looking over her shoulder for Tom. She needed to be alone right now, but knew she didn't have the strength to turn him away.

The doors swung open just as Tom turned the corner, but Abby was inside in a flash and watching the doors close in front of his hopeful face.

She bit her lip as the elevator slowly descended, trying hard to stop the tears that had already begun flowing down her cheeks. She tried not to let herself think of her mother, although it seemed to be the only thought that she could formulate.

The trouble was, just the thought of her mother made her ache. The concept of never hearing Anne's voice again was something she expected and had begun to prepare for, all the while completely unable to comprehend the actuality of it. The thought of never being able to call home and hear her answer the phone scared her to the point of tears, and as a result she found herself constantly calling home to see if she was awake, trying to get as much as she could out of whatever time they had left. She knew she'd never be able to look at the world around her and *not* see her mom—movies and songs they had watched or listened to together, traditions they had shared that she would have to forge alone. The impending loss was overwhelming and therefore incomprehensible, and Abby would have given anything to be able to ignore it for just a second, a minute, an hour. But no matter where she went, she found it impossible, so as a plan B she'd decided to keep herself busy. Busy and alone. Which was precisely her problem with seeing Tom emerge from the office building just as she was about to cross the street.

"Abby, hold up!" he called again, jogging now.

Jesus, she whispered—both a curse and a prayer—and continued her hurried pace.

"Abby!" Tom was exasperated, she could tell, by the time he grabbed her arm and spun her around. "What the hell is going on?" She saw a flash of anger in his eyes and suddenly realized that he must have thought she was angry at *him*.

"Nothing," she said as gently as she could, biting her trembling lip. "I just need to be alone, okay?"

"No, it's not okay, because *you're* not okay. I can tell." He crossed his arms across his chest in a stubborn gesture of defiance.

"Look, it's not about you. It has nothing to do with you. I just can't handle this right now."

"Abby, I'm not letting you walk by until you tell me what's wrong."

She could tell he meant it, and at the compassion and concern in his voice, she felt the resolve she'd been carrying disappear.

"It's...God, I can't even say it." She closed her eyes against the tears and turned away from him, trying to compose herself.

"Abby." Tom grabbed her arm again and spun her around to face him. This time the anger was hers, and she could feel it flashing from her eyes.

"Just leave me alone!" she cried, writhing out of his grasp. "How many times do I have to tell you, I just need to be alone? I don't want you seeing me like this—don't want *anyone* seeing my like this. It's unprofessional."

"Right now, I don't give a damn about what's professional," Tom yelled right back. "You're crying, Abby, and all that matters is finding a way to make it better."

"You can't make it better!" she fired back. "No one can! I thought for a while if I ignored it and focused on other things it would make it all right, but it's not all right! *Nothing's* all right! My mother's dying, and I don't think I'll *ever* be all right again." She brought both hands to her face to cover her tears.

"Oh, Abby," she heard a recognition in Tom's voice and wondered briefly if he'd ever lost a parent, before feeling herself being pulled into his arms. She let him hold her, glad for his embrace despite her earlier promise to be alone. "I'm so sorry, Abby. I'm so sorry."

It was then she knew that he *must* have been through this before, because he said no more than that, exactly what she needed to hear. He didn't try and tell her that she *would* be all right again someday; she just couldn't see it now. He didn't say anything like *She was so lucky to have you in her life* or *you were lucky to have the time that you did.* Those were the words of someone who had never experienced this kind of loss—the kind of loss with pain so deep that no words could take it away. And so he didn't even try; he just held her for as long as she needed. When she finally pulled back, she offered a weak laugh as she wiped her eyes.

"I must look like hell." She tried to hide her face from him, but he tipped her chin toward him with his forefinger.

"You look beautiful," he told her. There was nothing but sincerity in his tone—no flirtation, no come-on, just a simple statement. That's why she was surprised when she suddenly grabbed him and kissed him.

Only when her lips were to his, her hands on either side of his face, did she realize what she'd just done, and she pulled back, embarrassed.

"I'm sorry." She began to turn away. "I—" but she couldn't finish, because suddenly Tom's arms were around her and he was kissing her.

And there, on a busy city street, Abby kissed Tom with every emotion in her, the turmoil of the past months finally finding its release in the least likely of places.

∽

Steven

Steven was ready to lose it. From the get go this morning, his day had been off to a rough start and had only gotten worse as it progressed.

It was a thousand little things, but by the time he got in the car to head home, he was shaking in frustration. His lack of time or energy to focus on himself in *any* way was taking its toll, and things at home had been tense. The joy that Faith brought him and Laura was beyond compare, and he was grateful for her every day. But the stress of raising a toddler while working two full time jobs *and* attending medical school *and* dealing with the impending loss of Laura's mother had afforded Steven little time for anything but comforting his wife. He knew that was part of marriage, that he needed to be there for her in her times of need and vice versa, but there was only so much he could do, and lately it was never enough.

Even now as he slowly steered out of the parking lot, he flipped open his phone to reveal two angry texts from Laura, wondering where he'd been all morning and why he hadn't called. Angry, he threw his phone back into the center console and sped up, darting around cars before slamming on his brakes in frustration at a red light and pounding the steering wheel.

While waiting for the light to change he grabbed a CD and jammed it into his stereo, turning the volume up as high as it went and losing himself in the music, finally finding a little time for himself. It was the volume of the music that kept him from hearing his phone ring; it was the volume of thoughts running through his head that kept him from thinking to check it.

Whatever the reason, he missed three calls in a row and, as he pulled into the garage, was blissfully unaware of what awaited him.

"I'm home," he called wearily as he came through the back door and threw his bag down, already wishing he was back in the car.

"Daddy!" Faith came barreling toward him, and he suddenly forgot his former wish, trying hard to cherish every second with her, knowing how fast she was growing up. She'd turned two a few months before, and already he couldn't believe how much he'd been missing.

"Hi, baby girl." He held her tiny body to his and kissed the top of her head. "How was your day?"

"Good!" she shouted with a grin.

"What did you do?" he smiled back, loving her enthusiasm.

"Colored," she stated, her *r* coming out as a *w* sound, and proudly she held up a piece of construction paper covered in scribbles.

"Oh, wow, it's *beautiful*," he said, honestly meaning it, and resisting the urge to help her pronounce her *R*s. She'd grow out of it soon enough, and for now it was so cute and endearing he even found himself hoping she *didn't*.

"Hey, babe," he called into the kitchen, surprised Laura hadn't greeted him yet. When she didn't answer, he walked cautiously around the corner, only to find her sitting at the counter with a glass of wine in one hand and her head in the other. "Hey," he repeated, hurrying toward her. "How are you feeling?" He knew the impending loss of her mother was hitting her hard, but this was a position he was still not used to seeing her in.

"I want a divorce," she said calmly as she looked up at him through bleary eyes.

Steven felt as though the wind had been knocked out of him. "You what?" he asked.

"I want a divorce," she repeated calmly before rising to cross the kitchen and put a casserole dish in the oven, which had just finished preheating.

"Are you serious?" he asked her, eyeing the empty bottle of wine in the recycling bin.

"Mm hmm," she said calmly, closing the oven and turning to face him.

"Hey," Steven glanced quickly at Faith, who had gone back into the living room and was quietly watching TV, before grabbing Laura's arm and pulling her into the dining room. "What's this all about?" he asked her in a hushed tone so their daughter wouldn't overhear. "I mean, I'm frustrated too, but we've barely been married two years," he added, wondering as he said it why that was relevant.

"Two years and a month, Steven," Laura said loudly, and again he wondered why timing was such an issue.

"Okay, two years and a month," he said softly, hoping she'd take the hint and keep her voice down.

"Look," she said, "I just can't do this." Steven had never seen his wife so calm and unaffected.

"Are you okay?" he asked her, concerned. "I mean, did you take something? I've never seen you like this."

"No, I didn't *take* anything." Her eyes blazed, but their red rims and bloodshot corners told him two things—she had been crying, and she had been drinking.

"Okay, maybe this is something we need to talk about when you haven't had a few cocktails." He started to walk away, wondering when she had taken that up. She'd never been one for drinking—always ordering virgin drinks when they went out.

"No, maybe this is something we need to talk about *now*." She grabbed his arm and spun him around, all her earlier calm gone.

"Keep your voice down," he said sternly, rubbing his arm and gesturing in the direction of the living room.

"I will not keep my voice down," she practically shouted. "I am going to say what I need to say, so don't try to stop me." She stumbled sideways, spilling wine over the rim of her glass. Laura just stared down at the stained carpet before slurring, "Look what you made me do."

"Laura, this is absolutely uncalled for." Steven was angry now. "Have you been drunk in front of our *daughter*? Not only is this ridiculously inappropriate, but what if something happened to her? You are in no state to handle a crisis, and my God, what if…" He trailed off, shaking his head at all that could have gone wrong, grateful it didn't.

"She's fine," Laura stated. "Dad's here to watch her."

"John's here?" Steven glanced around the doorframe and into the living room, and sure enough, there was the back of John's head on his sofa.

"Why didn't he say hi when I came in?" Steven looked back at Laura. "And why is he here?"

"He came by this morning," Laura stumbled into him, "to try and get me to go see Mom. But I told him I couldn't, and he just stayed." Steven guessed there was more to it than that, but still he was glad for the older man's presence. "And he didn't say hi to you," Laura added, "because he's *mad* at you." She stumbled over the word mad, but this time it wasn't her drunkenness that made him angry.

"Why the hell is he mad at me?" he whispered.

"Because I told him you've been cheating on me," Laura said confidently.

"You told him *what?*" Steven was shaking he was so angry. "Laura," he backed up, pointing at her. "You and I have our problems, and I've been less than the perfect husband at times, but I've *never* cheated on you. There have been times I've been tempted, but at the end of the day, *you're* my wife and I'd never do that to you."

"Well, you may as well be cheating on me—you're never around."

"I'm never around, Laura, because I'm throwing everything I have into studying for a career so I can provide for my wife and daughter!"

"You never wanted me to be your wife," Laura was yelling now. "You only proposed because you got me pregnant."

"Laura, that's ridiculous!" Steven cried.

"It is not," she slurred. "Remember? You gave me your class ring?"

"Are you going to hold that against me forever? I was trying to do the right thing."

"The *right* thing would have been to just leave me alone and let me raise Faith myself. It's what I'm doing anyway, basically, and at least then I wouldn't be *heartbroken* while doing it!"

"Laura," Steven put his hands on her shoulders. "You know you don't mean that. I could never walk away from you, and I could *never* walk away from Faith."

"And what if we *hadn't* had Faith? Would we still be together?"

"Laura," Steven's tone held a warning. "That's enough."

"Oh, just say it." Laura stumbled for a step before righting herself. "If we never had Faith in the first place, we probably wouldn't be together, now would we?"

There it was. The one thing they had both thought, the one thing they could never say. But Laura had said it, the punctuation to their argument, and Steven couldn't find it in him to respond. Disgusted, he turned away from Laura, only to see Faith watching them from the doorway, her young face marred by confusion.

"Faith, honey," he began to shake uncontrollably, "how long have you been standing there?" But Faith just turned and ran up the stairs as fast as her little legs would carry her.

"John!" Steven called as he started after his daughter. "How could you let her come in here?"

"I'm sorry." The remorse on John's face was obvious, mixed with a confusion Steven didn't understand. "I lost track of her." John shook his head confused.

*God, they're **all** crazy,* Steven thought as he took the stairs two at a time. Faith was sitting on her bed, talking to her stuffed animals, and as he stepped into her room, Steven wondered how on earth he was going to handle this. She was still young enough that the words they had said had probably gone right over her head—thank God. But the tones they'd taken with each other were tones she'd never heard her parents use—the sight of her mother in such a state, though she wouldn't have known the cause of it—were all things that had affected her, Steven was sure.

Taking a deep breath, Steven sat down beside Faith and attempted to describe to her something that he didn't understand himself.

Later that evening, after tucking her into bed and reading to her, Steven made his way wearily down the stairs. Laura was asleep on the couch, John sitting in one of the chairs that flanked either side of it, his face drawn.

"I'm sorry you had to see that," Steven began, but John put his hands up.

"Look, what's going on between you two is none of my business," he began and then immediately contradicted himself. "What *is* going on between you two?"

Steven shook his head and made his way to the kitchen. "You want a beer?" He ignored his father-in-law's question.

"Yeah, I'll take one." John followed him into the other room.

"What happened today?" Steven asked, still avoiding John's question, and the older man sat down at the counter.

"I came over to see Faith, and to try and get Laura to come see Anne - and I could just tell something was going on with Laura. So after she put Faith down for her nap, I sat down and poured her a glass of wine and told her to spill."

"And she did," Steven guessed.

"Yep. Started talking about you having an affair—you're not, are you?" John looked up, his expression hopeful.

"God, no!" Steven ran his hands through his hair. "Look," he sighed. "It's been tough, sure. I'd be lying if I said I haven't been tempted." His mind wandered briefly before he continued. "And there have certainly been times where I've said something I shouldn't, or left when I should have stayed, but I love Laura. When it comes down to it, I'd never hurt her like that."

"Good," John took a sip of his beer and nodded, as if he'd known all along. "Anyway, one glass of wine turned to two, and then she started talking about Anne, and before I knew it she was in tears. By the time Faith woke up, she was pretty tipsy, so I took

Faith on some errands. When we got back, she was just sitting at the counter with a blank expression on her face."

"Like when I got home," Steven mused, and John nodded.

"Yep. Sat like that for almost an hour. Didn't say much at all...I didn't know what to do, but I thought it best I stay, for Faith. I called Abby to go stay with Anne, and now here we are."

"Here we are," Steven parroted, wondering where exactly "here" was and what came next.

༄

CHAPTER TEN

Laura

Laura let herself in the front door of her childhood home, leaning her head back against it when it closed behind her. The silence of the house was deafening—save for the ticking of the old grandfather clock in the front hall and the beeping from her mother's machines in the living room, all was quiet. Her father was out with Abby; they'd both agreed to give her some much-needed alone time with her mother.

Laura had struggled to get here. She hadn't been home since the day Anne's hospital bed had been moved into the living room—confirmation that she was dying and had requested to spend her time at home. That had been months ago. It had been almost three months since her horrible fight with Steven, and though they hadn't said a whole lot to each other in those three months, he *had* made a point of encouraging her at every opportunity to see her mother.

Still, she'd struggled. Laura wanted to remember her mother the way she'd been in her prime—not shriveled in a hospital bed. But at her family's urging and faced with the reality that there wasn't much time left, she'd finally agreed to visit. Now here she was in a house that she didn't even recognize. It struck her then and there that it was her mother who had made this house what it was. The smells coming from the kitchen, the soft music that filled each sunny room—that was gone now, and it felt cold and empty. Quickly Laura crossed the floor, tears springing to her eyes, and found the first CD she could, pressing the play button repeatedly with an urgency she didn't quite understand. It wasn't until the first soft strains of the classical music her mother had loved so much filled the room that she sat back and let herself relax a little, composing herself before getting up and looking, for the first time, toward where her mother lay.

Her body looked small and withered beneath the thin cotton blanket, and Laura felt her heart break in two.

"Hey, Mom," she said softly as she sat on the edge of the bed and picked up her hand. "It's Laura," she added, though Anne's eyes remained closed, her breathing shallow but steady. "I'm sorry I didn't come sooner," she began, but stopped herself as she felt her throat close up with emotion. She knew she didn't have to continue anyway; if anyone would understand, it would be her mother. She studied her face now, trying to memorize it while at the same time trying to remember how it used to look. She pictured her mother's mouth laughing across the table from her at holidays, her eyes soft and gentle the way they'd been when she'd sung lullabies to Laura and Abby as kids.

How many memories they'd had together, just the two of them. When Laura was little, they'd gone horseback riding together, long trail rides under the summer sun. As she'd gotten older, Anne had taken her out of school for lunches out or down to the city for a birthday celebration. In recent years, they'd bonded on more of a peer level—late night phone conversations had become frequent in the years since Laura had Faith, and she and her mother had spent many a late morning out for coffee, talking in-depth about things that they'd only touched upon in the past.

It struck her now that this may be the last time she and her mother had alone together, and something inside broke. She watched her tears fall onto the parchment paper of her mother's hand, their fragility astonishing her.

"I just want you to know that I love you." She pressed her forehead to her mother's and squeezed her eyes shut against the tears that were once again forming. "You've been the best mom anyone could have asked for. I hope you know that."

There wasn't much left to say, and so she just sat there memorizing Anne's every feature, committing them to memory and vowing to never forget a single part of her mother.

Somewhere in the soft afternoon light she fell asleep, her head on her mother's shoulder as it had been so many times before. When she woke up, she heard soft voices coming from the kitchen and wandered in to find her father and Abby sitting at the table, both of them somber.

"Hey," Abby stood up quickly and wrapped Laura in a hug. "How are you holding up?"

Laura shrugged, fresh tears springing to her eyes. "I'm not, really," she half laughed, half sobbed as she wiped at her eyes with more force than she intended.

For the rest of the afternoon they gathered around Anne's bed, taking turns telling stories, laughing, and crying. They were there when she took her last breath; somehow John found the strength to make the necessary calls and arrangements. Abby and Laura escaped to the backyard when it came time for Anne to be taken from the house, unable to witness it.

It wasn't until late that afternoon when they were sitting again at the kitchen table that John reached into his coat pocket with shaking hands.

"Girls," he started, his voice cracking and thick with emotion. He stopped for a few seconds and licked his lips, trying to regain control of his emotions. "Your mother wrote these for you." Again his throat closed with emotion, and he stood silent. "She wanted me to wait until…" Finally, realizing he wouldn't get through this, he simply handed them each a letter with her name on it. All it took was one look at the familiar handwriting for Laura to break into tears again.

John simply gave a curt nod and left the room. Laura met Abby's gaze across the table, and without a word, both got up and retreated to her own room.

Laura took in the familiar surroundings of her childhood bedroom—her mother evident in all the trappings. The curtains they had hung together, the bedspread Anne had quilted for her high school graduation, the window seat they'd had so many late night talks on. She wondered if she'd ever be able to look around and *not* see her mother.

Slowly she lowered herself onto the window seat and opened the envelope with trembling fingers.

My Dearest Laura,

This is a difficult letter to write. As I do so, I'm sitting on the window seat where I've talked with you so many times—where I picture you reading this letter when I'm gone.

It seemed like this was an appropriate place for our last talk.

I hope you know what a blessing you have been to me. I probably didn't tell you often enough; I should have told you every single day. Even so, I'm telling you now from the most sincere place I can imagine. You have made my life so special, so complete—as I know Faith is making yours.

There are so many things I love about you, Laura. I love the way your whole face lights up when you're happy, the way I never had to guess at your feelings, you wear them on your sleeve. You and your sister are so similar that way. I love your sense of adventure, your excitement over seeing new places, the color of your eyes.

There are so many things I love about you, but there are a few in particular that I think you need to know about now. I love your gumption, Laura. You have been handed some difficult situations, particularly over the last few years, but you tackle each one with fervor and determination, and I not only love that about you, but I respect it.

I love your kind heart and your gentle spirit. You've always been that way—always thinking about others first. That's a gift, and it's rare. I hope you never lose that.

I love your fighting spirit, and your courage and your conviction—always fighting for the things you believe in and refusing to give up.

I could go on and on, my dear, but there's something else to be said—something very important.

You've always had a childlike quality to you, and I mean that in the best possible way. You have a curiosity for everything, and see things as though you're seeing them for the first time.

But best of all, Laura, you <u>love</u> like a child.

Loss has the power to shape you and to harden your heart. So many people experience loss—breakups, divorce, death—and it changes them. They stop opening themselves up to the hurt, and therefore they stop opening themselves up to all that life has to offer. Loss has the ability to take away your capacity to love fearlessly, piece by piece. The loss you must face in order for this letter to reach you is a great one. I remember losing my own mother, and wanting to close off completely, but I pray that you won't. I pray that no matter what comes, Laura, you will continue to love the way that you always have—with your heart wide open.

Know that you and Abby have been the brightest part of my life, and know that wherever I am, I am missing you and loving you and waiting for you with open arms.

Love you always, my dear girl.

Mom

Tom

Tom had no idea what he was doing here.

His presence was completely inappropriate—that much he *did* have an idea of. Even if his presence itself had been appropriate, the way he was going *about* being present was not. He peeked out again from behind the wall he was hiding behind, craning his neck to get a better sense of what was going on. The group was huddled at the front of the room, and he saw Abby on the far side, standing next to a woman who looked exactly like her. She looked up, and quickly he ducked back behind the tree.

He felt like an absolute idiot.

Word of the death of Abby's mother had spread through the office almost immediately, and for the life of him, Tom couldn't comprehend the emotions it had brought forth in him. All throughout the day that he'd found out, his phone had been in his hand. He'd drafted text after text, unable to decide what he wanted to say and therefore unable to send anything at all.

He was in a tough position. His feelings for Abby were stronger than he cared to admit; based strictly on those, he'd be standing next to her right now, a figure of support. But their relationship was very new, and therefore he wasn't sure of his place. More than anything he wanted to be there for her, to offer her his shoulder if she needed it and his love if she'd take it. But nothing he could offer her seemed right.

I'm so sorry, Abby, he'd tried writing. *Please know I'm here if you need me.*

That's the closest he'd come to success, but when it came down to it, he couldn't press send. *If you need me*, he'd thought, sounded like he just assumed that she needed him, and that seemed bold and arrogant—two things he didn't want to be in this situation.

He knew he was overanalyzing it, that really she would have appreciated anything at all, but just couldn't do it.

Instead he'd made a significantly dumber decision—getting in his car and showing up at the funeral. Now he had absolutely no idea what to do.

Finally he heard the music starting and slipped around the corner to stand along the back wall. Abby was seated now, next to the same woman she'd been standing next to earlier, and Tom assumed this was her sister. Next to them was an older man who wore the grief of the world on his face, and the raw strength of that emotion told Tom that he must be her father.

The service was short, a sweet celebration of Anne's life, and Tom felt he knew Abby a little better through it, just by getting to know more about the woman who had raised her.

Suddenly a bagpiper stepped out from behind him, startling him. The lone bagpiper began to play "Amazing Grace," walking slowly down the aisle and pausing at the front before turning and making his way back toward him.

Abby, who had been holding it together remarkably well until now, literally crumpled in her seat, wracked with sobs. Seeing her in so much pain made him want to wrestle the bagpiper to the ground and make him stop playing. But he finished his song, and when he was done, the funeral procession rose and slowly began its way back up the aisle.

It didn't take Abby's gaze long to find Tom's, and once it did he suddenly knew beyond the shadow of a doubt that he'd made the right decision in coming here. The depth of the gratitude in those eyes was matched only by the depth of her visible despair, and it was all he could do not to go to her.

I love you, he mouthed to her—surprising even himself. They'd only kissed the once; he'd taken her on a few dates since then, and neither could deny that they had feelings for each other. But it had hardly been three months—the severity of his feelings and the fact that he was speaking them aloud now astonished him. He was suddenly panicked—worried it was the wrong time to say it, that she wouldn't want to hear it right now—or ever.

But at Abby's fresh onset of tears and the *You too* she mouthed in response, he knew he'd found the only thing he needed to say.

֎

Steven

"Are you sure your dad's going to be okay tonight?" Steven asked as he stroked Laura's hair back from her face. The two of them had collapsed on the couch, exhausted after the long day.

"Yeah, I think so. Abby's spending the night there tonight. I was thinking of going over and spending tomorrow night there," she offered tentatively, looking up at him.

Things had been tense between them since their episode, but Anne's death had brought them closer.

"I think that's a good idea," he confirmed for her, and she once again relaxed her head onto his shoulder.

"I feel so bad for him," Laura began to cry. "He's just lost the one person he loves most in the world." She wiped at her tears, and Steven felt her shoulder sag beneath his arm.

"Hey," he pulled her close, looking into her eyes. "Do you know that *you* are the person I love most in the world? You know that, right? Nothing's ever going to change that."

A slow smile started across Laura's face, the first he'd seen in weeks. "I love you too," she said softly, the gravity of the moment lost on neither of them.

"Today made me realize how much we have at stake here," Steven continued quickly, fighting emotions he hadn't known he had. "We've got to get it together, Laura."

Laura nodded her agreement. "I know," she said. "I know I have to lose you someday, but I'm *not* going to let that be anytime soon."

"I'm sorry I've been away so much," Steven began, but Laura stopped him.

"No, please don't apologize. I know why you're doing it."

"No," Steven took a deep breath. "You don't." Laura looked at him with a hint of fear in her eyes, and he plunged ahead before she could worry. "I mean, yeah, I'm working really hard to graduate on time and start a career for myself so I can provide for you guys. That's a priority, and I absolutely cannot fail—will not fail. But that's the thing." He paused before continuing.

"My career is something I *know* that if I work at, I will succeed at. There are mathematics behind it. You work hard—you reap the benefits. But being a husband and a father is different. I watched my father keep his distance. I hardly knew *either* of my parents, and I've been so afraid that I'll turn out like them, that I've been throwing all my effort into the one thing I know I *will* be good at. The thought of failing as a father scares me so much that I've been trying to avoid it, because if I'm not doing it, I can't fail at it."

He saw Laura nod in understanding. "But I realized, a little late, I guess, that doing so makes me *exactly* like my father. So I guess what I'm trying to say is that I'm still going to throw as much energy as I can into school, but I'm going to stop avoiding being home. It's not failing as a husband or a father that scares me anymore—it's missing out on fatherhood. Life's too short," he trailed off, the emotions of the day catching up with him, "to waste it being afraid."

Laura was silent, but when he finally met her eyes, he saw understanding and love behind her tears.

"I love you," she said to him. "Thank you for telling me all that."

"I love you too," he murmured, pulling her close and feeling like a weight had been lifted.

∽

John

John's vision was getting worse.

He'd noticed it with increasing frequency over the past few months. Colors, particularly the dark ones, were difficult for him to identify and differentiate between. Objects blurred in front of him, even when they were directly in front of him. *Especially* when they were directly in front of him.

He'd been able to ignore it throughout Anne's illness; her medical situation had taken precedence over his, hands down. At the funeral he'd written off the blur of his surroundings by blaming the tears that had filled his eyes, and later, when all of his tears were cried, by blaming their dryness. In the weeks that followed, he found several excuses. Fatigue, for one. Sleep had not come easily to him since Anne's death. Although she had spent her last few months in a hospital bed in their living room, her presence had still been there. Now the house simply felt empty, and John spent several nights sitting in his chair by the window and simply staring out it. The next morning his eyes would be red and puffy, and any vision problems, he'd blame on this.

Yet as one month passed and then another and his eyes didn't change, he couldn't disregard it any longer.

Still, he stayed away from the doctors and the hospital. He couldn't bear to set foot in there, not with all the terrible memories of Anne's diagnosis and progressing illness.

Instead, he busied himself with other things—things like Faith. His granddaughter had become his biggest joy. Each time he saw her, she looked a little more like her grandmother, and he found comfort and peace in their similarities.

At the moment, she was perched on his lap listening intently to a bedtime story. She laughed out loud at parts, and the sound warmed him to the core. As he finished, she peered up cautiously at him through impossibly long lashes. "One more?" she asked hopefully.

"No, sweetheart," he chuckled. "That *was* your one more—remember? In fact, I've read you three more books than usual, and now it's *way* past your bedtime."

He prepared himself for an outburst—they were less frequent these days but still happened occasionally—but this time she just nodded and climbed off his lap and into her bed. John wrapped her in a big hug before rising to turn the light off.

"Grandpa John?" she asked softly but with urgency, fumbling over her letters in that endearing way that made *r*'s sound like *w*'s and everything else sound like an *m*.

"Yeah?" Immediately he was back at her bedside.

"What's that noise?"

John strained to listen to whatever she was hearing. "That's just the water in the pipes, honey. Your mom's doing the dishes downstairs."

"I didn't kiss Mommy good night," she said, and immediately he knew it had been a mistake to mention her.

"Yes you did," he reminded Faith. "Twice."

"I want to give her one more hug and kiss." She sat up, stalling.

"Faith," John tried to make his voice as stern as possible, though he was melting inside. "No more tonight. I'll make sure she comes and gives you one more kiss before *she* goes to bed." He knew if Faith went downstairs now, getting her to bed would be another thirty-minute ordeal, and it was already past her bedtime.

"Grandpa John?" she asked again as he rose a second time.

"Yeah?" He paused in the doorway, not falling for it this time.

"Where's Grandma?"

Her simple question broke his heart and stole his breath, and he had to steady himself on the doorknob before turning back around and kneeling next to her.

"She's up in Heaven, honey. She's an angel now."

"Why?" Faith asked.

"Because God needed her," he said, the first thing that popped into his mind, wondering how on earth to go about answering this particular string of questions.

"Why?" she repeated.

"I don't know, honey," he said honestly, stumped for anything else to say.

Faith was silent, and John tried to fill the silence.

"Sweetheart, do you know what's great about having a grandma who's an angel?" Faith shook her head, contemplating.

"Because now she can be with you *all* the time. You never need to be scared or lonely, because you always have your grandma with you."

Faith nodded, looking a little confused, and John wondered what exactly you were supposed to say to a three-year-old about this kind of thing. Worried he may have confused her even more, he took it in a dew direction.

"And you always have *me* with you too, Faith. You don't remember this, because you were just a baby, but the day that you were born, I promised you that I was always going to protect you, and I will. It's my most important job."

Faith smiled slightly.

"I love you." He leaned down to give her one last hug.

"Love you," she repeated softly as he closed the door behind him, his heart breaking in his chest—the pain of it pushing any concern over the fact that the hallway blurred before swaying back into focus, or thoughts of how the words on the pages of that bedtime story had disappeared right in front of him—to the furthest corners of his mind.

༒

Tom

"I'll have the bone-in Ribeye, please." Tom handed his menu to the waiter and refocused his attention on the woman sitting across from him. Abby was absolutely gorgeous.

Tonight she'd swept her hair back from her face and had worn a soft grey dress that made her eyes look more blue than green. Her eyes were dancing in the candlelight, the stress and sorrow of the last few months hardly visible in the soft light.

"I think you're wrong," she was saying.

"I am absolutely *not* wrong," he argued.

"You *are!*" She was laughing now. "That's his natural hair!"

"No way," Tom retorted. "There's *no way* that's not a rug."

"Twenty bucks," Abby stuck out her hand.

"Done." He took it, shaking it once firmly before grabbing his glass of wine and leaning back in his chair and smirking at her. "You know men have a sense of these things."

The man in question tonight was a senior account executive who had recently started working at the same company that Tom and Abby worked for. He had suspiciously thick, brown hair that didn't *quite* match his sideburns. Abby was shaking her head.

"I would hope you don't spend *that* much time looking at other men."

"I thought you told me women check out other women more than they do men," Tom stated.

"Oh, we do," Abby agreed with him. "Mostly to see how our outfit for the day measures up with theirs. But clearly," she gestured to his bright orange golf shirt and khaki pants, "that's not something that concerns you in the least."

"You don't like my shirt?" He sat up, feigning shock.

"Oh, it's fine," Abby laughed. "If you're actually golfing. Or, apparently, deer hunting."

Tom looked around. Sure enough, every other man in the restaurant was in, at the *very* least, a shirt and tie. Now legitimately concerned, he looked at Abby, but she was just smiling at him from across the table, and he relaxed a little. "I didn't realize it was so dressy." He started to make excuses, but she laughed and grabbed his hand.

"You look great. I was just giving you a hard time."

He shivered at the touch of her hand, and as she began to talk animatedly about something her niece had said, he marveled at how *easy* this felt. To be arguing over something as insignificant as his shirt or a co-worker was a delightful change from what he'd faced over the last several years, and he was enchanted by their easy banter. But what shocked him even more was the depth behind it.

Her mother's death had bonded them in a way that for some couples took years. Their conversation went easily from serious topics to lighter ones, difficult discussions to easier ones, with absolutely seamless transitions and humor thrown in with most of it.

Sure enough, by the time their steak came, they'd gone from arguing about whether a co-worker's hair was real or not to talking seriously about religion and their own personal beliefs. Tom talked about the way he wanted to raise his kids, his goals for each of them, and Abby listened with rapt attention before disclosing her own future dreams for a family.

After their meal they ordered dessert, and by the time they left to walk home and he grabbed her hand, he had the feeling that he wanted to face his future with this woman.

The thought surprised him, so quickly after his last relationship—which happened to be a marriage, but he didn't fight it. Something about her hand in his felt right, and he missed its warmth when she pulled it away to rummage in her purse for some ChapStick.

"Need any?" She held the stick out to him, and he took it gratefully.

"So what do you want to do now?" she asked with a hint of invitation, and he was just about to answer her when his phone rang from his pocket. He saw a flash of irritation on Abby's face—though he had explained to her that he needed to keep it on in case of an emergency with one of the kids, he knew it still bothered her.

"One sec," he ignored her irritation, not because he wanted to but because he had to, and checked his phone. Sure enough.

"What's up, Beth?" He held the phone with one hand and reached for Abby's with his other, but she pulled it away, her frustration with the interruption evident.

"I need you to come out to the house," she said matter-of-factly.

"Why, what happened?" he asked, concerned.

"Well, as you can hear, Luke's having an absolute meltdown, and I can't get Ben to come out of his room."

"Why? What happened?" he repeated as he listened to the wails in the background.

"Look, I'll tell you when you get here, just get here," she said and, with that, hung up.

Tom hesitated, trying to buy time, trying to decide what to do. He'd promised his kids that he'd walk through fire for them, and he would. At this point, it was simply a matter of Beth's judgment – whether or not the kids actually needed *him* tonight, or whether she was just sick of trying to deal with it herself and wanted someone else to take over. Beth was a great mother—there was no doubt about that—but since their divorce she'd begun playing the martyr; all of a sudden, in her words, she was "single parenting" two children. Nevermind the fact that he was out there at the *very* least three nights a week, from the time the kids were done with school until they went to bed, and more often than not, he'd pick up the nights when Beth was out of town on business. Add that to every other weekend, and he wondered if he may see the kids more than she did. Therefore, as he looked at the woman standing next to him on the sidewalk—the hopeful expression on her face mixed with the fact that this was the first time he'd seen her in almost two weeks—his first instinct was to ignore Beth and stay with Abby.

But as he recalled the sound of his son's wails, he knew what he had to do.

"I'm so sorry," he began, reaching for his keys, but at the stony look that came over Abby's face, he knew he didn't have to elaborate much. "The kids need me," he offered, an explanation. He watched as her expression warmed slightly.

"It's okay." She shrugged, though he knew that it really wasn't.

"I know this isn't a situation you usually have to put up with, six months into a relationship," he said, and then realized that this was a deeper conversation for another time. "But I'll make it up to you," he finished lamely, giving her a quick kiss before hailing a cab for her. "I'll see you at work tomorrow," he said.

Abby didn't say anything—just climbed into the cab. He knew she'd understand in the long run—this had happened before, and she always did, after the initial disappointment wore off. Still, as he turned to head to his car, he didn't know what he was dreading more—what awaited him at the house, or trying to explain to Abby a situation that he was still trying to get his own head around.

∽

CHAPTER ELEVEN

Laura

There were a lot of feelings that Laura hated. She hated the feeling of a day at the height of summer, when a simple stroll around the block left her skin sticky to the touch, her hair pasted to her forehead in heavy wisps she couldn't scrape away.

She hated the chills and shivers that stemmed from her teeth and worked their way into her very jawbone after she bit into something cold.

She hated the minutes after a scare, when her heart actually started to pound *after* the fact, when the reality of what could have just happened set in. That had happened once when Faith was two and had been playing at the neighbor's house with their son Jeff. After returning from the grocery store, Laura had walked over to pick her up and had wound up chatting with Kim for almost an hour. They were adding an addition to their house, and she'd followed Kim from room to room as she pointed out new features, what this wall would become, what that empty space would house. Laura found herself getting lost in the possibility of it all, and by the time they made it to the back porch, her attention was anywhere but on Faith. She'd noticed too late that the second-story deck they stood on had no railings yet—those would complete the addition. She noticed too late that the kids were playing dangerously close to the edge of it. She noticed too late that Faith's shoes were untied. It wasn't until she heard Jeff's small voice screaming that she sprang into action, suddenly beside Faith in a speed only terrified mothers could accomplish, sweeping her daughter into her arms *just* as she was going over the edge.

It had taken her legs the rest of the afternoon to stop shaking, her heart rate finally dropping back to normal after what seemed like hours.

She hated that feeling.

But there was one feeling that Laura hated above all others. One feeling that no matter the reason behind it brought with it an onslaught of its insecure counterparts like inadequacy and abandonment. The feeling Laura hated most was falling asleep with somebody and then waking up alone.

Falling asleep together was a commitment, and waking up alone meant that at some point during the night, her partner in crime had decided she was not worth the commitment, and snuck out, leaving only his scent on the cold pillowcase that she woke up next to.

This was a ridiculous sentiment to hold on to, she realized, after years of marriage, when she knew full well that her husband had responsibilities that sometimes required him to rise earlier than she did. Still, old memories fade just as slowly as old habits do, and she couldn't shake the utterly abandoned feeling she woke up next to when the bed was otherwise empty.

This was how she'd woken up this morning, and it had been the first clue that her day was off to a less than ideal start. The second happened almost immediately after, when she glimpsed the red letters of her bedside alarm clock blinking 9:07. She couldn't remember the last time she'd slept past 7:00, probably before Faith was born, and the fact that her three-and-a-half-year-old had not woken her yet was cause enough for alarm. Scrambling out of bed, she shoved her feet into a pair of well-worn slippers while simultaneously pushing her arms through the sleeves of her robe, already out of the bedroom door as she was cinching it around her waist. She hurried through the upstairs hallway and was almost to the bottom of the stairs when she paused. Faith's voice carried above the hum of the electric mixer, which she was shocked to discover, Steven had known where to find. The sound of a child's voice, *her* child's voice, warmed her heart, and for a second she forgot her crabby mood. She loved the inflection at the end of every sentence that, although she knew was simply childlike enthusiasm, still made it sound like Faith was asking a string of questions, one after another. This morning, Faith sounded like this:

"Hey, Dad! Once? Mom and I were making breakfast? And I spilled the flour all over the counter? And I thought she was going to be mad? But instead? She took her finger and drew a heart with my name in it!"

Laura brought a hand to her mouth and smiled at the memory, her daughter's recollection making her forget completely any negative emotion from minutes ago.

"Do I hear voices?" she asked, taking the last two steps at once and sweeping Faith into her arms. "Good morning, sweetheart!" she crooned, kissing the top of her head before sending her back to the counter and crossing the kitchen to give her husband a kiss. His lips were pursed and tight, and he turned his head away a moment too soon after a cold and unwelcome kiss. Laura's sudden good mood vanished. "Why did you let me sleep so late?" she asked confrontationally, turning her back on him to grab a coffee mug.

"Mom!" Faith interrupted. "I was just telling Daddy about that time I spilled the flour all over the counter! Remember?"

"I heard, honey. Of course I remember," she replied, looking pointedly at Steven to let him know she was still waiting for an answer.

"I've got it covered down here," he replied, not really answering her question at all. Perhaps that was his intention.

"You know I hate when you do that," Laura said, knowing full well how petty it sounded, and how many mothers would kill for the chance to sleep in. She knew it wasn't worth picking a fight over and wondered for a moment what on earth she was doing.

"Laura," Steven suddenly put the mixer down and spun to face her. "I am not a college fling. I am not just some guy, who spent the night with you and got what he wanted, and is going to leave in the morning. I am your husband, and I love you, and you need to get over those insecurities, and let me do something nice for you. Faith and I were down here trying to make you breakfast in bed."

Laura's shoulders slumped underneath his hands, and she let herself be folded into his arms, as Faith continued to chatter at them both from her perch on her stool, mixing spoon in hand.

"That's the position you were in the first time I realized I wanted to spend my life with you," Steven whispered, turning Laura so she could see her daughter gesturing with a mixing spoon. She knew the night he was referring to—she had made him dinner, which they had never got around to eating, they were so hopelessly in love with each other.

That had also been the night Faith was conceived.

And she wondered, as she apologized for being so cranky and thanked Steven for such a kind thought, when she had become so mistrusting, why it was obvious to both her and Steven that she was sabotaging their relationship, picking fights at every available opportunity.

Things had been great between them these last few months; they'd both been making a continued effort to make each other more of a priority. What was wrong with her, then?

"Maybe you're so used to drama in your relationship that you're picking fights just for some semblance of normalcy," Abby suggested later, plopping her head into her hands as the two of them watched Steven and Tom playing with Faith the backyard.

Laura was amazed at her sister's clarity and insight, and she figured she might be right.

"I think I'm just frustrated with the bigger picture, too," she added to her sister, and at Abby's questioning look, continued.

"This is the life I've always wanted, Abs," she began, "ever since I was a little girl. All through high school and college, I watched the other women in my class 'make something of themselves' by becoming journalists and advertising executives, lawyers and doctors, nurses and teachers. I saw my friends buy their first 'power suits' the week before graduation and head off to conquer the business world, collect their paychecks, and make a name for themselves. I watched all this with admiration and awe, and always a little bit of envy, because I never aspired to any of it for myself. I watched Mom raise us, and *that's* what I always wanted to be—a mom. I'm sure feminists everywhere are dropping dead and rolling in their graves to hear me say this, but to stay at home and raise a family has always been enough for me."

"You're a great mom!" Abby interrupted, trying to follow where Laura was going with this. "And the women's movement was about choice. If your *choice* is to be the best mother you can be, then that's great! And hey, I'm with you—it's what I've always wanted too," she said, and Laura could see the longing in her eyes as she watched Tom in the yard.

"Right, I know, but here's the thing—all this time I've been forgetting to consider that Steven is just as much a part of this family as Faith is. We've both been so wrapped up in Faith and our desire to be good parents that we've forgotten about each other. And I'm frustrated with it. We've been doing better, both of us making an effort, but we really only do the big stuff. Steven sends me flowers once a month and takes me on a few really nice dates, and he figures he's done his part. Like this morning—little things. I hate waking up alone—he knows that. I love spending mornings with them. He knows *that*. It wouldn't have been so hard to just wake me up - even just to give me a kiss, then let me go back to sleep."

"Laura, I think you're overreacting." Abby shook her head. "He was just trying to do something *nice*."

"Exactly!" Laura cried, leaving Abby looking completely lost. "Something *nice*, but not something nice *for me*. Look, everyone knows that sending your wife flowers is something nice to do, but what if you send her flowers she hates? What if you despise carnations, and Tom sends you a bouquet of them? It's nice that he did it, but it's not nice for *you*. Because he should at least take the time to find out what you like or not. It's *nice*, very nice, that Steven wanted to make me breakfast in bed. But come on, how long have we been married? He *knows me*—at least he *should* know me—well enough to know that given the choice, I'd rather be up early and spending time with the two of them *any* day than getting breakfast in bed. *That* would have been the nicer gesture."

Abby laughed, shaking her head at her baby sister. "My god, you're impossible. I get it, I do, but try to focus on the positive. Try not to say *one* negative thing about Steven for the next two weeks, and I mean it. No cheating. See if you can do it, and I think you'll start to see the good in everything he does instead of the bad."

Laura considered this as Abby gave her a quick kiss on the cheek, collecting her purse.

"Looks like the men have it covered, I'm going to run to the store quick before lunch with Daddy. I forgot to get him a card," she grimaced.

"You're a terrible daughter, the worst ever!" Laura called after her, feigning shock, bringing her attention back to her husband, laughing with Faith in the backyard, and committing herself to Abby's challenge. *Two weeks,* she thought. *I can do that.* Yet by the time she'd left fifteen minutes later, she'd already broken her vow three times, stopping herself from stomping into the backyard to yell at him again for the crooked way he parked his Jeep in the garage. *This is going to be harder than I thought*, she realized as she backed out of the drive toward lunch with her father.

She wondered just how quickly she'd fallen into the habit of dwelling on the negatives, and just how quickly she could pull herself out of it.

John watched as his daughter waited for the light to change, her honey-blonde hair catching the August sunlight and sending it straight back heavenward. His throat tightened watching her— her mannerisms were the same Anne had possessed—the dainty way she held her hands in front of her as she waited, the way she repeatedly pushed herself on to her tiptoes, and then lowered back onto her heels, too antsy to stand still in one spot and completely unaware of the habit. Her usually hazel eyes squinted against the midsummer sun, turning an unusual sea green in its light. The red light changed green to match them, and she hurried across the street and into the restaurant, flip-flopped feet smacking as she saw him and waved.

"Hey, Dad," she smiled, kissing his cheek as she slid into the booth beside him. "Is Abby here yet?"

John shook his head and refolded his hands in front of him. "For a minute there, I thought you were her!" He smiled, trying to play it off like he was kidding. The resemblance between the two was uncanny, and besides, his eyes weren't quite what they used to be.

Laura laughed, unaware. "Very funny. We're easier to tell apart than that."

"Not lately," John said, suddenly serious. "You've both been walking around with that same ridiculous scowl on your face all the time."

"Not anymore," Laura squeezed his hand. "I'm turning over a new leaf. But let's not get into that now, Dad! It's your birthday!" Laura smiled, handing him a white square with "DADDY" printed neatly in the middle.

"My favorite word," he smiled, running his thumb along the ridge to tear it open, marveling that no matter how old his daughters got, they were never too old for the familiar sentiment.

He opened the card, one of those musical numbers that sang at you as soon as they were unfolded, and he flashed an embarrassed smile as the other patrons looked up to locate the source of their interruption, and then looked back at the card in front of him, secretly pleased that Laura had picked a card that played one of his favorites, touched that she would have remembered.

He focused his attention on reading the sentiment that he was sure would match the thought, but the words blurred before his eyes, and he squinted, trying to focus. No luck.

"Dad?" Laura asked, noting his silence.

John looked up and grinned, and from the look on Laura's face, he knew she was aware he was overcompensating. He was banking on her not knowing what he was overcompensating *for*. Since their mother's death, his daughters had become mother hens when it came to his health, and he didn't want them squawking over this. "That's very sweet," he lied, reaching across the table to pat her hand. The dejected look on her face vanished, and she flashed that beautiful grin he loved so much. Just as he was thinking of a way to change the subject, Abby showed up, and as he watched his daughters, who acted so much like their mother, talking across the table, he knew that Anne was with him today after all.

CHAPTER TWELVE

Laura

"Faith," Laura leaned her elbows on the table, bringing her nose within inches of her daughter's. "How can I explain this to you so you understand? Let me see..." She paused, scratching her chin for effect. "Okay, look at this picture you just colored. You did such a good job! Are you proud of it?" Faith nodded, her eyes trained on Laura, curious. "What if..." Again, she paused for effect, removing the cap from a thick black Sharpie. "What if I took this marker and colored *all* over it?" Faith immediately wrapped her arms protectively around her drawing, pulling it away from her mother. "Would you be happy with me? Or would you be angry with me?"

"Angry," her four-year-old responded quietly.

"Good. Why?" Faith shrugged, so Laura filled in the blanks for her. "Because I'd just ruined your project, a project that you worked very hard on, and one that took you a lot of time. You've spent all afternoon coloring that, and what if I just came over here and started coloring all over your hard work? You'd be angry, wouldn't you?"

Faith nodded, so Laura continued.

"Okay. Well, this clean kitchen," she gestured toward the spotless kitchen, "and this clean living room," she motioned toward the neatly vacuumed carpet, "and this table," she pointed at the table underneath Faith's elbows, covered in glitter and glue, marker and paint, "this is all *Mommy's* project. This is what I spend a lot of time on, just like you did on your drawing. And this is what *I'm* proud of, just like you're proud of your drawing. So imagine how I must feel when you don't clean up after yourself. I feel like you've just taken a big marker to my project. Do you understand?"

Again, Faith nodded.

"I'm sorry for yelling before," Laura continued, sinking to her knees in front of Faith's chair. "And I understand making a mess—that's half the fun!" She smiled and touched her finger to Faith's nose as she said this, bringing forth that giggle she loved so much.

"But you need to respect Mama's project, okay? After you're done, you need to help clean up the mess. Okay? Can you help me do that?"

Faith nodded, this time enthusiastically. "Good," Laura said, enveloping her daughter in a hug. Within a matter of seconds, Faith was chattering away again, and as she stood up she wondered why young children completely lost their voice when being scolded.

"I don't know where you find it in you to be so patient," a deep voice said behind her, and she spun on her heel to see Steven standing in the doorway.

"Hey," she glanced at her watch, startled. "What are you doing home so early?"

"I took the afternoon off," he responded, bringing his hands from behind his back to reveal a bouquet of roses, Peruvian lilies, and yellow solidago. "The florist said this would be a good bouquet for this time of year..." He trailed off, suddenly embarrassed, probably mistaking her temporary paralysis for something other than complete and utter shock, Laura realized.

But her feet were cemented to the floor. This was so *completely* un-Steven. Her first reaction was doubt; she wanted to ask what he had done that had guilted him into buying her flowers. She opened her mouth to ask him, but something stopped her. She thought about what Abby had said—maybe he *did* really want to try to make this work. Maybe things *could* change. One look at his face told her she was right; he looked as vulnerable as she'd ever seen him—not the least bit guilty. Suddenly her face broke into a huge grin, and she reached for the flowers.

"They're *gorgeous!*" she exclaimed, holding them out and inspecting them. *"Perfect!"* Thank you, Steven." She gave him a quick hug with her free arm, suddenly shy. "You have no idea how much this means..." She trailed off, emotion suddenly caught in her throat, and she turned before he could see it, busying herself with putting her flowers in a vase and arranging it in the middle of the counter. She turned back around to look at Steven, who was bent over the kitchen table admiring Faith's artwork. He looked up, almost surprised to see her still standing there.

"What are you waiting for? Go change!"

"Change?" Suddenly self conscious, she ran a hand over her rumpled oxford, noting her unkempt hair in the reflection of the microwave. "Why?"

Now it was Steven's turn to grin. "You and I, my dear," he began, taking her in his arms, "have a reservation tonight at the Drake, and we need to be checked in by 4:00."

"The Drake?" she parroted, dumbfounded.

"Yep," Steven continued, "and dinner reservations at Japonais, followed by drinks at the Violet Hour, followed by..." He trailed off, aware of their daughter sitting behind them. Laura followed his gaze.

"What about Faith?" she whispered

"It's all taken care of," he said with confidence. "Abby will be here in twenty minutes."

Laura was speechless. With a grin, she kissed her husband and ran upstairs to pack.

Standing in her closet, she mentally vetoed everything she owned. It had been so long since they'd been out like this. Then suddenly she remembered the dress she had gotten the Christmas before last and had never gotten a chance to wear. She found it hanging in the back of her closet, long forgotten and still in its hanging bag. Pulling back the plastic, she carefully took it off the hanger and stepped into it, praying it would still fit. The zipper slid up her back effortlessly, and she stepped in front of the mirror, momentarily stunned at her transformation. Where a frumpy mother had stood minutes ago, there now stood a sophisticated woman. The green satin clung to her in all the right places and turned her eyes the color of the early spring leaves. She brushed her hair and pulled it into an elegant twist, taking her time applying the makeup that she so rarely wore, finishing her look with a touch of lip-gloss. Tiptoeing back into her closet, she selected a pair of matching silk heels and slid her feet into them, throwing a change of clothes for tomorrow and a pajama set for tonight into a small duffel, at the last minute replacing the pajama set with a silk negligee. *What the heck,* she thought with a smile as she turned off the closet light and shouldered her overnight bag. When she got to the bottom of the stairs, Steven was waiting there for her, and she saw Abby sitting at the table with Faith.

Steven looked up at the sound of her footsteps, and his mouth fell open, his eyes widening to the size of saucers. *"Wow,"* he said, letting out a low whistle. "You look absolutely amazing." At his praise, Abby looked up and echoed his sentiments, standing up to give her sister a hug.

"Have fun!" Abby said enthusiastically, turning to hug Steven as Laura picked up Faith and gave her a kiss on the forehead.

"Be good for Aunt Abby, okay?" she instructed, and as Faith nodded enthusiastically.

Minutes later she and Steven were heading down Lakeshore Drive toward the city. Taking his eyes off the road for a second, he glanced over at her and smiled when he caught her looking at him, reaching over to grab her hand.

"When did you all of a sudden get so romantic?" she asked with a smile, shaking her head in disbelief, *still*, that this was happening.

"I've always been romantic!" he countered with a grin. "I've just been too…selfish, I guess, lately, to do anything about it. I'm sorry, Laura." He sobered suddenly, squeezing her hand before he drew it to his mouth and kissed it. "I really am. I've been stupid, and I know that's not an excuse. It's an admission—I'm stupid. I've *been* stupid."

"You need to expand your vocabulary," she laughed, and she could tell by the relieved smile that came over his face that he was grateful for her light banter.

"Seriously though," he continued. "When I first met you, I promised that I'd do *anything* for you, that I'd do anything to make sure you were always happy. And somewhere between then and now I've lost sight of that promise…and I never want that to happen again. And if you'll let me, I want to spend the rest of my life showing you just how much you mean to me. Will you let me?"

Laura lay her head on the headrest behind her, letting her gaze drift to the homes that passed them by as they drove. She wondered briefly if the families inside were as happy as the façade made it seem—the glow of their lights blinked at her as if to say *we're a happy home*.

Turning to smile at Steven, she said the only thing she could think of to say.

"Anything for you, mi amore."

Steven simply laughed as he returned his eyes to the road. "Don't be so cheesy," he teased.

"You started it," she grinned back.

Abby

Abby lay in bed trying to familiarize herself with the guest bedroom. She'd stayed there before, of course, but it was always an adjustment sleeping somewhere new. She stayed still and listened to the sounds of the house. The gentle hum of the dishwasher in the kitchen below her, the whir as the heat kicked on, the gentle pitter-patter of little feet that came closer and closer to her door, finally pushing it open a crack so that the hallway light she'd left on for Faith spilled onto her floor.

"Aunt Abby?" Faith's little voice asked gently.

"Yeah, honey?" Abby pushed herself up onto her elbow and rubbed her eyes, squinting at the small form in the doorframe.

Faith didn't say anything in response, just walked over and climbed into bed next to Abby, cozying up next to her before resuming the thumb sucking that Abby remembered Laura mentioning. They'd been struggling to get her to stop doing it, but Abby couldn't find it in her to scold Faith now. Instead she lay, with her niece in her arms, breathing in the berry scent of her shampoo. She choked back a sob, wanting this life so badly for herself, and then suppressed the feeling, remembering her earlier vow to herself that she wanted to put her own desires aside in order to be a good sister and aunt. She couldn't very well do that when she spent every visit wondering when this would all happen for her. After all, that was part of loving someone, wasn't it? Putting aside your own selfishness to support that person in what he or she chose to do, even if that meant being reminded on a daily basis of a life that you wanted, but weren't assured of ever getting?

She reached to the nightstand and grabbed her phone, careful not to wake Faith, but needing to hear Tom's voice. She wasn't surprised that he didn't answer; though when she checked the bedside clock, it seemed a little early for him to be asleep. She knew exactly how their conversation would go the next day.

She'd ask him why he hadn't called her before he'd gone to bed, to say good night. He'd respond with something about how he just passed out after he put the kids down, that he hadn't expected to fall asleep so quickly. She'd remind him that it meant a lot to her—especially on nights when he was at Beth's with the kids—to have him call at the end of the night. He'd roll his eyes, exasperated that they were having the same conversation again, as if he had no control over the situation at hand. Then he'd finally promise that he would, from now on, make a greater effort to do so.

Yet she had a feeling that a week from now, a month from now, they'd be right back here again. And she wondered, not for the first time that night, if she was wasting her time with Tom. Actually that answer was easy—she knew she was—she knew Laura, Steven, or any of her friends and family would say the same. But the question that followed was the tougher one. *Did she have the strength in her to end it?*

She'd gotten to know his kids over the last several months, and she thought now of never seeing Luke or Ben again, of never sitting on Tom's couch, watching TV with him again. That part was stupid, she knew, but she just got so *comfortable*. There was something about a night with him that felt like coming home. She was completely herself around him—something, she realized, she rarely was around others. She thought of never cooking dinner together again, of never feeling his lips against hers, of never feeling his hand in hers. She thought of all the things she'd miss—the way he said good morning, the way he laughed, the way he spoke to his children, the way that when he took her into his arms, her world could crumble around her and she wouldn't even notice.

It wasn't until she shifted on her pillow that she realized there were tears running down her cheeks, and she let them come, occasionally lifting her hand to wipe them away before they reached Faith, as if her pain could be transferred to her niece with so little as a tear.

The next morning Abby checked her phone almost before she was awake, as she always did, hoping for something from Tom. But as she'd known there would be, there was only a blank screen to greet her. She felt her anger welling up inside of her as she sent him an angry text, asking him where he was or what he was doing, when she knew full well that he was only with his kids. What she really wanted to ask him was "Why, after all this time, is it so hard for you to fathom that your girlfriend would like to hear from you when you're spending the night at another woman's house?" But even that wouldn't satisfy her.

What she really wanted to know was when he was going to find some semblance of balance in his life. Their relationship had been so amazing those first few months. It was as if they'd seen nothing but each other. They laughed and joked, held hands and held each other. Then, almost overnight, Tom had realized that spending all of his time with Abby had meant not spending enough time with Ben and Luke, and had immediately set out to make it right.

And though Abby had agreed that his kids needed and deserved more of his time, though she supported his decision to dedicate more of it to them, she knew that "making it right" had turned into overcompensating. He now spent every free minute he had with the kids, and not only that, he was deliberately out of contact with Abby when he was doing so. If Tom was on a pendulum, then he had swung from her to his kids and then some, and the aftermath left her feeling like she'd been little more than a novelty. Only the words he said, those sweet sentiments, managed to convince her otherwise, but today even that couldn't help her.

Finally, after she'd gotten Faith her breakfast—after she'd gotten Faith her lunch, for that matter—Tom responded.

Sorry babe, his text said. *Passed out last night after I put the kids down.*

That was it. No "I'm sorry," no "I'll call you later," nothing at all.

She didn't know what else to tell the man. He knew it as well as she did—there was no balance in this, just as there had been no balance when he'd spent all his time with her. And just like his kids had, she deserved some made up time now. But going back and forth, making up for lost time, was no way for a man to live. She just wanted him to balance it out—try and work out a schedule he could stick to. She wanted to be able to reach him if she needed him. She wanted—she didn't know what she wanted, she realized. She wanted a conventional relationship. She wanted nights out without having to worry about babysitters and schedules. She wanted Tom to enjoy their time together, carrying nothing but a smile. But Tom carried nothing but guilt.

The thing was, Abby understood it all. She understood how Beth must feel—wondering why Tom thought he could make another work when he hadn't made them work. Though she didn't pretend to understand the depth of Beth's pain over the matter, she could easily sympathize with how each move must make her feel. She could understand Tom's guilt over how this might affect his kids, although they both adored Abby. She understood it all, except for where it left her.

"Abby? Hello?" Laura's voice cut through her thoughts, and Abby stared at the phone in her hand. She didn't even remember it ringing and didn't remember picking it up.

"Laura? God...I think I'm losing my mind." She sank onto the couch, running a hand through her hair. "I didn't know I'd answered the phone—I didn't even know it rang." She managed a small laugh, but she knew it sounded pathetic.

"Is everything okay?" Her sister's concern was obvious, but Abby knew it was more concern for Faith than for her.

"Yeah," she said wearily. "She's napping." *I wish I was napping*, she wanted to add. Sleep seemed to be the only way to turn off her mind these days.

"I was talking about you." Laura surprised her. "You sound awful."

"I feel awful," Abby heard herself say.

"Are you coming down with something?" Again Abby wondered if the concern in Laura's voice was directed at her or the potential illness Abby had inflicted on her daughter.

"Just a cold," Abby lied. It was easier than telling the truth. She knew exactly how Laura would respond to what she really wanted to confess. It was what her friends and family had been telling her for months now. "You deserve so much better," or "you deserve someone who can give you what you need," or "you deserve someone who has time for you." You deserve, you deserve, you deserve.

Abby knew exactly what she deserved—she knew what she was worth. She knew full well that there were men out there who would drop everything to give her exactly what she wanted—everything that Tom couldn't. Rational thought told her to go find it. Objective opinions told her to wait for what she deserved. But rational thought and objective opinions are no match for emotions. Because no matter what she deserved, it didn't matter. What she wanted, what she needed, was Tom. Tom, who she knew like the back of her hand. Tom, who with one word could make everything all right again. *Everything that he made wrong in the first place*, a little voice told her, but she quieted it.

"Well we're on our way home," Laura was saying. "Thank you again for staying with Faith. You don't know what a night away did for us." Abby could hear the joy in her sister's voice and struggled to push down a pang of jealousy.

"Not a problem," she found herself saying. "Thank you."

"Why on earth would you thank us?" Laura sounded thoroughly confused.

"Because I like spending time with my niece!" Abby said quickly. It wasn't a lie; she loved spending time with Faith. But she knew the real reason she'd thanked Laura was because it had given her a necessary distraction. Again she wondered if finding different ways to distract herself from her MIA boyfriend was the way she wanted to spend the rest of her life, but pushed the thought away.

She'd barely had time to hang up the phone when it rang again, and she wasted no time quieting Laura's fears. "Look, I promise it's just a cold, and no, I didn't give it to Faith, and yes, she ate a good lunch, and no, she hasn't been seriously injured."

"Well that's good to hear," a deep voice responded, and Abby scrambled upright, clutching the phone to her ear.

"Tom! Sorry, I thought it was Laura calling back. She never stops worrying."

"Sounds like someone I know." Abby could hear the smile in Tom's voice, and she smiled despite herself. "How are you?" he asked.

"Fine," she lied. This was really becoming a bad habit.

"Did you say you're coming down with a cold? That's a bummer. I was going to suggest we do something fun tonight, just the two of us."

"No!" Abby cried, a little too quickly. "I mean I'm fine, just a little tired. But yeah! Just tell me when and where!"

"No, don't worry about it," Tom said. "Rest up and feel better, and we'll do something some other time."

"No, Tom," she argued. She knew she was pushing now, and that he hated that, but she wasn't about to miss this opportunity to see him. "I'm fine."

"All right," he didn't sound convinced. "Well, I'll call you later."

Abby wanted to push it further—to ask for a time, an activity—any firm plan she could hold onto. But she knew from experience that all that would come from that would be him changing his mind.

So instead, all she said was "Okay. Love you. I'm excited!" But what she heard was, "Please, please don't back out on me again, Tom."

And as she hung up, she let herself wonder if rational thought, objective opinions, and everyone else was right. After all, here she was, a young woman (she emphasized the young part to herself), lying on her sister's couch and doing everything in her power to hold her boyfriend to his invitation, because if he backed out now, she didn't know when she'd see him next.

⁃⁃⁃

Tom

Tom hung up the phone in frustration. Suddenly he didn't want to see Abby tonight. He did, of course, but he knew what was coming. She'd had the pushy tone to her voice, which meant if he backed out now, he'd have hell to pay. But he'd really wanted to have a relaxing night to unwind after spending so much time with the kids the last few days. He'd found himself almost relieved that she hadn't been feeling well, but hadn't caught himself in time when he'd mentioned his idea for a date. He should have known she'd jump all over it.

And he knew she had good reason to. He hadn't seen much of her lately, but he didn't know what to do about that. She was right. The pendulum had swung back the other way, but he didn't know how to make it right. This had happened right after the divorce—out of guilt, he'd spent almost every night out at the house. It had taken a huge toll on him both physically and emotionally, and it hadn't been until Abby had come along that he'd rediscovered the joys of having time to himself. Of course, back then, time to himself had included Abby. He'd wanted nothing more than to be with her every waking moment. He *still* wanted nothing more than to be with her every waking moment, but he'd come to realize that just wasn't a possibility. Abby realized it too, he knew, and understood, but no amount of understanding changed the fact that she still wanted to spend every moment with him. So he didn't blame her for jumping at this chance, and though he wanted to be with her too, he wished she hadn't. No matter what he wanted, he needed to be alone tonight. Except for the slow drives to and from the suburbs (slow not by choice but by the force of heavy traffic), he hadn't had a minute to himself in—he couldn't even remember how long. If it wasn't the kids it was work—if it wasn't work it was Abby, and he found himself wondering more and more frequently if he'd bitten off more than he could chew.

Everyone had told him he was stupid to rush into this so fast—just as he knew they'd told Abby—but neither of them had cared. He still didn't care, he was pretty sure. It was none of their business. But he did wonder if maybe they'd been partially right. Hindsight is 20/20, and looking back he knew that he shouldn't have rushed into things so quickly with Abby. His divorce had barely been final when they'd starting dating, and as a result, there had been no time to fall into a schedule, to work out his timing and by default his life. It would have been so much easier to have worked that out and then started dating someone. Then he could have said, "This is my life. This is where you would fit into it. That's either okay with you or it's not—make your decision." Saying it to himself now, he realized how completely unromantic a sentiment it was, but it was practical. Tom had said this very thing to Abby a few weeks ago, and it had left her in tears. "It makes sense," she had said, "but facts and sense have no place in emotions." He saw her point—there had been no way to stop what happened between them—and in some way, it had been just what he needed at the time. She had reminded him about emotions he had long since forgotten about, and he knew that if not for her, he probably never would have rediscovered them.

She had reminded him that love can become something more than two names on a set of divorce papers—that there was still a shot at that kind of love for him. *With someone like her.* He knew exactly how lucky he was. She was beautiful and smart, caring and kind, hardworking and loyal, and on top of that, she threw everything she was into him. There's nothing she wouldn't do for him. He'd never take advantage of that, but it was flattering. Still, despite all this, he just wished she'd be more understanding. He knew that she was in theory, but he wanted her to be more understanding in practice.

He sighed. He was going around in circles and needed to stop thinking about it. Flipping on the radio, he tried to drown his thoughts in his music. Loud and blaring, he was sure every other car on the highway could hear it, but he didn't care.

He pressed the accelerator harder and harder, picking up speed and weaving in and out of traffic like he was driving the damn Batmobile. And he smiled slightly, blatantly ignoring the phone vibrating in his center console, enjoying those stolen moments just to himself, passing them the only way he knew how.

∽

CHAPTER THIRTEEN

Laura

"Sorry I'm late," Laura rushed into the restaurant and sat down across from her sister. "Steven and I got a little ... distracted," she felt herself blushing as she flashed Abby an embarrassed smile, and suddenly Abby was in tears.

"Hey, what's wrong?" she reached across the table to take her sister's hand. "Are you ok?"

"No," Abby sobbed. "I'm breaking up with Tom."

Laura pulled her hand back and shook her head. "For real this time?" she asked, in a more accusing tone than she'd intended, and Abby immediately bristled.

"What's that supposed to mean?"

"Come on, Abby, you've told me that about ten times in the last six months. I'm sorry, but I just don't believe you actually will do it this time, just like you've never followed through with it in the past."

This brought fresh tears from Abby, and Laura quickly regretted being so harsh.

"Look, I'm sorry," she said, far more gently. I remember how hard it is to end a relationship you always knew was wrong. Just because you know it's not a good idea, that doesn't mean you can end it that easily."

"It wasn't *always* wrong," Abby argued. "For those first few months it was fantastic."

"And he's treated you like crap for an entire year, since. I think you need to weigh which has had more of an effect on you - those great first few months, or the terrible months since."

"Well when you put it that way, it sounds like an easy choice."

"So why are you sticking around?" Laura questioned, and Abby shrugged.

"I don't know. I love him. I'm comfortable with him."

"Maybe you've gotten so used to the drama in your life, that you're keeping it around, just for some semblance of normalcy," Laura suggested with a smirk, parroting the very words her sister once said to her. But the words were lost on Abby, who just shook her head.

"Look, I love you," Laura told her, "and I'm here for you. But you know where I stand on this one, and there's really not much more I can tell you. So, can we just enjoy our lunch?"

To Abby's credit, she put on a smile and tried to enjoy the rest of their weekly lunch, but Laura could tell her relationship still weighed heavy on her mind.

She truly didn't know what else to do, though. Although they'd all been a little wary of Tom's situation, they'd welcomed him with open arms when Abby introduced him as her boyfriend. And Laura legitimately liked Tom - she just didn't like the way he'd been making Abby feel lately. She didn't think it was a reflection on him, personally, it was just the way he was choosing to handle the situation he was in, and Laura didn't think he was doing it very well. He'd completely separated the two aspects of his life - except for a few occasions where Abby had gotten to spend time with his kids, she'd never met another member of his family She'd yet to met his parents or his ex, even after over a year of dating, and Laura knew how that, more than anything else, hurt her sister.

She'd been there for Abby every time Abby called crying, vowing that she was going to end it, but months had passed and she still hadn't, and at this point, Laura was sick of hearing about it.

But she cared about her sister, and so she spent the afternoon trying to take her mind off of Tom. She took her to get a pedicure, then took her shopping, and by the time she hugged her goodbye, saw a renewed spark in her big sister's eye.

She crossed her fingers as she watched Abby drive away, hoping that this time she'd actually find the strength to make the difficult decision she needed to make.

∽

Steven

"Hey," Steven called as Laura walked in the door, turning to give her a quick kiss before turning back to the fajitas he was making.

"Yum!" Laura cried, grabbing a pepper to munch on before sitting down at the counter. "Where's Faith?" She looked around.

"Time-out," Steven said.

"What'd she do?" Laura looked curious.

"Oh, nothing—that's the problem. I asked her to clean up her toys, and she didn't. I asked her again, and she didn't. I told her she'd get a time-out if she didn't, and *still* she didn't. Then she broke down crying like it was completely unfair when I finally gave her one."

Laura smiled ruefully. "She's testing you."

Steven nodded. "I know. I just wish I knew how much longer it was going to last."

Laura laughed before walking over to give him a kiss. "It will pass. And then it will be something else, and you'll be wishing for the simple days of her testing you."

"Yeah, I guess," Steven conceded, and then smiled. "Plus, she looked pretty darn cute, giving me those puppy dog eyes, once she realized crying wasn't going to work and just tried apologizing. I almost caved."

As if on cue, Faith appeared at the top of the stairs. "Daddy?" she said softly. "Can I come down now?"

Steven went to the base of the stairs. "Will you clean up your toys, please?" His little girl nodded enthusiastically, and he waved her downstairs. She ran down them as quickly as her little legs would carry her, running straight to Laura.

"Hi, Mommy." She climbed up into her lap.

"Hi, baby." Laura gave her a kiss on the forehead, but lifted her out of her lap and set her feet back on the floor. "What did Daddy just ask you to do?"

"Okay," Faith said, outnumbered, and retreated to the living room to pick up her toys.

"How was Abby?" Steven changed the subject.

"Wrecked." Laura shook her head. "She and Tom got in another fight, and this time she really thinks it's over."

Steven had to fight the urge to laugh. "I feel like I've heard that before, with those two."

"Be nice," Laura warned, but she too was smiling.

"Why do people get so crazy over relationships?"

"Because," Laura answered, "maybe we know on some level that of all the things in our lives, our relationships are the only ones that are worthwhile."

Steven was silent, marveling at his wife's insightfulness. And she was right—he cared about the medical field, but his job would *never* mean as much to him as the people in his life. He longed for nice things one day, but the loss of a nice car or even a house wouldn't devastate him to the extent that losing a loved one would.

Before he could say anything, Faith came barreling back into the room. "Done!" she cried, and then resumed her spot on Laura's lap.

The three of them enjoyed the peace of a quiet evening together, and as he watched his wife and daughter, Steven couldn't help but feel like he'd never been quite so content.

༄

CHAPTER FOURTEEN

Abby

Abby blinked hard, trying to stop herself from seeing red. But as she focused her sight on Tom again, she found it impossible to keep the anger and hurt from welling up inside of her.

"You're doing what?" she asked, trying to make sure she was clear on what he was telling her.

"Abby..." Tom started. "The kids asked me to go, and how can I tell them no? What am I supposed to do? I can't disappoint them like that. It's just a week. And I'll call you every night. Beth and I will be sleeping in separate rooms, and it's not like we're going to be the only ones who are there."

Abby nodded slowly, fighting against the quivering in her lip with all of the strength she could muster. "Tom," she began, choosing her words carefully. "I understand how much you love those kids. I understand that you want to spend time with them. And I understand that you don't want to disappoint them. Believe me, I get all of that. But what about me? What about hurting me, and disappointing me? What about all of the steps I have taken to try and be a good girlfriend to you, despite the ups and downs of your divorce? This may be the way you and Beth choose to handle your divorce, but right now, this soon, it's not something I am comfortable with. Why did you even get a divorce, if nothing's going to change?"

"Well, I..." Tom began, but Abby cut him off, continuing.

"Those kids are always going to ask. They're not going to magically turn a year older next year and suddenly realize what this divorce means in terms of boundaries. If you don't set those boundaries now, it's just going to get harder. I know I've never been through a divorce, so maybe I'm out of line here, but the way I see it, the more things stay the same, the harder it will be to change them. I know the kids are asking you to go, but if you say yes to this vacation, they're just going to keep asking. What makes you think saying no to the next one is going to be any easier? The way I see it, there are alternatives that will make everyone happy. This is about you spending time with your children—I think there are ways for you to do that that will make me comfortable as well, and you claim to care about me, and about my comfort. Well, do you or don't you? Because it has to be one or the other, you can't keep going back and forth. And no matter how you rationalize this and what you say, what I hear is 'Sorry, Abby, but you don't mean enough to me for me to try and find an alternative that would allow me to still spend time with my children *and* not risk our relationship.'"

Tom sat across the room, watching her as she spoke. His expression was tough to read—anger, frustration, understanding, stubbornness, selfishness, love, fear—Abby couldn't tell. She stared right back at him, unwavering. Finally, she shrugged. "Look...I know what I'm worth. But I can't sit here, across the room from you, and convince you that I'm worth having in your life, that

I'm worth fighting for. That's a decision you have to make for yourself."

"Abby," Tom couldn't hide the tenderness in your voice. "I know what you're worth. You're one of the most amazing women I've ever met—kind, generous, thoughtful, selfless, funny, sweet, creative, smart..." He trailed off as he struggled for words. "I know there are guys out there, probably most guys, who would call me dumbass for treating you the way I am right now, for putting a future with you at risk for something like this. But they're my kids...I just don't know what to do."

"Well...I guess that's that, then." Abby wiped a tear from her cheek. "You make your decision, and we'll see what happens." With a smile, Abby rose and poured them both a glass of wine. "Now..." she changed the subject. "Tell me about your weekend!"

With a wary look, Tom began to recall the events of his weekend, relaxing with every word, blind to the fact that with every minute that passed, Abby was desperately building a wall around her heart between them. She knew he didn't notice the tears that fell silently from her eyes that night as she slept in his arms, knew he didn't see the subtle changes in her demeanor over the next week. In fact, it wasn't until two weeks and six phone calls, which she didn't bother to return, that Abby began to get the impression that Tom actually understood he might have lost her.

∽

Tom

Tom snapped his phone closed and set it back on the table, deciding against leaving another voice mail. There were three from him already. Tom sat back and rubbed his eyes in frustration. *What does she expect me to do?* he thought angrily. *This is ridiculous.* In his anger, he stood up too quickly, and his shin met the side of the coffee table with all too much force. He winced and bent to rub his leg where he had hit it. As he did so, he caught a glimpse of the two coffee table books he had sitting out. One on the founding fathers, and one on the city's history. Opening the first, he read the inscription from Abby—"Hey, love, Happy Birthday! Here's to a shared love of history...I've had fun discussing it with you these last few months. Can't wait to see what's to come!" He opened the second one and found a similar message—"Tom, I so enjoyed our date at the museum. Saw this and it made me think of you. Thanks for an amazing two months." Closing the book, Tom sighed and sat back down. He looked around the room—at the rich colors on his living room walls. He pictured her standing there months before, splattered in paint, blisters on her hands, but grinning at him. "Doesn't it look great?" She had swooned. "It feels like home!" Tom hadn't wanted to paint his walls, at least not so soon, but Abby had refused to let him host his children in a white apartment stacked with boxes. "This divorce is going to be hard enough on them as it is. They need to be visiting their father at a place that they can feel at home in."

He ran his hand over the leather of the couch beneath him and remembered her excitement at helping him pick it out. The glass he was drinking out of had been handpicked by her to match the rug she had helped him get for his kitchen. As he took in his surroundings, he realized there was not one thing in that apartment that she had not touched. He walked to his closet and opened the drawer where he kept his mementos, and found letters, cards, and notes from her. The Post-It she had attached to the coffee she had brought for him when she knew he had a long night ahead of him. The card he had found waiting for him only a few hours after he had called her to complain about his terrible day. He smiled at the comical image and read what she had written inside—"Here's to tomorrow being a better day! Cheer up, I'm thinking about you." The note she had slipped inside his pants pocket when she picked them up from the dry cleaners for him—"You look amazing in these…love you." As he read, a fear he had never experienced before began to grab hold of him. What was he thinking? He stood in place, completely surrounded by a woman who had thrown her all into making his life better, not only for him, but for his children. Crafts that she had done with them littered the refrigerator; he could still hear their laughter as they sat together on the kitchen floor, their hands wrist deep in paint, Abby not the least bit concerned that Luke had gotten it all over her expensive blouse. He knew at that moment that he could search the world over and never find another Abby, and something inside him began to race. His heart, his pulse, his brain, everything jumped into overdrive, and before he even realized what he was doing, he was slamming the door behind him and running for the elevator. *Come on, come on,* he thought, pressing the down button repeatedly. Sometimes the elevator took up to twenty minutes to arrive, and tonight he didn't have that kind of time. Turning on his heel, he burst through the stairwell door and started down the thirty flights, two at a time. Ten minutes later, out of breath and out of patience, Tom finally hailed a cab and gasped out Abby's address to the baffled taxi driver.

Tom had never bothered to find out who "Murphy" was, but his law was in full effect as they rounded the first corner to find themselves trapped behind a slow moving line of cars. He stared out the window and impatiently drummed his fingers on the door as he thought about Abby. How could he let her get away? He couldn't begin to number the ways that she had shown him over the past year how much he meant to her. Two hands would be *more* than sufficient to count the times he had done the same for her. He shook his head, disgusted with himself at his selfishness, and prayed that it wasn't too late. After what seemed like hours, the cab came to a halt in front of Abby's brownstone, and he threw a twenty at the driver as he dove out of the car, unaware of whether or not that even covered the fare. He didn't care about that—all he could see was the possibility that he was losing the most amazing woman who had ever come into his life. He was so focused on it that he didn't notice Abby coming down her stairs until he nearly knocked her over.

"Abby!" he gasped, breathless and suddenly at a loss for words, shocked by her appearance. To a passerby, she wouldn't have looked any different. But those green eyes that usually held such love and sincerity when they looked into his were now cold and indifferent, and regarded him with little more than slight curiosity.

"What are you doing here?" she asked, her voice calm and level, and he found himself wondering how it had gotten to this point so quickly without his knowledge.

"I've been trying to call you," he stated, still struggling for words.

"I know."

"Did you get my voice mails? Why didn't you call me back?"

"I've had some thinking to do," she replied coldly.

"About me? About us?" Tom tried to control the fear in his voice.

Abby ignored the question and pushed passed him. "Look, I've got an appointment to make. If you come back later, maybe we can talk then. Otherwise, shoot me an e-mail or something."

With that, she left him standing on her stoop, mouth agape and heart heavy.

∽

John

"Well?" the doctor prompted.

John focused on the Amsler grid, willing the lines to straighten. But they remained wavy. He cleared his throat.

"Um," he took his hand from his eye and checked his watch. "You know what, I completely forgot I have somewhere to be. Can I reschedule this appointment?"

As he said it, he was already moving to put on his raincoat and hurrying toward the door.

"John," his doctor called after him, a warning. "You really should come in for some more thorough testing. If you're struggling with the grid, it may point to a more serious problem, like AMD and a loss of central vision."

John waved his hand over his shoulder, letting the doctor know that he'd heard him. "I'll reschedule," he called, unsure even as he stormed out why it pained him to admit that his eyes might be failing him.

He burst from the dim light of the office to an even dimmer May sky, overcast and gloomy.

"Hey, John!" a familiar voice called, and he spun to see someone walking toward him.

Just who it was, he couldn't tell—his, or her, face was blurred, and it wasn't until she was nearly on top of him that he recognized a woman who had been in Anne's monthly book group.

"Oh, hi Gina," he fumbled. "Look," he continued in a rush before she could say anything, hardly slowing as he continued walking toward his car. "I hate to be rude, but I'm in a bit of a hurry. My granddaughter's got ballet." It was the truth after all, and though he hadn't planned on attending, he thought now that it may be just what he needed to distract him.

"Oh, how sweet!" Gina called after him, intent on starting a conversation. "She must be getting so big—how old is she now?"

John waved as he neared his car, pretending he hadn't heard her. Anne was probably rolling in her grave right now at his behavior, but he needed to be alone. Climbing into the car, he tried to regain control of his breath. *Macular degeneration, Loss of central vision*, he heard again, and his hands began to shake on the steering wheel.

∽

Laura

"Abby!" Laura cried, shocked at what her sister had just told her. "That's it? Just like that? You just left him standing there?"

"Yes," Abby responded calmly. "Look, either I'm worth it to him, or I'm not."

Laura shook her head, surprised by her sister's resolve.

"I'm proud of you, Abby, but don't you think you need to sit down and talk about this, and officially end it? Otherwise I'm afraid you'll just end up taking him back."

"Maybe, but I need some space first to distance myself from him emotionally. Otherwise, one look from him and I'll be tempted to believe him this time."

"Alright," Laura said. "I guess that makes sense, but I still don't think you should have lied to him and told him you had an appointment."

"I didn't have an exit plan!" Abby laughed. "I wasn't expecting to run into him, and just couldn't talk to him yet."

"Well," Laura winked at her. "Thanks for choosing me. I actually *do* have somewhere to be though—Faith has ballet this afternoon. But you're welcome to stay. You know where everything is. Are you going to be okay?" One look at her sister's face and she knew she would. Despite the pain in her eyes, Abby exuded a strength and resolve that Laura had never possessed and could only hope to emulate one day. "Hey." She took Abby's face in her hands, a strange gesture as the younger sister who was used to receiving counsel from her sister, not the other way around. Nonetheless, she looked straight into Abby's eyes and said, "This isn't about *you*. I know it feels that way, and that it's nearly impossible to separate yourself from the situation. But you can't let yourself believe that it's personal. He could be dating the most beautiful woman in the world, and he'd still struggle with this. It has nothing to do with his feelings for you."

Abby stared back at her sister, feigning shock and hurt. "You mean…I'm not the most beautiful woman in the world?"

Laura laughed and let go of Abby's face. "You know that's not what I meant. All I'm saying is try to stop taking this so personally. I'm glad you're ending it, believe me. But just don't think that he's doing any of this because you're not good enough. I've seen the man look at you…he's crazy about you."

"Well, he sure picked a strange way to show it." Abby snorted, leaning back and putting her feet up as her sister walked out the door. "I'll be right here when you get back!" she called after her, unable to see Laura roll her eyes in amused exasperation.

Laura steered through the early May rain, eyes occasionally darting to the backseat to check on Faith, who gazed quietly out the window from her booster seat. The dark clouds gave an evening feel to what was actually early afternoon, and the streetlights were already on, reflecting off of the wet roads and reminding Laura of the city. The windshield wipers droned rhythmically, mesmerizing them both to the point where the usually talkative Faith hadn't said a word in minutes, finally breaking her silence to ask about the rainbows on the road.

"That's oil that's being washed off the road by the rain, sweetheart," she explained patiently. "Cars run on gasoline, and sometimes that leaks onto the road, which creates those puddles you're looking at." She actually had no idea if what she was telling Faith was true or not; she was simply guessing and prayed that the questions would stop there, though she doubted they would. But Faith amazed her and stayed quiet. For almost five seconds.

"Does it look like a rainbow when it's in the cars?" she inquired.

"No, but I wish it did! It's actually kind of plain and ugly."

"Then why does it look like a rainbow on the road?"

Where's Steven for these kinds of questions? Laura thought wryly "I don't know, honey," she replied honestly. "Maybe it has to do with the way the light reflects off of it. But I *can* tell you this— oil like that can make a road *very* slippery, especially if it hasn't rained in a while," she said, adding, "You have to drive *extra* carefully," for emphasis, proud that she had *something* informative to tell her inquisitive daughter. She knew other parents let some of the questions slide, but Laura believed in fostering the curious nature of her daughter. Too many traits were lost on the youth, and she wanted to encourage the ones like this to grow, and stay, in Faith.

Satisfied with her mother's answer, Faith contemplated the new information for a few minutes before finally saying, in the insightful way that children can, "So when the oil is helpful it's ugly, and when it's dangerous it's beautiful?"

Laura almost choked on her gum.

"Sometimes things aren't quite what they seem," she recovered quickly. "Do you remember last summer, when we were picking the cherries out of the orchard, they looked round, red, and perfect?"

"Yeah," Faith responded.

"Do you remember when we cut them open, there were *worms* inside of them?"

"Ew!" Faith squealed, the memory obviously fresh in her mind. "Yeah! And we had been eating them all morning! You thought we should go to the doctor, but Daddy said we didn't have to."

"Yes! I remember," Laura replied. "Well, we were acting off of blind faith that those cherries were good, because they *looked* good. Sometimes in life, you can't do that. Things that look nice aren't always good for you, and things that look bad aren't always bad for you. That's why you should always stay curious—just like you are—and make sure you ask a lot of good questions before you make decisions."

Faith nodded her little head in the backseat, completely trusting of what her mother told her. "What is to act off blind faith?" Laura knew she had explained the word "Faith" to her daughter several times, knowing she had always been interested in what her name meant.

"Well, you know what *faith* means, right? It's believing in—" she paused to see if Faith could remember.

"Something you can't see," she finished, to Laura's delight. "Faith is believing in something you can't see."

"That's right, honey. So acting off of blind faith means that although you can't see *all* of something, you're judging by what you *can* see and making your decision based on that. For example," she paused, willing herself to come up with something quickly, "chocolate chip cookies. Your favorite, right?" Faith nodded. "Well, when I make a new batch of chocolate chip cookies, do you *know, for sure*, that they're going to be good?"

"Yes!" Faith responded, without pause.

"How do you know?" Laura challenged her.

"Because I've had them before!" Faith cried, clearly exasperated that her mother would not know this.

"Yes, but what if this batch I used something different? What if this time, I put in too much baking powder, and they're going to be sour? How do you *really* know?"

Catching on, Faith mulled over this for a second before replying, "Well, they smell good. And sometimes you let me try the beater—"

"Batter," Laura corrected.

"Batter? You said beater!" Faith replied, sounding confused and slightly betrayed.

"The *batter* is the cookie dough. The *beater* is the tool that I use to mix it. So you're eating the batter off the beater!"

Faith giggled. "That's like a tongue twister!"

Laura laughed too, and then continued their conversation, explaining to Faith, "So when you decide that you're going to eat a chocolate chip cookie, you don't know, at least not for *sure,* that it's going to taste good. But you're using things you *do* know for sure, like the way they've tasted before, and the way they smell, to tell you that it will probably be okay! *That's* acting off of blind faith. A lot of people feel that way about God. They can't see him, but they're surrounded by such beautiful creations that they have faith that he is there."

Faith nodded, and Laura was sure she understood completely. "And that's why you named me Faith!" She threw her hands up with a grin.

"That's right! Daddy and I were very young, and we didn't know *what* we were going to do to get by. But we knew, without a *doubt*, that we would love you more than anything, and that you would be absolutely the best thing that would happen to us. So when we found out we were having a little girl, the only name we could *possibly* name you was Faith, because that's what we had in you, from the very beginning. Faith that you would be the biggest blessing we'd ever receive."

Faith smiled in the backseat. "What if I'd been a boy?" she suddenly wondered, horrified that a boy would be named Faith.

"I don't know!" Laura replied, stumped herself. They'd never even thought of it. "Faith-o, probably!" The sound of her daughter breaking into a fit of giggles warmed Laura's heart, and she grinned at her in the rearview mirror. "What would you have liked to be named, if you were a boy?"

"Traugott," Faith replied without skipping a beat.

For the second time that day, Laura almost choked on her gum.

"Traugott!" she recovered. "That's..." *find a euphemism, find a euphemism*, "an interesting name! Do you have a friend named Traugott?" Laura went through a mental checklist of Faith's preschool class, trying to remember if Faith had met a boy named Traugott.

"No, I kind of made it up," Faith replied.

"*Kind of* made it up?" Laura inquired.

"I mean, I've never *met* someone named Traugott. But that's the name of the boy in my dreams."

Oh god, it's started already! Laura fought panic. *Did she say boy of my dreams, or boy in my dreams?* "You have dreams about boys?" she asked, feeling like somehow they had skipped childhood entirely and there was a teenager in her backseat.

"No, *a* boy. A baby. Sometimes I have dreams that I have a little brother. At least I think it's a little brother—it's just a baby, and you're holding him, and Daddy's there too."

Laura breathed a quick sigh of relief as she slowed, cresting a small hill, the grocery store coming into view at the bottom of it. "Oh, I see," she said, suddenly distracted. Blinker on, she waited for an opening in oncoming traffic. At this point, it was looking like that would take hours. "And his name's Traugott?"

"Yes!" Faith cried, frustrated. "I think so. It's either that or Sammy."

"Sammy, huh?" Laura decided not to ask how Traugott could be confused with Sammy. "Sam is a good boy's name."

"Yeah," Faith nodded. "If I ever have a brother, I want to name him Sam."

"I'll remember that."

"Will you name him that?" Faith pressed.

"I'll think about it, honey. But I don't even know if we'll ever have a boy."

"But if you do, will you name him Sammy?"

Laura laughed. "You're persistent."

"What's persistent?"

"Persistent means that you don't give up, especially when you want something really badly."

"I want a brother really badly," Faith said matter-of-factly. "Like the one I have dreams about. I like those dreams."

"I'll try to do that for you," Laura said only half paying attention. To be honest, she hadn't even thought about another child until just now, and she wondered if the timing just might be right. Steven was settled into his residency, she was receiving her master's degree this month and would be settling into a full-time job. It had been a long road, but they were finally there—and she made a mental note to broach the subject with Steven tonight.

"What does *anything for you me a moray* mean?" Faith questioned, and Laura smiled at her pronunciation of the words.

"Where did that question come from?" she asked.

"You said you'd try to do that for me, and whenever Daddy says he'll do something for you, he says *anything for you me a moray.*"

"He says it to you, now, too," Laura reminded her, and Faith nodded. "*Amore* means love, in Italian—which is a different language," she added quickly. "It just means 'Anything for you, my love.'"

"But what does it mean?" Faith pressed.

"It's just something he made up," Laura began, unsure of how to explain to her daughter the concept of doing *anything* for somebody. "Do you understand?"

"Yes," Faith answered, though Laura wasn't sure she did.

Laura slowed as she approached the upcoming stop sign, trying to think of how to explain this to her daughter, wishing the questions would be over. She raised her eyes to the rearview mirror to explain further and found instead the horrifying sight of headlights careening toward their car. She was vaguely aware of Faith saying something, but couldn't hear over the blood rushing through her head, pounding in her ears, the sound of sheer panic as she watched the car fly closer. For a split second, time passed in slow motion—the car was close enough for Laura to watch the surprise register on the driver's face as his familiar eyes locked into focus, even closer as she watched him try and recover, swerving in an attempt to miss them, and finally, so close that she watched as his front left bumper came flying through the right side of her back window.

Straight into Faith.

And the world went black.

PART II

CHAPTER FIFTEEN

John

John Baxter dialed Steven's number *one* last time, praying that this time he would answer. He was about to hang up, knowing that Steven's machine would be the only answer he received, but his son-in-law surprised him and picked up.

"H'lo?" Steven's voice slurred.

He's drunk again, was John's first conscious thought.

"It's me," John began. *"Don't* hang up."

There was only silence on the other line. "Steven?"

"Yah." John could hear the disinterest in the younger man's voice and fought the urge to hang up on *him.* He was in no state to hear this, anyway. Still, John opened his mouth to tell Steven what he had called to say.

"She's crashing."

The silence on the other end of the line was deafening, and he waffled back and forth between wondering if Steven was simply shocked or he had passed out.

"She's what?" Steven's voice, suddenly clear, cut into John's thoughts.

"She's crashing. Abby was just there, and so was I, and was just on my way home when Dr. Anderson called me. Nurse Harris walked in just a few seconds after I left, and…" He trailed off, still not wanting to believe it himself. "Laura's not answering her cell. Is she with you?"

He barely had time to finish before Steven cut him off. "I'm getting into my car. I'll meet you there," Steven said without hesitation.

"No!" John barked, exasperated in his fear. "You can't drive. Listen to yourself. You can barely string two words together. Stay there. I'll turn around and pick you up. And try to sober up." He hung up the phone with an urgency that betrayed his calm demeanor and whipped his car around, speeding back up Sheridan.

Minutes later, Steven appeared in his driveway, a coffee mug in hand, and it took John a second to recognize him. His face was unshaven, his eyes red rimmed, squinting against the sun so hard that John wondered when he'd been outside last. His face was pale and gaunt, his clothes hanging far more loosely than they had been the last time they'd seen each other.

My God, John thought, silently chiding himself for giving up after simply calling. He should have come over here; he should have broken down that door. *Where has Laura been? How could she let him get to this point?* His thoughts were interrupted by a gust of cold air as the passenger door opened.

"Hey," Steven said more habitually than out of interest, sliding into the seat beside him and deliberately avoiding John's gaze.

John nodded his own greeting, backing the car out of the driveway as quickly as its long curve would allow him.

They passed the drive in silence, and while John focused on getting them to the hospital as quickly as possible, Steven focused on God knows what. Pressing the accelerator as far down as it would go, John flew through a yellow light just as it turned red, barely missing a sedan making a right turn. He could feel Steven's glare on him from the passenger seat, and he turned to look, shocked at the pure hatred radiating from the younger man's eyes. "Still making the same mistakes, I see," he said coldly, turning away and staring out the window at the scenery that flew by in a blur. "If you get pulled over, they'll take you straight to jail."

John swallowed hard, torn between stopping right there and telling Steven to find another ride to the hospital, or answering him:

I wish they would.

○∽

Laura

Laura hit the hospital doors at a dead sprint, their gradual slide so slow that she had to turn herself sideways to squeeze through. She continued her mad pace down the hallway, a male nurse flattening himself against the wall, hands up in a pose of surrender, his clipboard clattering to the floor, to let her pass. She ducked into the stairwell and took the flights two steps at a time, arriving at the top long before the elevator would have gotten her there.

As she continued toward room 403, she cursed herself for leaving the hospital that morning. She'd barely been home since Faith had been admitted, but the nursing staff had assured her that everything would be all right for a few hours, she should go home, get outside for a bit. When she'd adamantly refused, they'd practically ordered her out of the hospital, telling her that she could come back that afternoon for regular visiting hours. Reluctantly, she'd gone home for a quick shower, taking a long walk to kill the time before she could go back to the hospital. She hadn't even felt her phone vibrate—luckily she'd left her watch at home and had used her phone to check the time when she saw her father's missed calls. The drive alone from Winnetka back to Children's Memorial in Lincoln Park had taken her almost an hour as she flew past drivers on their way back to work after the lunch hour, cell phones pasted to their ears. Where had they been going that was so important? More important than her daughter's life? *Please don't let me be too late,* she prayed feverishly as she slowed her pace, nearing her daughter's room. As she burst through the door she found Steven and her father talking to Dr. Anderson. Neither made a move toward her, and she went straight to Faith's side.

"What happened?" she asked.

"They've got her stable, now—" her father began answering her.

"I'm talking to the *doctor*," she snapped, silencing him. "And give it to me in language that I can understand, none of your medical bullshit," she continued, focusing her gaze on the man standing between the two men who had each, at one point, been the man in her life.

Dr. Anderson cleared his throat in his discomfort. "Laura, basically..." he paused, his search for the right words registering in his furrowed brow, "her body's giving up the fight. She suffered a traumatic head injury in the accident, and the swelling in her brain just hasn't gone down the way we hoped. Now, you know we've done all we can to relieve the pressure on her brain and her skull, but her body has taken a beating trying to adjust to it, and it's just not recovering the way we hoped."

"No," Laura barked, more a command than a statement. "There's got to be something else that you can do. What about—"

Steven cut her off, coming to her side and placing a hand on each shoulder.

"B, look at me," he instructed her, more gently and with more sincerity than she had heard from him in months. Reluctantly she turned to look at him, shocked at what she saw—the weight he had lost in recent months that had gone completely unnoticed by her. The five o'clock shadow that seemed more a general darkening of the skin than stubble itself, the hollows of his eyes. "What made Faith who she is has been gone since May. It's just a machine keeping her alive now. Dr. Anderson's been saying this for months—and I agree," he added reluctantly, gulping down his tears and trying to find it in him to say this next part, "that it's time to let her go."

"No," Laura repeated, collapsing into sobs in his arms. The physical contact was almost foreign to her, and she felt his hesitation for a moment before he wrapped his arms around her.

"It's time, honey."

"No!" she cried, twisting out of his embrace and running out of the room.

Laura didn't slow her pace until she was safely out of the view of Faith's room. As she walked, she caught her breath. The news that Faith was in a coma had hit Laura the way air comes into an open car window. Often when she was driving, she'd roll down her window for some fresh air, and it always struck her how it took a moment—a second, a full beat—for the cold, sweet smell to find its way into the car. She supposed she'd just assumed that it was there, pressing against her window, waiting for any chance to get inside, and its hesitation never failed to surprise her.

That's how it had been when Dr. Anderson had delivered the news that her baby was in a coma—that there was a chance she might not wake up. She'd known it, in the back of her mind, known it as she waited, pacing the waiting room that horrible day last May. She'd known it the way she'd known all of Faith's pain before it was announced—the way sometimes in the middle of the night she shot up in bed, wide awake and ears trained on Faith's room, and sure enough, minutes later, she'd hear the frantic murmurs of her daughter awakening from a nightmare. She'd known it the way she could know, on a playground full of children, Faith's cries from the rest. Yes, she'd known, and she'd been sure that given Dr. Anderson's confirmation, it would rush in through the opening of truth. What *it* was, she wasn't really sure, but she'd just known the news would hit her like a Mack truck.

That's why she was so surprised when the news finally came, when it swirled outside her head for a moment—a second, a full beat—its bitter taste souring the corners of her mouth before it entered, its force knocking her to the ground, unconscious.

For a second she wished she could do that again, faint right here and right now, dead to the world around her, dead for a moment to the searing pain that enveloped her now.

∽

Abby

One of the lights in the waiting room flickered once before sputtering out, casting a shadow over the figure that was hunched in the corner. Abby approached her sister's shape with caution, afraid of what the slightest movement might invoke.

When she'd arrived at the hospital, she'd gone straight to Faith's room, but had found only Steven there, bent over his daughter's bed. She'd gone to him immediately, wrapping her arms around him. His face had crumpled when he pulled away, sniffing hard three times before finally allowing the tears to come forth. He'd told her about what the doctor had said, about Laura's reaction, about how John had gone off in search of her. Tom had arrived moments later, and after giving Faith's hand a gentle squeeze, she'd left him with Steven and gone to look for Laura herself.

She'd finally found her, in the waiting room four floors below her daughter, slumped in a chair in the corner. Her back was to Abby, but she could see her sister's right shoulder blade shaking, and she knew immediately that she must be writing something.

"Laura..." Abby took a cautious step toward her. Her sister unresponsive, Abby slowly lowered herself to her knees in front of the end table that Laura was writing on. "Hey..." She looked up into Laura's face, but her eyes remained trained on the paper that she wrote on. Abby glanced at it, reading the words Laura had scrawled sloppily on an insert she'd ripped from a magazine.

The way she said Yew Nork instead of New York

The way she still can't pronounce "specific"

The way she said good night to every one of her stuffed animals individually before she went to bed, so none of them felt left out

The way her right pigtail always flipped out at the end

The scar on her thumb from the time she tried to make me breakfast in bed

She had Steven's eyes

The way she was curious about everything

The forts she made under the dining room table

The way her hair always smelled like summer

The sound of her giggle when you tickled her

Her first word was "yes"

Her last word was "yes"

"Laura," Abby said sternly, finally commanding the attention of her baby sister, who looked at up with her from eyes so pained they cut Abby's heart in half.

"I'm forgetting her," she said numbly. "I'm forgetting my own daughter." The realization of it wracked her body with sobs, though no tears fell from her eyes, and she put her head in her hands, elbows on her knees, and rocked. "She has such a good little heart..."

"I know," Abby cut her off, tears streaming down her own face. Laura looked up, suddenly angry.

"You don't know! She's *my* daughter. You don't know her at all!" The words cut Abby deep, and she struggled to remind herself that it was her sister's anger she heard.

"I loved her just as much as—" she started, but before she could finish, her head whipped to the right beneath Laura's palm.

"Don't talk about her like she's gone!" she cried as Abby raised a hand to her stinging cheek, shocked. Laura raised her hand to slap her again, but Abby caught her wrist, first her right, and then her left, until she held both of her sister's hands.

"Don't do this," she warned, anger flashing from her eyes, amplified behind the tears the pooled in them. "Don't lock us out. We're all we've got." Laura struggled for a minute before collapsing to the floor, the tears finally flowing.

Abby tightened her arms around her, pulling her in close, kissing the top of her head. She felt the scar on Laura's forehead from when she'd fallen in the bathtub when she was three, felt the bump on her arm where she'd broken it falling from a horse, felt her sister's every pain as if it were her own.

This one ripped the very heart from her chest and laid it at Laura's feet, an offering. *What's mine is yours. Use it until yours can beat on its own again...*

And she wondered, as the weight of her sister's head fell into her shoulder, *How do you lean on someone already hunched over in pain?*

CHAPTER SIXTEEN

Tom

The soft shuffle of feet behind him brought Tom's gaze to the doorway, where Abby was leading Laura slowly into the room. Laura's eyes were bloodshot and downtrodden, her shoulders stooped, her hair a mess. It occurred to him that appearances were deceiving; she looked as though she could be as drunk as Steven. Or maybe he looked as though he was distraught as Laura. *Maybe drunk and despair aren't too far apart,* he thought, glancing over his shoulder at Steven who was sobering up with a cup of coffee as he stared blankly out the window.

Laura went straight to Faith's side, on the opposite side of the room from her husband, and like he did every time he visited Abby's niece, Tom wondered how *he* would handle losing a child.

The very thought of it had just about torn Steven and Laura to pieces. Faith had been in coma since the accident, as the doctors did all they could to reduce the swelling in her brain, but it hadn't worked the way they'd all hoped—Faith hadn't woken up and had fallen deeper into her comatose state. It wasn't long before the doctors began counseling Steven and Laura on next steps, and it was no secret that they strongly believed it was in the little girl's best interest to be taken off life support. Though Tom could see that it pained him, Steven had been in agreement, arguing that Faith's quality of life would be nothing if they kept her living as a vegetable.

But Laura had refused. She'd gone through every emotion in the book—anger, fear, sadness, guilt—and most of all, hope. Unjustified, in Tom's mind, hope that there would be some sort of miracle, that Faith would wake up. For a long time she refused to even discuss it with Steven, driving a wedge between the two of them that, over the past five months, had done more damage than he figured either of them knew how to remedy. She'd spent her nights here at the hospital, and Tom wondered when the last time she'd even seen her husband had been.

Now, as he watched them, Laura reached for Faith's hand and lowered her face to kiss its soft skin, resting her forehead on her daughters shoulder. Tom glanced at Steven, who watched his wife with an emotion that he couldn't read.

"Tom, Dad," Abby said softly and motioned toward the hallway. The three of them stood outside the doorway, Abby dictating her conversation with Laura in hushed tones. "It was tough," she was saying, "but I think she's ready to let go. It's looking like it will be today, so..." Her voice caught, but she spoke through her tears. "I think we need to say our good-byes. Can I propose we take shifts with the two of them in the cafeteria, so we can all have a moment alone with her?"

Tom and John nodded their approval, and for the next two hours, they took turns sitting with Steven and Laura. He marveled over how much he had come to care about these two in the time that he and Abby had been together. They'd been on the brink of disaster themselves, until that fateful day in May, but the tragedy of the accident had brought him and Abby back together with a force that surprised him. Now here he was, waiting for her to come back from saying good-bye to her niece.

Tom was the last to go in, and he lingered with the little girl, telling her everything he hadn't been able to while she'd been alive, and left the room teary eyed and exhausted. Nodding to Abby, she told her sister gently that they'd be out here in the waiting room for as long as they needed.

With that, Tom sat down wearily and watched two of the people he'd come to love most in the world move slowly toward saying good-bye to the one person *they* loved most in the world.

∽

Steven

Steven sat at Faith's bedside and looked across her tiny body at his wife. Shoulders hunched and head down so that the tip of her nose touched the bed; Laura had been silent for what seemed like hours. With a sudden gasp she looked up, red-rimmed eyes meeting Steven's. She bit her lower lip, fighting the emotion in her shaking voice.

"Why her," she began, pausing in an attempt to keep her emotions in check. Steven felt a sudden rush of compassion for his wife, a foreign feeling. All these months he'd been harboring a growing resentment, blame, and animosity for her. The compassionate tug at his heart was a surprise, and he impulsively reached for her hand across the bed. "Why her," Laura continued, "and not me?"

There it was, the question he knew she'd been asking herself all these months. There was nothing to say except the question he had been asking *himself* this whole time.

"Why her at all?"

There were tears streaming down both of their faces now, and suddenly he had to be near his wife. He jumped off of his perch, overturning his chair in the process and flew around the bed to kneel next to her chair and pull her into his arms. The unfamiliar gesture opened a floodgate of emotions in them both, and Laura wept into his shoulder, piercing, unhindered sobs wracking her body. Steven looked up long enough to see a nurse pause in the doorway momentarily, but he nodded to her and she continued on by.

And there, on the cold floor of their daughter's hospital room, Steven held his wife for the first time in almost six months. All at once he felt complete again, and he wondered what had taken him so long. This was *their* daughter, not his and not hers, but *theirs*. How could they have forgotten that so easily? Both had retreated to their corners, unable to see the other's grief through their own.

Laura opened her mouth to speak, but no words came out, and she sat like that, mouth agape, for minutes until she found the stability to ask Steven what she wanted to ask him.

"Why did it take you so long?"

The accusation in her simple inquiry stung, and Steven squeezed his eyes shut in pain.

"I don't know," he began, pulling Laura into his lap and stroking her hair mindlessly as he kissed the top of her head. "I was angry. I had so much anger, and nowhere to direct it. I was angry, mostly, at your father, and every day I pray for the grace to forgive him. I was angry at God, for taking her. Why her? He gets her for eternity—why not let us have her a little longer? Why give her to us at all if he was only going to take her away? I thought we'd made the right decision in having her, despite what we were up against. I guess I thought that, somehow, that we would be rewarded for that. That God had great things in store for her because of her circumstances...that there *must* be a higher purpose for her in this life. And then that life was extinguished. Her heart's still beating, Laura, but that's not Faith in there. She could live a long life, probably outlive both of us, but how? Hooked up to some machine? That's no life for a child, for a girl, for *our* girl. I waited for you, to make a decision, despite my better judgment. And I found myself angry at you for your adamant opposition to what I thought was best for Faith. And that tiny window of anger allowed all of my other anger, anger with John, with God, and anger with myself, to flood out. And I poured it onto you." He shook his head sadly, knowing he had been wrong but struggling to find any other way that it could have played out. Laura was silent for a long while, and he wondered if he'd said too much—if he'd just severed the bond that they had rediscovered. But Laura's words had a clarity to them that rendered him speechless, and he wondered if it was really that simple.

"I just figured that it's hard to support someone else's pain when you can't even support your own."

As she continued, her words brought fresh tears to his eyes.

"I love you, Steven. I'll never stop loving you. And I understand your anger, every bit of it."

Steven closed his eyes and pulled her closer, wondering if all husbands were this lucky. If all mothers, in the face of losing their child, could find it deep within them to be this selfless. He listened as Laura continued.

"But Steven, try and understand." She turned to face him, the intensity in her green eyes burning right through him. "I was angry too! Angry at myself—think of my *guilt!*" she cried. "There were nights when I couldn't breathe for feeling so guilty! And I was—*am*—so mad at my Dad—*he cost Faith her life!*" Her emotions poured out of her now, passion personified. Steven expected tears, but she had cried them all. Now there was nothing but crystal clear clarity in her eyes, the clouds of pent up frustration and anger temporarily gone. "And I know now that my anger was misdirected as well. It's no one's fault, really, no matter how hard I try to spin it that way. I've gone through everything in my mind, time and time again—if only I had acted faster, checked to make sure no one was running a red light—she'd still be with us. But despite all that, it's not *my* fault. And as much as I want to blame my dad...*God, I want to blame my dad.*" She fought to control the emotion in her voice. *It's his fault,* she wanted to scream. But she swallowed hard and suddenly a peace she'd never experience overtook her, and words she never thought she'd say left her mouth—words she knew she'd have to repeat to herself every day for the rest of her life. "Steven, the fact of the matter is...God had a plan. His plan involved Faith, and we don't know what it is. We probably won't ever fully know. But we have to believe in it. We have to do our daughter justice, and have *Faith*, blind faith, that there is a bigger reason for all of this."

Steven shook his head, dumbfounded at his wife's wisdom, wondering what had finally brought her around. He waited for the *buts*, knowing in his heart that she'd *still* find a reason to wait. And when she opened her mouth to speak, he closed his eyes, praying for the patience to deal with this again.

"We need to say good-bye," she said, so softly he almost didn't hear her.

Steven's embrace loosened in his shock, blinking hard to focus his vision. "We *what?*"

Laura turned to look at him, pulling her legs Indian style beneath her. She reached out and smoothed his hair back above his ear, finding the strength to offer a weak smile. "I'm ready."

Suddenly faced with the reality of a decision he thought he'd been ready for for months, Steven panicked. *I can't. It's too soon. She might still wake up—might still be okay. It's happened before; there have been miracles. I read about them every day.* He found himself repeating every argument Laura had ever thrown at him, finding new justification in them, suddenly believing them wholeheartedly. But as he rose to his feet and stood on trembling legs to look at his daughter, he knew his wife was right. It was time.

"Should we call your father? Abby, Tom?"

Laura shook her head, biting her lip. "No."

Steven's head jerked up in surprise. *You're not going to let your family say good-bye?* he thought, and opened his mouth to say just this when she beat him to it.

"They said good-bye this afternoon. They were able to say their good-byes."

Steven nodded, his blurred memory recalling their presence that afternoon when they had arrived, their presence now, in the waiting room, where they offered their silent support, and returned his attention to Faith. As he watched her, the beeping of her monitor blurred into the background, and soon everything faded but her. His beautiful daughter lay below him, and not for the first time since she'd been born, he saw her not as a four-year-old, but as everything she'd ever been. He looked at his daughter and all at once saw every stage she'd been at. He saw her as a newborn, her mouth held the same way now as it had been then, relaxed and turned up ever so slightly at the corners to reveal the smile just beneath it. He saw her as a toddler, chubby and giddy, learning to use her limbs and waddling everywhere as a result of it, her entire lower body thrown into her run before she learned to isolate her legs. He saw her on her first day of preschool, those braids that he'd flipped over her shoulder, later laughing as he told Laura how cliché they were. He memorized her now, committing to memory her tiny hands, her ski-jump nose, her soft skin. He didn't want to forget any of it, yet knew he would. He'd already lost her voice. It came back to him once in a while, but when he tried, like now, he couldn't recall it.

The realization that this would be the last time he saw her alive hit him with a force he didn't know existed, and he found his feet cemented to the floor. He picked up her warm hand and squeezed it. How could he, in just a few minutes, let go of that hand and *walk away* from her? How did that moment happen, when a parent walked away from his child knowing it would be the last time? He suddenly understood what had been causing Laura to hesitate all these months, and he wondered if he was really ready for the decision they'd come to. Yet as he looked down at Faith, he was overtaken by the kind of love that only a parent can feel. He knew, beyond all comprehension, that he loved her enough to do this. The logic of it never added up; if he sat trying to rationalize it, he couldn't. Loving someone enough to take that person's life from them, it just didn't make logical sense. But he knew as a father that he hadn't understood real love until that little girl had been born. She had blown it out of the water. Suddenly there wasn't an ounce of selfishness in love. Suddenly he found himself caring about someone's happiness, someone's safety, someone's quality of life, more than he cared about his own. And he knew that keeping Faith alive would be something he did only for himself, and for Laura. He couldn't do that to her; he loved her too much. Through his tears he looked up to see Laura smooth the hair back from Faith's forehead and plant a kiss in the middle of it.

For years after that moment, he would swear he'd felt Faith's hand flinch as she did so, squeezing his as he held it. Laura's tears fell onto Faith's face, and he reached over and wiped them off of her cheek, imagining for a minute that they were hers, that she had awakened and would be looking up at him with bright eyes.

But her eyes remained closed, peaceful and dreamlike, and he knew it was time. Steven circled the bed to stand behind Laura, to say good-bye to their daughter together. He wrapped his arms around her, placing his hand over hers as they both enveloped Faith's tiny hands, eyes closed in silent prayer and farewell. One at a time, Mother and Father leaned down and kissed their daughter good-bye, watching as the nurse who had been summoned entered the room and turned off the machine, not hearing a word she said as she explained to them what would happen. Steven was vaguely aware of the slowing beeping of the monitor, watching Faith's chest rise more slowly as the seconds passed, until finally, with a tiny gasp from her mouth, it stopped entirely. He tightened his grip around his wife, fully expecting her to collapse to the floor as she'd done the first time she saw Faith in this bed, but her legs held firmly beneath her. He stole a glimpse of her face and almost collapsed himself. Through her tears, Laura had a look of peace on her face.

The first time they'd been in a hospital room together, Laura had been giving birth to Faith, and Steven remembered wondering how women got so strong—where they found the strength to breathe through pain that immense and focus on the good that was surely to follow.

Tonight, as he watched his wife say good-bye to their daughter, he found himself wondering the same thing all over again.

Back home, flowers of all shapes and colors lay piled on the front steps, their cellophane wrapping crinkling in the breeze. Teddy bears that had been placed there sagged underneath the weight of the water they'd attained from the rainstorm the night before.

Inside, the house was still, the red light on the answering machine beeped, fourteen messages waiting to be heard.

Upstairs, a small satin blanket lay crumpled on the floor, the same place it had been lying for months. A pair of tiny jeans and the purple fleece with the flower on the hood lay on the end of the bed where Laura had tossed them. The Disney Princess clock next to the bed blinked a red twelve o'clock, forgotten after a brief power loss back in July.

A child's vanity sat in the corner underneath the windows, the toy lipstick and eye shadow spread across its surface, a compact's open mirror reflecting the rain on the window.

A single raindrop started its slow trek across its cold panes, leaving not so much as a trail behind it as it gathered more water on its way down. Somewhere in the middle it stopped, trembling in the wind—or was it hesitation?—before joining an existing trail of water and vanishing from sight.

And just like that, Faith McCord was gone.

༄

John

John wrung his hands nervously and checked his watch one last time. Only a minute had passed since he'd last checked it, but it felt like hours. Stamping his feet impatiently, he shoved his hands back into his pockets, trying to keep them still.

Finally he saw the glow of headlights at the base of the drive, and he straightened anxiously. Laura and Steven had been busy in the immediate aftermath of their daughter's death. He knew that after a long day, all they'd want to do was go inside and sleep—that sweet escape from the reality of all that had happened.

He knew neither of them would be happy to see him. Though they all had been assured in the aftermath of that horrible day last May that it was an accident—that he'd seen them and braked in enough time, and it was the slipperiness of the road that caused his car to hit theirs—neither Laura nor Steven had spoken to him since the accident. And he knew that what he'd come to tell them would further damage their relationship, maybe forever, but he had to come clean. The truth had been eating at him for months now, and his daughter deserved at least that much after all she'd been through.

After all he'd taken from her.

The car slowed as it approached him, and even with the glare of headlights in his eyes, he could see the weariness on Laura's face as she put it into park and slowly climbed out. She looked disoriented, as if the reality of what had happened today still hadn't hit her, despite the arrangements she'd spent the evening making.

She knew that tomorrow she and Steven would spend the day at the funeral parlor, readying a burial neither of them had ever planned for. It was a funeral that could have been avoided, if it wasn't for him. That's why he was here, he reminded himself as he took a tentative step toward his daughter, and then a second.

"Hi," he offered cautiously.

Laura said nothing, just sniffed and nodded. Her eyes were red rimmed, both from crying and exhaustion, but they held an icy clarity that told him she still blamed him.

"Laura, I need to tell you," he began, but she shook her head and took a step back.

"Don't, Daddy." She fumbled for her keys. "I understand now. There was nothing you could have done differently."

John was about to open his mouth to stop her, when her words registered. "What?" He looked up, surprised. This was a change, and one he hadn't been expecting today of all days.

Laura found her keys, and when she met his eyes, there were tears in them. "I'm so mad, Daddy. I'm mad she had to die," she spit out the word like poison, "and I'm mad at the way it happened. But…" She hung on that last word, as did John—the closest she'd come to forgiveness yet—before she continued.

"But I've heard it from the police, from the doctors, from everyone—it was the conditions. You did all you could to stop in time." John could see that it pained her to admit that—that she so badly wanted to blame him—and wondered at her change in heart.

"Do I wish you hadn't been driving on that particular road at that particular time?" she was saying. "Of course. But that's no one's fault, really. And as nice as it would be to have *someone* to blame, I can't do that. If *any* good can come out of losing my daughter, it's not going to be by alienating family—by alienating you. I owe my little girl that much—she loved you so—" she stopped as a sob bubbled into her throat. "So much," she choked out as John rushed forward and threw his arms around her, crying as well.

"I'm so sorry," he repeated, over and over.

"It's okay," she soothed, a foreign feeling to be soothed by his own daughter. "Now," she pulled back and forced a sad smile. "What are you doing here? You said something about needing to tell me something?"

John opened his mouth to offer the confession that had been weighing on him, but something stopped him. Maybe it was the fact that she'd finally forgiven him—he didn't want to make her angry so soon. He wanted to be allowed to be here to comfort her and Steven—to grieve with them—during such a hard time. Perhaps the time to tell them would be later, after things had settled down a bit.

"Nothing," he lied. "Nothing at all. I just wanted to let you know I'm here for you."

"Thanks," Laura replied. She seemed awkward, as though she wasn't sure how to act, the months of silence between them gone in an instant.

"Where's Steven?" John looked around, willing his mind to think about something else, and not the lie of omission he'd just committed.

"Inside," Laura answered.

"I can't believe how he looked," John said before he thought better of it, but Laura didn't seem offended. Instead she shook her head sadly.

"I know. I've been spending all my time at the hospital," she began, and suddenly John understood her earlier look of disorientation. "I hadn't noticed his change—we hadn't even talked in the last few months. We were so angry at each other…" She trailed off, and John couldn't decide whether she was thinking of all that had passed between her and Steven, or about how odd it felt to be confiding in her father after so long. "Anyways," she shook her head briskly. "Now more than ever we need to reconnect."

John nodded. "You're right. You'll need each other—and us, now more than ever." He tried to convince himself that those words—that sentiment—were the reason he couldn't tell her the truth yet. "What can I do?" he added sincerely.

"Just asking," Laura's lip quivered, an attempt at a smile. "That helps. But I think we'll be okay tonight." She looked toward her house as if afraid to go in. "I'll call you tomorrow, okay?" she said as the tears came again.

"Okay," John nodded, stepping forward to give her an awkward hug before turning to go.

He walked the short distance between her house and his, telling himself all the way that he'd done the right thing by not saying anything.

༄

Laura

Late the next morning, Laura walked into her house numb. The last few hours had been a blur; she could remember surprising herself with her decisiveness, picking this and that, leaving Steven to pick the headstone while she went home to get clothes to bury Faith in.

What do you bury your daughter in? Do you put her in that dress you loved but she'd hated, or those pajamas she'd refused to take off for weeks at a time, much to your chagrin? Did you bury her in something nice, that those who came to pay their last respects would remember her in, or did you opt for comfort?

Laura stood in front of her daughter's closet staring at the clothes, suddenly lifeless. The holiday dress that Faith had worn for their last Christmas card picture together suddenly could have been any of the dresses hanging in Macy's. The skirt she had worn on her first day of pre-K could have been any old skirt. She looked around the room and took in her daughter's items, seeing her in all of them but at the same time feeling as though she was looking at a stranger's things. She became vaguely aware of Abby's sudden presence, and with tears, the two of them picked out Faith's funeral clothes.

With promises from Laura that she'd meet her at the funeral parlor within the hour, Abby took the clothes and drove across town, leaving her sister just where she'd found her—standing in front of her daughter's closet.

She gingerly touched the items hanging in there, sobs welling inside her like the distant rumble of a freight train. Suddenly dizzy, she crumpled to the ground, wrapping her arms around Faith's favorite purple fleece and weeping.

And there she lay, spinning with the earth, as it gradually made its progress toward the longest night of the year.

∽

CHAPTER SEVENTEEN

Laura

Laura didn't have to look up to know that she was headed in the right direction. She watched the same tragic landmarks pass by underneath her, and realized that her head had been bowed in the same defeated pose every time she came here. She passed a fresh bouquet of flowers on her left; on her right was a stuffed penguin that looked as though it had been there for years, weather worn and looking defeated. This was no place for stuffed animals. They belonged indoors, in the arms of the children who loved them, not out here, silently keeping watch over their former possessors from cold limestone perches. At the third oak tree she made a sharp left, and there, at the crest of the hill, came to rest at the base of it.

Before her, a small stone cast a shadow in the pathetically dim light of the lanterns burning through the dusk. Steven had picked it, she realized, and it looked wrong. The edges were sharp, not rounded, the stone rough around the edges, not safe for a child. The etching in the stone itself was far too shallow—Laura worried that it would be worn away in less than a decade, the name and dates gone forever. Raising a trembling hand, Laura reached out to run her thumb across them. The icy chill of the stone was enough to jolt her back to reality, and finally the thoughts she had been suppressing flooded to her mind. She felt each letter beneath her fingers—F-A-I-T-H-M-C-C-O-R-D—and marveled at the way a name could change, just like that.

When they'd first found out that they were having a girl, it hadn't taken them long to choose the name. It represented the kind of faith they had in each other, in God, in the future of their daughter, who *must* be fated for something spectacular, to be conceived as she was, against the odds. The name had held little more than a hopeful excitement then, etched into gifts and inscribed in children's books as they anxiously awaited the birth of their daughter. When she was born, the name had taken on a life all its own; suddenly there was a person attached to it. Faith was a name that cried for three hours the first time it saw a street cleaner, and plugged its ears every time since, a slightly panicked look on its face. Faith was a name that loved Christmastime most of all, a name that sang its carols months before the radio was even playing them. Faith became a name that loved to hear the story of how it was born, not just on its birthday, but time and time again. And now Faith was a cold name beneath her fingers, alive only in etchings and stone, floating in memory, poised to fly away at any moment and be lost forever. Only then did Laura realize there were tears streaming down her face, black dots growing in the dirt before her like ripples on the lake. She was gripped by a searing pain so deep that she felt as though her insides were shrinking, creating a void so large in her chest that even her lungs couldn't expand past the density of loneliness, and she found it harder to breathe with each passing minute. Her daughter lay beneath her, little more than bones at this point, and she was *here*.

It had been her job to protect Faith, and she had failed her. It was that simple. Faith should be at home right now, curled up in her favorite fleece blanket in front of the TV. She would have just woken up from her afternoon nap. Laura had always marveled at how she could go down at three, wake up at five, and was still able to fall asleep again by eight o'clock. She had been a great sleeper. And like so many other parents, Laura had plopped her daughter in front of the TV while she prepared dinner. It kept her occupied and out from under foot. Plus, one look at her daughter's sleepy face as she stumbled down the stairs after her nap had always told Laura that she had little energy for anything else at the time. She pictured her there now, eyes sleepy and unfocused yet still riveted on the television, transfixed by the animated characters. This time of year, it would have been Barbie Nutcracker. Her hair would have been mussed, a kink at the back of it from where her elastic band had been holding it in place earlier. In five minutes she'd find her energy and wander into the kitchen asking for a snack. Laura would balk, explaining that dinner was soon and she couldn't spoil her appetite, but would usually cave in and give her a small bowl of pretzel Goldfish, her favorite. Faith would plod back to her perch on the couch, and hours later, when the dinner dishes had been put away and Faith had long since been asleep, Laura would find the plastic bowl balanced between the couch cushions, just as full as it had been when she'd handed it to her. With a smile, Laura would pour the Goldfish back into their box. She'd wondered if Faith had ever made it through a whole box before they went stale. She'd wander into Faith's room before going to bed herself, the nightlight casting a comforting glow on the bright pink and green area rug, illuminating her daughter's peaceful face as she slept deep under her quilts.

That's where she should be sleeping now, not underneath Laura's cold hands that dug into the earth with fervor. Sobs shook her body, and she missed her husband's arms around her. She needed a comforting embrace. But all that found her was a cold wind, circling around her, fluttering her hair and blowing dead leaves over the gift she had brought her daughter. Laura straightened, wiped her eyes, and gingerly picked up the small, tin-wrapped package she'd brought with her. The brightly wrapped chocolate turkey seemed trivial and petty now, in this place, but she couldn't come empty handed. Laura had always made a big deal of the holidays, and Thanksgiving was no different. She wasn't ready to see Faith's empty chair at the table tomorrow, wasn't ready for the family. Her cousin's children would only remind her of Faith—each step they took would be a painful reminder of each one Faith would never be allowed. Each word they uttered would be meant to be supportive and encouraging, but would only scratch at a deeper wound. Part of her would want to tell them that it was okay to talk to her—she was still human. A broken one, yes, but she still walked among the living. And somehow she knew they were dreading it too, afraid of what to say to someone who had lost a daughter, if anything at all. All too suddenly, Laura longed for the simplicity of her daughter. The childlike curiosity, the simple pleasures of easy entertainment, and the way the world melted away when that little girl was in her arms. Her hands shook uncontrollably as she placed the chocolate turkey on Faith's gravestone. *Happy Thanksgiving, baby,* she half-thought, half-whispered as she sat back on her heels, thinking again about the tragedy of such a childlike item resting against such a permanent stone, succumbing to a new wave of tears and to the fact that this was going to be a long, long night.

⁐

Abby

If she had to field one more "Where's Tom?" from an unwitting cousin, Abby was going to scream.

"He's with his family," she said, wincing at the words. *One of the casualties of dating a divorcee with kids*, she wanted to add, but she kept her mouth shut. Truth was, she felt guilty for even thinking about herself or her own problems. Laura had lost her daughter and was across the kitchen gallantly trying to put on a brave face for the first holiday without her, and here she was feeling sorry for herself over having to share her boyfriend for a day.

But she'd been "sharing" him for the entirety of their relationship, and despite their recent bonding over the past few months, as she looked around the room today she finally allowed the realization that she'd been fighting with for so long to materialize— it wasn't what she wanted. *I need you today,* she'd said to him that morning as he got dressed to go to Beth's. *Faith hasn't even been gone two months. It's our first holiday without her ... you don't seem to understand how hard this is.* Tom's mouth had set in a firm line. *Oh, I understand,* he'd said. *I understand perfectly, Abby. Don't you remember? I've been here with you every day, every night—through her coma and since her death? Which means I've been completely neglecting Ben and Luke, and now Beth's pissed at me."* Abby had interrupted him there. *Does Beth know about me?* she'd asked. Tom had told her to stop being ridiculous, that of course Beth knew about her, but Abby had found herself wondering about the extent of the other woman's knowledge. She'd known, early on, that they'd been dating, when the kids would tell her about their weekend after spending it downtown with Tom and Abby. At one point she'd flipped, and insisted that if Tom wanted to see the kids, he do it at the house, and since then, there hadn't been many problems. Abby couldn't help but wonder if it was because Tom was hiding their relationship from Beth—or at least the depth of it. Of course, Beth had to know Abby was still in Tom's life, especially these last few horrible months, but in the back of her mind, she had a feeling that Tom assured Beth that it was only a friendship, or at most, a casual relationship. She doubted Beth knew that late at night, Tom confessed his desire to spend his life with Abby, or that as he'd held her hand in the waiting room, he'd whispered over and over how much he loved her. She doubted the other woman knew that sometimes Tom wondered aloud what his and Abby's children would be like or what their wedding would entail. But despite the dishonesty on Tom's part, or the lack of knowledge on Beth's part, she knew that wasn't what bothered her most of all.

The truth was, she didn't want a boyfriend—and someday a husband—who would have to be somewhere else on important holidays. What *if* they had children of their own? Then how would he decide where to spend his time? It just wasn't a situation she wanted to deal with at all.

Suddenly Abby smiled sheepishly at her cousin who had been standing there since asking the question, unaware of just how long she'd been lost in thought. "He's with his family," she repeated, and then politely excused herself.

She didn't want to think about it anymore; she needed some air.

Letting herself out onto the back porch, Abby breathed a deep sigh of relief, but immediately the breath was sucked right out of her. Strewn across the back patio were several of Faith's toys—her

Disney Princess bike, the Fisher Price roller skates she'd gotten for her last birthday. Abby assumed that Steven and Laura had simply not been back here all these months—or perhaps they had and couldn't bring themselves to move anything. She knew that Faith's room remained untouched.

Suddenly a wave of guilt washed over her like nothing she'd ever experienced, and for the first time, she thought she might know what Tom was going through—his own emotions telling him one thing, tempting him to do one thing, but someone else's emotions winning out—someone who was his flesh and blood, someone whom he cared about almost more than he cared about himself. She knew who played each role in Tom's life—she may be the person his own selfishness urged him to spend his time with, but the well-being of his own children would ultimately be what won him over. And here she was, wanting to wallow in self-pity, when inside there was her flesh and blood, bleeding. Laura.

Immediately she was on her feet and rushing back into the house, looking around the kitchen and living room frantically for her sister—not understanding the sense of urgency that had overtaken her but surrendering to it just the same. Laura was nowhere to be seen; Steven stood in the corner looking miserable but surrounded by family. Her father glanced at her in surprise as she came breezing through, but she was past him before he had time to say anything.

Flying around the corner, Abby reached the staircase and breathed a sigh of relief. Laura sat in the middle of them, arms crossed over her knees, her head resting on top.

"Hey," she said, quietly sitting down next to her sister. "You okay?"

Laura smiled bravely, but her lips trembled and she shook her head.

"Honey..." Abby put her hand on Laura's. "Why on earth did you offer to host everyone this year? I know we've had Thanksgiving here every year since Faith was born," she stopped herself short, wishing she hadn't said it. But Laura continued to stare straight ahead, seemingly un-phased, so Abby continued. "We all would have understood if you hadn't wanted to do it this year. More than understood..."

She watched Laura's face carefully, and after what seemed like hours, she slowly turned her gaze on Abby. Her eyes were red and puffy, swollen from the effort of holding back the tears that Abby could see in them now. "I just...I had to do it. I don't know, Abs...it just would have felt like we've moved on, like we've forgotten her, if we'd done anything differently this year. I know that sounds really stupid—"

"No, it doesn't." Abby offered quickly, and then hesitated. "But there's more to it than that, isn't there?"

"I didn't want to come home to an empty house. I needed to have people here," Laura responded, but Abby wasn't convinced. She looked pleadingly at her sister.

"I can't help you, Laura, if you don't let me in."

Laura's face finally crumpled as she admitted what Abby had known she was hiding. "I don't trust myself behind the wheel!" she sobbed, wiping ferociously at the tears that finally came.

Abby was silent; she truly didn't know what to say to that. "It wasn't your fault," she ventured. "Nobody blames you—you couldn't have done anything differently." Abby didn't say whose fault it was—she didn't add that there was someone in attendance that day who would have been well-advised to stay home. She didn't say anything, because Laura already knew.

"That's not what I mean," Laura said. "What I mean is I don't trust that I would try and get myself there in once piece. Without Faith, what is there to live for?"

Abby was silent, searching for words, but as she struggled for the right thing to say, a movement caught her eye. She locked eyes with her father, who was listening from the hallway and had clasped a hand over his mouth at Laura's words. Shaking his head slowly, he backed away from his daughters, his eyes conveying to Abby what she knew he couldn't say:

What have I done?

CHAPTER EIGHTEEN

Laura

The snow was floating above the floodlights—ever so slowly earthbound and twirling in what Laura was sure was a bitter breeze. It was late, and morning was clearly in no hurry to arrive, but Laura couldn't sleep. She sat curled in the chair next to the fireplace, her head resting against its back, eyes halfheartedly open and staring out the frosted pane in front of her. She was vaguely aware of the strains of Christmas music that surrounded her as they wafted from the speakers. "Panis Angelicus," always one of her favorites, had a sadness to it she'd never noticed before, but as she listened now, she was sure of it. She wondered what the words meant. No matter how she tried, "Panis Angelicus" to her sounded like "Angelic Pain" and it occurred to her that she personified that contradiction. Here she sat in her living room, warmly decorated for the season, watching the peaceful snow as it fell outside, and she'd never felt more pain than she harbored right now. The tears in her eyes blurred the white lights of the tree in the corner, and she blinked them away to focus on the ornaments. She had barely noticed that the tree had been decorated; Abby and Tom had come over to decorate for the holiday, knowing that Laura would be in no mood to do so, but knowing that it needed to be done. She took in the familiar ornaments of her childhood, collected over the years. There was her "My First Christmas" ornament, the train her father had bought for her, with a matching one for Abby, the year they took their first train trip out west, the airplane ornament he'd always pointed in the direction of their next vacation, a cross-stitched ornament her mother had made for her and Steven on their first Christmas together.

She noted similar ornaments of Steven's, years of memories and loving gifts, but as she searched the tree, she saw none of Faith's. Her eyes darting frantically, she searched for "Baby's First Christmas" with Faith's baby picture, grinning and happy—the rocking horse she'd received as a gift from Abby. Knowing that they had left the ornaments off for her benefit, but angry all the same, Laura flew out of her chair, sliding across the floor in her socks and scrambling down the basement stairs. She hurriedly rummaged through the shelves until she found the pink memorabilia box she was looking for, gasping in this reassurance that her daughter *had* existed.

She slowly climbed back up the stairs, cradling the box like it was Faith herself, finally sinking to the floor in front of the tree and gingerly removing the lid. The rush of memories that flooded her as she looked inside took her by surprise, and for a moment she had to remind herself to breathe. She took the objects out one by one, handling them carefully, as though they would break at the slightest pressure. The top of the box were things that Faith had made—her day care picture framed in the middle of a lace doily, glued on top of a folded piece of wrapping paper and made into an ornament. The Santa she had created out of red construction paper and cotton balls. The noodles and glitter that made up countless shapes, the pipe-cleaner reindeer. And beneath that, the ornaments that commemorated all her years on earth—and a gaping hole where the fifth should have been. Laura brought her knees to her chin. She was well beyond tears, but the pain in her chest was so crushing that she thought that her heart might not stand the pressure. Through half-closed eyes she pictured Faith as she would always see her—laughing on Christmas morning, the joy and excitement in her eyes unmistakable, and possible only in children. She pictured her bright smile, caught in a sunbeam of early morning light as she tore open a present. She saw her in the snow on Christmas Eve, laughing in delight as the snowflakes caught on her tongue. Her arms ached for her, and she could almost feel the sleeping child beside her, curled up asleep after Laura read to her from her favorite Christmas stories. She had loved those nights and had always lingered by the fire long after Faith had drifted off, the heat of the fire warming them both.

Tonight, the fire had died, and the hearth was as cold as her heart. With shaking hands, Laura placed the ornaments, one by one, on the tree. She didn't bother standing up to do so—this was the level they would have been hung at if Faith had done it herself. She almost smiled as she pictured the trees these last few years, Faith's enthusiastic decorations crowded onto the bottom of the tree.

Almost as soon as she'd put the last ornament on the tree, Laura took them all off again—they didn't look right. It wasn't right that they were up, when Faith wasn't there. She placed them hastily back in the box, suddenly not as careful. All she knew was that she needed to not see them anymore—they needed to not exist. Placing the lid back on the box, she hurried back down to the basement where she hid it, behind the other boxes, where she wouldn't find it for a long, long time.

Returning to her perch in front of the tree, Laura curled up in a ball, and though there were no tears on her face, she knew she was crying. Feeling all too much, and not enough, she closed her eyes and waited for this, too, to pass.

Steven

Steven lay in bed and watched the snow float slowly past his window, for some reason focused on the fact that his wife, a floor beneath him and probably just as awake as he was, watched the same snowflakes he did, only seconds later. He got to see them first. Why this was important he didn't know, but it had occupied his mind for a moment, and he was glad for it, glad for an interruption to the thoughts that were a constant, seeping through his skull from the outside world, thoughts induced by the simplest of things around him. He turned over, wrestling with the pillow beneath him that had *never* felt this lumpy and marveling at the fact that for whatever reason, his bed was the one place he *couldn't* sleep these days. He found himself dozing at work, definitely something they frowned upon in the medical world. His colleagues had finally convinced him to take some additional time off, and he'd nearly fallen asleep behind the wheel on his way home, drained from the emotions of these last few months. Yet now he was here, in bed, and couldn't fall asleep to save his life. *To save my life*, he thought, and again his mind wandered back to his little girl. He couldn't save her, no matter what he did. He'd prayed, and when he'd felt God hadn't answered his prayers, had prayed to every other god he could think of, even stooping to make a deal with the devil if he'd just give him his daughter back. He'd sat by her bedside, convinced that a father's love was enough to bring her back, but nothing had worked, and now she was gone. And her mother was a story below him, staring lifelessly at the same snowflakes he was— seconds later—as he lay in a bed as cold as they were. He rolled over again and focused on their slow descent, letting them finally mesmerize him into a fitful sleep where he dreamed, as he'd done so often these days, of the past.

The house was warm and inviting as he drove up to it, his headlights illuminating the snow covered driveway. I'll have to shovel tomorrow, *he'd thought as he turned off the ignition and dashed through the cold into the house. Immediately the smell of rosemary and sage entered his nostrils.* Laura must be roasting a chicken *was his only thought before the bright flash that was his daughter came barreling toward him.*

"Daddy!" she cried, hurling herself full speed into his arms. If nothing else kept him from retiring early, this would—the sight of his baby's excitement to have him home at the end of the day.

"Hi, sweetheart." He kissed her forehead and set her back down on the ground, removing his boots and overcoat and walking into the warmly lit kitchen. Laura stood at the far end of the island, her apron covered in flour, pieces of dough in her hair as she alternately kneaded her hands through sugar cookie dough and tried unsuccessfully to tuck her hair behind her ear with her elbow. She offered him a huge grin, and he smiled right back, marveling at how far they'd come in restoring their relationship this last year. Watching their daughter reclaim her spot on her stool and dig her hands right in with her mother's, he couldn't imagine not *having put that effort in with Laura. He walked over to inspect their work—one tray of cookies already cooling and filling the kitchen with its enticing aroma. Shapes of all kinds covered the tray— stars, Christmas trees, Santas, candy canes, bells. He noticed a jar of frosting sitting next to the bowl, along with brightly colored sprinkles and decorations, and half smiled at the mess he knew the kitchen would be within a matter of minutes.*

"Hey, babe." Laura kissed him on the cheek. "How was your day?"

The two talked for a few minutes about each of their days, before he asked if it would be all right if he crashed in front of the news for a few minutes with a beer. "Of course," Laura had replied, and within minutes he was sitting in his favorite chair, the news just about to start. Yet he found his thumb moving for the mute button within seconds, and he lay his head back and closed his eyes, listening to the sounds of the two people he loved most coming from the kitchen. Soft Christmas music was coming from the speakers, and he heard the two of them talking, punctuated by Faith's giggles and exclamations. The smells of the house overwhelmed him, and he couldn't imagine being more content than he was at this moment.

His daughter, as she'd done so many times, proved him wrong as she carried, very carefully, a cookie that she'd made just for him into the room and presented it to him, climbing into his lap as she pointed out what made that particular cookie so special.

"These are his eyes," she was explaining, pointing to the two black dots that sat on either side of the reindeer's face, "and this is his nose!" She pointed proudly to the cinnamon candy she'd placed strategically in the middle of his head. He hardly noticed the fact that she'd given the reindeer whiskers, or that his antlers were frosted with green frosting, and saw only the effort she'd put into decorating this for him.

"Can I try it?" he asked, and she nodded enthusiastically, giggling as he bit off the animal's antlers. "Faith," he declared, "this is the *best cookie I've ever had," and he meant it, pulling his little girl close and inhaling the scent of her, all sugar and daydreams and innocence.*

At some point, Laura came in with dinner for the three of them, and they sat there in the living room, eating and watching The Grinch, *Faith laughing out loud at times as she watched him try to steal Christmas. Later, he held Faith on his lap and read her favorite Christmas stories to her, the house hushed around him except for the crackle of a fire in the fireplace, the Christmas music, and a light snowfall outside. After Faith had dozed in his arms, he gazed out the window at the softly falling snow,* and startled awake.

Had his eyes even been closed? The memory of his daughter was so vivid in his memory, and his arms ached with emptiness as he realized they held only a pillow.

And the house that had been so warm in his memory was now cold, so cold it chilled him to the bone.

Padding softly down the hall, he ducked down the stairs to find Laura curled up in front of the Christmas tree, sound asleep and shivering. It was only after he'd covered her with a blanket and smoothed the hair back from her face that he realized she was crying, and his hands moved to his own face to betray *his* tears.

And he wondered, as he made his way back upstairs, just how many nights now he'd been crying in his sleep, completely unaware.

∽

Tom

"Who are you taking to the holiday party?" To anyone else, Beth's voice would have simply sounded curious. But Tom knew better. He'd been on his way out the door after dropping the kids off, needing to get back downtown and pick up Abby for the party, when she'd casually dropped the question. "Or should I even ask?" she added, animosity in her voice.

Yep, there it was. Just as he expected.

"If you're not going to like my answer, then why do you ask?"

"Why would you feel the need to hide it from me?" she retorted. "Everyone else probably knows who you're taking. As usual, I'm the last to find out anything, and I have to drag it out of you. It's like pulling teeth—"

"Abby," he cut her off, frustrated. "I'm taking Abby. There, is that what you wanted to hear? Glad you asked?" He tried to control his temper, taking a deep breath and reminding himself that he didn't need to be baited into that.

"You told me you weren't dating her anymore," Beth cried, almost shouting.

"I never said that," Tom replied. "You heard what you wanted to hear."

"So you're still talking to her? You're still dating her? Have you slept with her? God, you're such a liar."

"*Beth*," he said sternly. "Enough. Seriously, if I keep you up to date on her, you flip out, so I just choose not to talk about her with you."

"You know what," Beth waved her hand. "Don't bother coming out here tomorrow."

"It's my weekend with the kids," he began, but she cut him off.

"Well, I don't want to see you. And if *you* want to see *them*, you better think about being honest with me. And cutting that woman out of your life. She ruined our marriage, Tom!"

"*That woman* has a name, Beth. It's Abby. And she did not ruin our marriage. Our marriage was over before she came along—come on, the divorce was *final* before I even met her. You're just looking for somewhere to place the blame."

"*Just get out!*" Beth cried, and Tom turned on his heel.

"Gladly," he muttered under his breath, slamming the door behind him.

Angry, he threw his car in reverse and squealed out of the driveway, making a sharp turn at its base to fly down the street. He waited until he stopped at a stop sign, until the house was out of sight, to take a moment and collect himself.

No matter what he did, he couldn't seem to please everyone. Abby wanted time from him, Beth wanted time from him, and neither wanted to hear about the other. Beth in particular—any mention of Abby sent her flying off the handle. She had herself convinced that it was Abby who had driven him from his home, but they both knew that wasn't true. Meanwhile, he knew Abby resented the time he had to spend out at Beth's because of the kids—and on the increasingly frequent occasion that Beth joined him and the boys for the day, in an attempt to maintain civility in their parenting and present a united front, it was sure to lead to a fight with Abby.

At the moment, leaving one and driving toward the other, he felt trapped to the point of wanting to keep on driving straight past Chicago, straight out of Illinois, and as far as his wheels would carry him. He almost laughed at the thought of what *that* would do to the women in his life. He'd be in fights for the next month. With a sigh, he exited, eased off the brake, and started a slow drive toward Abby, hoping *she* wouldn't be angry with him for something too.

He was at his limit.

Yet as he neared her apartment, he worried that she would be upset—he was fifteen minutes late; he'd been at Beth's all day and had barely contacted Abby. That was usually the kind of thing that made her nuts. But to his surprise, her face lit up and broke into a huge smile when she saw him. His first thought was that perhaps she knew how close he was to the end of his rope and how another fight with her could be the last. His second thought was that she had never looked so beautiful. He'd never been in such a conundrum before—lately he'd been thinking of leaving her, just to simplify his life—yet he'd never loved anyone more. And that's what kept him coming back. Just when he thought he'd hit his limit and taken more than he could take, he looked at her, and all of that melted away. She climbed into his car and gave him a quick kiss on the cheek.

"You look handsome," she told him.

He thanked her, told her she looked beautiful, and waited. He sat and waited for her accusations, her *How come I didn't hear from you all day,* or *just this* once *you couldn't be on time?* But she said nothing, and he began to relax. He'd almost succeeded until he remembered the last time she'd been acting like this. Those two weeks back in May, after their fight about him going on vacation with Beth and the boys, she'd been eerily calm, not her passionate self. Usually Abby said what she was thinking, and what she meant, no matter how heated. But for those weeks she'd been docile, reserved, guarded. He'd thought it was great; finally she understood how to communicate with him and what he responded to—until she stopped returning his phone calls and he realized that calm was really indifference, and she was quickly falling out of love with him. The day he had realized it had been the day of the accident, and in her grief Abby had seemed to have forgotten her loss of feelings for him. Things had been back to normal for months now, Abby getting upset and flustered over the smallest of things, Tom backing off as soon as she did.

And now that she wasn't, he suddenly missed that. He should have been relishing her calm acceptance of how things were in his life and where she fit in, but instead it made him anxious. Something had changed, he could tell, and the thought of losing her made his chest hurt.

"Are you okay?" he asked, trying to keep the tremor from his voice.

"Yeah!" she said, sounding a little too enthusiastic.

"Are you sure?" He glanced over, but the smile on her face seemed sincere.

"Yeah, why?"

"I don't know. I was expecting you to be upset about me being late."

"Hey, it happens. No worries."

Now he was really concerned—that was unlike Abby. She had the capacity to be very understanding, but usually not in matters involving his ex-wife. "All right," he said, still unconvinced.

Still, he reached for her hand and squeezed it as he steered toward the party.

Just breathe, Abby told herself as Tom's grip on her hand tightened. He could tell something was wrong, but she was determined not to ruin tonight.

And she was determined not to fight with him again. After all, it was useless.

They'd had this fight a million times. She knew that was a common expression, an exaggeration, but she wouldn't have been surprised if it had actually *been* a million times. Time and time again, she told him how she felt, why it bothered her.

It just doesn't make sense to me, she'd say. *One minute you guys are fighting, and I'm your go-to vent girl. You call me and vent for your entire commute back into the city about how she's mad about this or being unfair about that. And I listen, try to be there for you, give you advice—something not many girlfriends do when their boyfriend calls to talk about his ongoing tumultuous relationship with his ex. Then, two days later, on* your *day with the kids, Beth tags along to the petting zoo, or on a picnic, or the museum. Can't you see how hard that is for me to follow? How frustrating it is? Or, most of all, how it could lead to me questioning how you can change your mind so easily, whether or not you'll change your mind about* me *like that?*

Tom would tell her it wasn't like that. He was as confused by Beth as she was, he just didn't want to say no to her coming along on those types of things and start yet another fight with her. Abby would accuse him of taking the path of least resistance because it was easy for *him*, and would urge him to think about the kids, and how confusing it must be for *them* to every third weekend be a complete family unit again, only to go back to one parent at a time and fights in between. About that point, Tom would shut down, refuse to say anything, tell Abby he had to go.

Two days later they'd make up, things would be great for a week, and then they were right back to this. The last time it had happened, Abby had vowed it would be the last. *One more of these fights and we're done*, she'd told herself. It felt, after all, like she was just wasting her time. She was dating someone she barely saw, and when she did, he was exhausted from whatever stage his relationship with Beth was at.

She was perfectly willing to accept the unique challenges that dating a divorcee with kids would bring—but she didn't agree with the way Tom and Beth were handling theirs, didn't respect it, found that she hardly respected Tom at this point because of it.

And that was a deal breaker.

But the holiday party was tonight, and she'd committed to going with Tom—and although her heart was breaking to see him, knowing it would be the last time—she wasn't going to back out on him now.

Still, she worried as his thumb trailed the back of her hand, that it would be easy to fall back into him tonight. So many times she'd promised herself she'd end it, had even taken the steps to do so a few times, but one look from him or one touch of his hand brought her right back to where she'd started—wanting to be near him with every ounce of her being.

Fighting it, she pulled her hand away before turning to smile broadly at him and pulling a tube of moisturizer out of her handbag.

"The winter makes my hands so dry," she said as she rubbed it in. It was both small talk and an excuse to pull her hand away, and she kept going. "Did you know that it's not actually the cold weather, but the dryness of the heat you have on inside, that makes your skin dry in the winter?"

"I didn't know that," Tom said, moving his hand onto her thigh. She could see on his face that he knew something was bothering her—that something had shifted—and was trying to stop it with all his might.

Sure, as soon as I lose interest, he can't give me enough attention, but when I'm into him, he ignores me for days at a time. She put her moisturizer away, biding her time until he was parking the car so that she wouldn't have to hold his hand again.

Her job for the rest of the night was to put up a good front, and she did just that—dancing with him, laughing at his jokes, letting him drape his arm across her shoulders as he talked to a colleague. Yet about the time she let him kiss her under the mistletoe, she felt that old familiar pang and couldn't keep the tears from springing to her eyes.

Not because, as she looked up at this man she loved with all her heart, she'd have to end it, but because in that moment she'd once again lost the strength—and will—to do so.

Here we go again, she thought, happy, angry, and sad all at the same time. But most of all, feeling very helpless. Or was it hopeless?

Maybe they're one and the same, she thought.

CHAPTER NINETEEN

John

Christmas was different this year.

He'd known it would be. He'd actually bought Anne a gift—the perfume he got her every year—and had been halfway to his car in the parking lot before he'd remembered that she was no longer around to receive it. Still, he couldn't bring himself to return it. It sat on her side of the sink, and he wondered how many more bottles would accumulate there over the years—when he would be able to break a habit thirty years in the making. She'd wanted him to remarry, and truthfully, he'd like to, if only for the companionship. But he couldn't fathom loving someone else as much as he'd loved Anne, and even if he could, he wondered what she'd make of his peculiar Christmastime habit, one he doubted he'd ever break.

Anne had singlehandedly made this holiday what it was to him. Christmas had been a nonevent in his family growing up; his extended family didn't live close, and therefore it was just another day with him and his parents, a few presents thrown in. But Anne had taken it and made a *season* of it. She started listening to Christmas carols months ahead of time, and throughout the whole month of December, the house had smelled of evergreen, cinnamon, and baked breads, pies, and cookies. Her spirit had been infectious, and by the second year of their marriage, he'd been looking forward to the holiday almost as much as she had. Over the years they'd created Christmastime traditions together, ones they had continued every year of their marriage. Last year he had added something to it—both of them knowing it may be her last Christmas. Each year she'd talked about wanting to take a sleigh ride, and each year they'd gotten too busy. Finally last year he'd made the arrangements, and they'd glided gracefully across the fields, Anne's beaming face all he needed to know it had been a great gift—to wish he'd done it so much sooner. She'd happily sung "Jingle Bells" as they went, laughing and holding tight to his hand. He'd tried to ignore that it was shaking, tried to ignore the tears in her eyes despite her laugh. The snow had been falling in huge flakes—as it was again tonight as he stared out the window.

Every day he missed her, but today he felt her absence profoundly. Faith's too. Christmas took on such a magical quality when children were involved. Steven had been great in that regard—leaving bits of red lint in the fireplace for Faith to find in the morning, convinced Santa had torn his coat.

He dreaded the Christmas season in a way he'd never dreaded anything, but his daughters did everything they could to make it cheery.

Abby was amazing, the way she came in and took charge. The day after Thanksgiving she'd gotten and decorated trees both for him and for Laura and Steven; she had made all of Anne's traditional dishes—and had even wrapped his presents when he'd asked. She hadn't inquired as to why he'd wanted her to do it, and he was thankful for that. He wasn't ready to explain yet—wasn't ready to tell them how his eyes no longer focused on what was right in front of him. Most of all, he wasn't ready to tell them how long he'd known.

"Daddy?" Abby appeared in front of him now, dressed for Christmas Eve service in a red turtleneck and khakis, her hair pulled back neatly into a barrette. "You ready?" They were going to Christmas Eve service together, along with Steven and Laura, who would meet them there and then come spend the night at John's.

"Yep." He pushed out of the chair slowly, his bones stiff after sitting for just a few moments. He wondered if losing Anne hadn't aged him more than he realized. "Tom with the kids?" he asked and saw a pained look flicker across Abby's features.

"Yeah," she said softly. "Big holiday, and all."

Unsure of what to say, John just patted her hand. Who she dated was her decision, and he thought Tom was a great guy. Still he thought Abby deserved someone who had the ability to be with her on the big holidays. He hated to see her lonely today of all days.

"Do you mind driving? I'm a little groggy," he lied.

"No problem," Abby responded, and he was glad she didn't push the issue any further. She drove slowly, expertly navigating the slippery roads. Steven and Laura were there when John and Abby arrived, surrounded by other members of the church congregation who had become extremely attentive since Faith's accident. They never had to want for support here, and John was glad for it. His youngest daughter looked calmer than she had in months, a peace about her that he didn't know how to explain.

Steven stood next to her holding her hand tightly, and he smiled to see them once again close.

The four of them made their way into the chapel, clinging together in the pew like survivors on a life raft and trying to ignore the absence of the two people who had really made this holiday what it was. Both Abby and Laura had tears streaming down their faces as they sung "Silent Night" with candles in their hands.

That night in bed, both of his children under his roof again but his wife and grandchild gone, the house felt strangely empty and full all at once. He moved his hand to his side of the bed—the sheets were cold and smooth. Since the day Anne had been moved to the hospital bed downstairs, he'd slept on her side of the bed. Not because it was the side he'd really wanted, but let her have—which was true—but because it smelled of her, and he felt closer to her that way. Even now, months later and the sheets washed countless times, he swore he could still smell her.

He finally fell asleep, missing Anne so much it hurt, but when he awoke the next morning, he swore he could feel her presence there.

Both Laura and Abby were surprisingly upbeat—Abby missing the love of her life and Laura missing the love of hers, but happy to be together, to be with him. He actually heard Laura laugh, a sound he hadn't heard in ages. She looked surprised herself, but relieved somehow, perhaps just now finding out that she was still among the living.

Abby had prepared Anne's famous egg casserole and surprised him when she raised her coffee as they gathered around the Christmas tree to open presents.

"I just want to toast Mom and Faith," she said. John cast a worried look at Laura to gauge her reaction, but her face remained peaceful, though a brief look of sorrow came across it. "To Mom, for making this holiday what it's been for thirty years—we'll keep your traditions alive for years to come. And to Faith, for reminding me just what that word means. We'll get through this."

She lowered her mug a bit awkwardly and took a sip, and Laura and Steven both raised their mugs. "To Mom and Faith," they said in unison before exchanging a private glance and then turning to John.

"Daddy," Laura began, "we have something for you." She handed him a heavy flat package, and he was overwhelmed with gratitude. "We were horrible to you," she rushed on, "in the aftermath of an accident that hurt you just as much as it hurt us. We were angry, but not at you like we thought. We were angry to lose our little girl, and because of the obvious roles in the situation, took it out on you. Anyway," she waved a hand, "I've talked about that before and could go in circles for hours. My point is, I know we can't get the last seven months back, but hopefully this can be a start in amending what was torn."

John wanted to stop her, to tell her the truth, but again felt that now was the wrong time. Instead he ran a thumb along the line where Laura had taped the wrapping paper together, tearing it slowly. He pulled the paper away to reveal the back of a picture frame, and he turned it over gingerly in his fingers.

There beneath the glass was a child's picture, drawn on bright yellow construction paper, of a woman and a child. They were walking away, toward a wall of flowers, and beneath it Faith had scrawled *Me and Grandma*. He felt tears spring to his eyes and didn't even try to wipe them away, watching them plink onto the glass of the frame.

"It's Faith and Anne. She drew it right after Anne died," Steven began. "She kept saying that her grandma had promised her they'd go on a walk through a garden once the snow melted. We found it again a few weeks ago, when we started the process of going through Faith's things, packing some of them up." His voice was thick with emotion. "We wanted you to have it. It's kind of how we picture them now, together and walking among the flowers."

John looked up, his eyes blurred this time by something besides his illness, as his tears fell freely from them. "Thank you," he managed, opening his mouth to tell them more—to tell them everything, but nothing came out. He clamped it tightly shut and looked back at the picture, watching his two girls walk away from him toward a place so beautiful there was no earthly description—a place where they could no longer feel pain—and wished, not for the first time, that he could join them.

༄

Laura

"I think he liked it, don't you?" She snuggled closer to Steven in bed that night, her head on his chest, listening to the steady beat of his heart.

"I do," came his distant reply. "Laur?"

"Hmmm."

"Is it always going to be like this?"

"Be like what?" Laura sat up and leaned on her elbow, looking at Steven. She realized there were tears in his eyes.

"This. This day. Every holiday, every birthday, every anniversary of the day she died—will I ever be able to think of something *besides* Faith?"

Laura thought for a moment before speaking, repeating words she'd heard her own mother say years before. "Steven, it's not a bad thing to think of Faith. What happened was horrible—ours, and every parent's—worst nightmare. But it happened, and now we have to choose what we do about it. You're never going to stop thinking about her. Maybe you'll go a day, maybe even two, without consciously doing so, but she's always going to be there. What matters is what you do with that memory—if you dwell on the tragedy or make something better out of it."

"Like what?" Steven was crying freely now.

"Like becoming the best pediatrician in Illinois, and opening a wing, or maybe someday a whole hospital, in her memory, dedicated to children's trauma—and saving all the lives you can." Even as she said it, Laura knew somehow that someday, Steven would do just that.

She was sure he knew it too, but as he held her now, she could feel his body shaking with sobs.

"I couldn't protect her," he cried. "I couldn't save her ... from the minute she was born I was so concerned about not becoming my father, and I tried so hard ... but even in the end ... I couldn't save her."

"Steven," Laura placed her hands on either side of her husband's face, crying herself to hear him so torn up, as she had so many times since the funeral. "You are not your father. You were a wonderful dad. Faith loved you with everything she had. Don't forget that."

"But I couldn't protect her," he sobbed.

"Of course you couldn't," Laura soothed, wondering where her own calm was coming from. "No one could. She was never really ours, Steven. But we were so, so lucky to have her for the time that we did."

"It's not fair," he said, sniffing loudly. "God has so many angels—why take ours?"

"I don't know," Laura admitted. "I don't know."

Steven

Steven didn't know where Laura found it in her to be so wise and understanding, but he had a feeling all of that would diminish as soon as he passed this along to her. *He* was certainly about to.

"I'm sorry." He sat down heavily on the couch, pinching the bridge of his nose with the hand that wasn't clutching the phone to his ear. "Can you run that by me one more time?"

Abby dutifully repeated what she had just told him, about how she'd gotten a call from the police department, that John had gotten pulled over, and when the officer had realized he'd been driving without a license, he'd taken him into the station, and that now he needed a ride home.

It was the *reason* he'd been driving without a license that gave Steven's blood the feeling that it was about to boil—something about test results showing a loss of central vision—something about macular degeneration, and something about the symptoms having first presented themselves well over a year ago.

Which meant his vision had been declining when he'd gotten behind the wheel that day—when he'd careened into the back of Laura's car.

The day he'd killed Faith.

Abby was on her way to get him now and was hoping Laura and Steven could meet them at John's.

"Laura won't be home for another hour." He checked his watch. "But I'll leave a note for her to come meet us as soon as she can."

Steven steered toward John's, anger and disbelief growing with every mile. By the time he arrived, he was too worked up to bother straightening his car in the drive before slamming his door and storming into the house.

"John!" he cried, but the older man was already within his sight, sitting at the kitchen table with Abby—regret and sorrow etched in his face. Steven walked toward him as though he might hit him, and it looked as though John expected it, his face suddenly scrunched on one side. Instead he simply slammed his hands onto the table in front of his father-in-law. "You damn fool! You damn, stubborn fool!"

John's eyes had already welled; Abby simply sat with her head in her hands, shaking it from side to side. "Why didn't you say anything?" She finally looked up at John.

"Why didn't you *do* anything?" Steven added. "I want a goddamn explanation."

"Steven," Abby said gently, but she looked just as angry as he felt. Both looked expectantly at John.

"I'm sorry," John began, and Steven cut him off.

"I'm sorry doesn't cut it," he boomed. "A little girl is dead because of you, because you were selfish and stubborn." He could see that his words hit John with almost a physical force, and for a minute he almost regretted them.

"Look," John continued softly when he had recovered. "For a long time I knew things were getting worse, but I just thought I needed a new prescription, a stronger prescription. But for so long Anne's illness took precedence, and after she died I couldn't bear to set foot in a doctor's office or hospital. It just brought back too many memories. Finally I did, that day ..." He trailed off, all three of them knowing exactly which day he was talking about. "The doctor was having me look at an Amsler grid, which has these lines—"

"I know what an Amsler grid is," Steven shot back, impatient.

"Well, the lines were all wavy, and then he started talking about a potential loss of central vision, and I just didn't want to hear it. I had already lost so much ... so I ran out of there before he could officially diagnose me."

"So you *weren't* diagnosed with it *before* the accident?" Abby clarified.

"No, if I was, I swear I wouldn't have gotten behind the wheel. I swear it. Even if I had, I'm sure there would have been legal trouble—and then this would have come out a lot sooner."

"But it didn't, and so you've been hiding it from us." Steven spat. "For almost a year."

"I tried to tell you—*so* many times I tried to tell you, but I just couldn't. You were already going through so much..."

"Because of something you did," Steven finished for him, but to his surprise, John didn't hang his head as he had so many times before. Instead, he looked his son-in-law straight in the eye.

"Steven," he said calmly. "I understand your anger. If I were you, I'd be mad at me too. I'd probably hate me, probably refuse to *see* me. But there's something you should know. I love Faith more than any grandfather ever loved his grandchild—and there will not be a day that passes the rest of my life that I don't live with the guilt and regret of what I've done. You and Laura can punish me *all* you want, but I hope there is a day you realize that *that* is punishment enough, just knowing what I've done and that I can't undo it."

Steven didn't know what to say to that, and so he was silent, and in a moment John continued, his voice thick with emotion.

"My eyes were failing me. I shouldn't have gotten behind the wheel, but I did. I shouldn't have been driving in the state that I was—scared and angry—but I was. It was raining, and the roads were slippery. I made the last minute decision to try and catch Faith's ballet practice, knowing how seeing her would cheer me up. There were so many factors, such a combination of events that had to happen at the same time—that all happened. It could be because of my vision, that my depth perception was off and I didn't stop soon enough."

"But the police said you did," Abby said quickly, and John nodded.

"Yes, they did. I stopped in enough time, but skidded due to the rain. Just another fender bender, except I slid right through a red light, and into oncoming traffic. It could have been the rain, could have been the roads. It could have been that I was going too fast—could have been a million things. But after the investigation, it was ruled that I couldn't have done much more. My vision hadn't progressed *that* far yet. I hadn't been speeding at the moment I applied my brakes—the law cleared me of any fault—declared it was just an accident. I, of course, will never feel that way. You, of course, will never feel that way. I will never forgive myself, and you will probably never forgive me. But—"

John didn't get a chance to finish before Laura flew in the door.

"What happened?" she cried as she rushed in. "I got your note." She looked at Steven and, seeing the tense looks on everybody's face, froze in her tracks.

As John repeated everything he had told Abby and Steven, Steven watched his wife's face. He watched the shock register, watched the emotions play across it, finally watched it settle into an expression he couldn't read as John finished.

"So you knew about this before the accident," she repeated slowly, and John nodded.

"And you didn't do anything about it," she said, and again John nodded, closing his eyes in pain.

Laura was silent for a long while, and Steven watched her carefully, waiting for her outburst. Yet despite his close observation, when she finally stood, it was so abruptly that he jumped in his seat. Slowly she walked around Abby's chair to stand before her father. Steven wondered if she was going to hit him, as he almost had, but instead he watched as she threw her arms around him. "I forgive you."

He heard the strain in her voice, knew how hard those words were for her to say, and wondered if he'd heard her right. Evidently, John did too.

"What?"

"I forgive you." Laura repeated, pulling back and looking him in the eye.

"But," he started, but Laura shook her head and brought a finger to his lips.

"If there's anything I've learned from this, Daddy, it's that our children are never actually ours. They're given to us, the greatest gift, and they can be just as easily taken away. We do all we can to protect them," she looked at Steven before continuing, "but sometimes it's just not enough. But harboring anger, harboring guilt—that's not going to do a *thing* to honor my little girl's memory, is it? I know they're emotions we'll continue to deal with, probably forever, but what would I be if I didn't at least *try* to move past them? I learned a lot from Faith in her short time here, and one of the most astounding, was how she loved."

Now she looked at Abby, tears streaming down her face.

"Mom put that in my letter," she said, and Steven knew exactly which letter she was talking about, though she had never let him read it. "She said that you and I had always been able to love like children did—with our hearts wide open—no matter what kind of circumstances life put us through. I didn't want to see it at the time—I was so upset over losing *her*, but I see it now. Faith wouldn't even have known what a grudge was—what it meant to be angry, to harbor any feeling other than unadulterated love for someone else. And if I can do *anything* for her, it will be to try every day to love like she did."

She looked around the table, first at Steven, then Abby, and finally her father.

"I love you," she took his hand. "Always have, always will." With a deep breath, she said something that Steven would continue to wonder about for years. "*Nothing* you do will ever change that."

༄

CHAPTER TWENTY

Abby

"Your call has been forwarded to an automatic voice messaging system—*Tom Reynolds*—is not available." Tom's voice interrupted the woman of the recording, and Abby closed her eyes and caught her breath. It was the most he'd said to her in days, and it wasn't even directed at her—although she'd felt better acquainted with his voice mail this weekend than she did with him.

The woman was now telling her to press *five* for more options, and she quickly hung up without leaving a message. That one would probably go unreturned anyhow, just like the others.

She knew he was busy; it was Luke's birthday weekend, and although they had been dating for almost two years now, he still asked her to stay away from family functions where Beth would be present. *Things will calm down eventually; it won't always be like this,* he'd say, promising that soon things would be "normal." But he'd been saying that for the entirety of their relationship, and it still hadn't happened. Although she knew and loved his children, and they her, and Beth knew about her and was apparently even dating someone herself, Tom still couldn't bring himself to bring the two aspects of his life together.

This meant that whenever he was out there, living the other aspect of his life, she was left completely and utterly unable to reach him.

Which left her—despite the pictures of the two of them that covered her apartment, despite Luke and Ben's artwork that donned her refrigerator, despite the many letters from him that she kept in the second drawer of her dresser—feeling like nothing more than his mistress.

Shaking her head, she knew what she had to do. She flipped her phone back open and shot him a text that simply said: "Meet me, our spot, 8:30 tomorrow night." It pained her that she chose the time only because she knew he'd be back in the city by then—that if she ever needed him for something important, the other aspect of his life took precedence.

She was almost surprised when he responded eight hours later, *"Okay. What's wrong, babe?"*

There were a lot of ways she could have answered. *I haven't heard from you in three days? You're my "in case of emergency person" and I can't reach you, ever?* But instead, she said nothing and lay in bed all night knowing what she had to do and finding it impossible to find the courage to do so.

The next night, Abby tried to smile bravely as Tom walked toward her, but her mouth quivered and she had to close it again and turn away to wipe her eyes.

"What's wrong, babe?" he asked, concern registering on his face. As if he didn't know—as if he'd had nothing to do with it—as if one touch of his hand to her cheek could make it all better.

And it almost did.

"Let's just cut the bullshit." Her breath came out in frosty puffs in the cold air. She could see him taken aback by her anger; it surprised even her.

"Babe, if this is about me taking so long to respond to you, you have to cut me some slack…you can't imagine how crazy it is to be in charge of a nine-year-old's birthday party."

"*No*, you're right. I can't, because you won't let me be a part of it." *Don't let him talk his way out of this one,* she told herself. He had a way of twisting her words, every time, to eventually lead her to believe that *she* was being unreasonable, and he simply deserved a little more flexibility. *What about what I deserve?* she said to herself, before continuing.

"Tom, sit down." He sat on the bench, *their* bench, and looked at her quizzically, as if he had absolutely no idea what was wrong or the role he'd played in it—even though they'd had this discussion at *least* a dozen times. She took his hand between hers, tears welling in her eyes as she realized she'd probably never hold it again. Hands trembling, she let it go and looked up at him. "This thing between us…it's over." She was surprised at the bluntness of her comment, and so was Tom, shock registering uncharacteristically slowly in his eyes. He opened his mouth to say something—perhaps to protest—but Abby cut him off. "There was a point, early on, that I realized I was never going to be number one in your life, that your kids would always hold that place. And that's how it should be. The problem came when you factored in the fact that they weren't your kids with *me*, which meant that there would be another woman attached to that, and so by association, she too would be number one in your life. It took me a while to get used to that, to accept it, but eventually I did. I told myself that I may not be first in your life, but that your second might be better than someone else's first. Am I making sense?" Tom nodded, and before he could interrupt, she continued. "Well ... it's not. Maybe it's your fault and maybe it's not—maybe you can give me more, and are just stubbornly refusing to do so—or maybe you really can't. But I can't tell you how many times I've told myself I have to do this...how many times I *have* done it, only to take you right back the next morning. This time, Tom, I have to stick to it." Her tears were flowing freely now, and her voice caught as she finished her sentence. "I love you, and I always will...but I need more than this. I need someone who is willing and able to give me what I need. And I know what you'll say. You'll tell me that you *can* give me what I need, and you *will*...at least until you feel like we're back on solid ground. But then your attention will go back to other things, and we'll end up right back here...and I just *can't* be here. I can't live this way—you can't give me what I need."

Tom was silently staring at the ground in front of him, and she stood up slowly. He still hadn't said anything. Abby didn't know if that meant that he agreed with her, and if so, what was there to say? Or was he angry? She couldn't bear to look at him. The hurt on his face would be enough to make her sit back down, make her take him in her arms and take it all back, tell him that she didn't mean it, that she'd do *anything* for him. She had told him that before, that she'd do anything for him. But as it turned out, what she'd meant was *anything but feel this way constantly*. And when he'd told her the same, what she'd needed to hear was *anything to **keep** you from feeling this way constantly*. It was over.

⁓

Tom

There were so many things he wanted to tell her. He wanted to tell her about how kissing her that first time had felt like coming home. He wanted to tell her that she brought a sense of comfort to him just by being there. That standing beside her, he could have done anything.

But all of this he kept to himself.

He didn't trust himself to speak, and he wouldn't let her see him cry. Instead he watched her face—her eyes caught the sunlight in a way that turned them the most beautiful green he'd ever seen—her hand moved so quickly and quietly to brush the hair off her face—her motions so familiar to him that it didn't seem real that he wouldn't see her again.

Finally he opened his mouth. *Don't go*, he almost said. *You're wrong. I can give you what you deserve.* But instead, he said, "You're right. I'm just a man, and this is all I can give you. You deserve more. I know you do, and I wish I could give that to you, but I just can't."

He saw the surprise register on her face—all this time he'd fought for her to stay. Now he'd given her the go-ahead to walk away. Surprise turned to hurt, and he watched tears spring up in those beautiful eyes. He wanted to wipe them away so badly his hands shook, but he kept them in his pockets. *Cruel to be kind*, he repeated to himself, closing his eyes. No matter how much he loved her, wanted her, needed her, he wouldn't be the one to make her cry. He wanted to be the one to make her happy, and if he couldn't do that, he wouldn't do any of it.

Abby

Abby's shock that this was really it—it had really just ended—quickly gave way to hurt. *Why isn't he fighting for me?* she wondered, at the same time knowing that if he had, she wouldn't be able to walk away, and she needed to. She didn't know if it was her feelings or her pride that were more bruised by his decision to let her go—but felt hypocritical for thinking that way since she was the one who had let *him* go.

Lips trembling and wet with tears, she took his face in her hands and kissed him softly—just like she had so many times. She didn't know how to define the power this man held over her, but for a moment almost begged him to reconsider. She wanted to tell him she hadn't meant it—that she *was* just pissed he hadn't gotten back to her. She wanted to tell him that she couldn't imagine life without him—couldn't imagine waking up the next morning and not being able to hear his voice.

But despite all this, she somehow found the strength to slowly rise on shaking legs and turn to face him a final time.

She paused for a moment to lay a hand on his head before turning on her heel and walking away, wiping her eyes and pulling her coat tighter around her trying to keep out the chill, when all along she knew it wasn't the wind that was making her so cold.

CHAPTER TWENTYONE

Abby

Every so often, Abby let herself think about Tom.

If you love something, let it go. If it comes back to you, it was meant to be, people always told her. It had been her favorite quote as a girl, scrawled in neat cursive in the margins of her high school notebooks.

But now she wondered about it. What about the ones that you let go because you know it's *not* meant to be? What if letting someone go is the ultimate way of showing him that you love him, the ultimate kindness you can do to someone you loved so much?

And what happens when *he* comes back to you? Does that mean that somehow, suddenly, it *was* meant to be?

After their talk, Tom had called, telling her he'd been wrong to let her go, that he hadn't meant it, that he needed her. When she hadn't responded, he'd called again, and then again, almost frantically. She'd taken another job - the thought of seeing him every day at work too much to bear, and had moved her things out of the office late at night, while Tom was away. He'd called her new office, he'd e-mailed her several times and, finally, had come to her house. She'd watched him from her window, unwilling and unable to buzz him in. The lights were off—he wouldn't have seen her—but she watched him shift his weight from side to side on the stoop, looking first right, and then left, and finally up. Though she knew it was impossible, she imagined he caught her eye as he did so.

Her heart did that same old flip, and she had to grip the windowsill for stability. That's the thing about that kind of love, that kind of passion—it never really leaves you. Even if the object of it is long gone, the love itself lingers on.

It burrows into the darkest corners of your mind, ready and waiting to remind you of its presence, a presence that will always be as real as it ever was.

She watched Tom that day, watched him as he sat on the steps to wait for her, watched him check his watch as the hours rolled by, and finally watched as he reluctantly walked away, looking back only once to her window, and at that moment, she knew he knew she was there. Saw her shadow watching him from the window, maybe even saw her fingers pressed against it, wanting so badly to run to him.

There were no more phone calls after that, no more letters or e-mails, and she never saw him again.

But as she knew she always would be, Abby was still haunted by him. She found him everywhere. In the chuckle of the man behind her in line, in the unkempt waves of a stranger's hair, suddenly she was back there, standing with him, loving each other in the face of a future both of them had foreseen, but ignored, for so long. She'd hear a child's laugh and would be convinced that when she turned around she'd see Luke. She passed the history museum every day on her way to work and still saw him standing in the rain, umbrella held high, waiting for her that day. She heard his voice call her name in the dark of the night, and as she lay shivering in bed, waiting for sleep to rescue her again, she wondered if ghosts were real after all.

∽

Steven

Steven squeezed his wife's hand as they walked out of the cemetery, and suddenly she stopped short just before the gate.

"Do you want to walk around?" she asked. It's so beautiful in here, especially this time of year..."

Steven nodded and let her lead him back into the cemetery where their daughter was buried, meandering slowly down the path. It was beautiful, she was right. Summer was almost gone; he knew they wouldn't have many more days like this. The trees were leafy overhead, blocking the early afternoon sun but doing nothing to muffle the sound of cicadas. He breathed in the sweet, heavy scent of summer, willing it to memory, marveling at all that had happened. They had flown past the anniversary of Faith's accident, and were flying towards the anniversary of her death.

He still struggled every day, but somewhere in these last few months he'd found it in him to start living again. Every morning he had to remind himself to do so – remind himself that there were still people in his life worth living for – the woman next to him being one of them. Somewhere along the way they'd stopped clinging to each other only in grief and started once again simply clinging to each other, in the secret corners of the night. He smiled at her now, kissing her cheek softly before focusing again on the path ahead of him.

"You're beautiful," he said to her, meaning it more now than ever. Her face was absolutely glowing.

"I'm late," she spat out, seeming surprised at the blunt delivery.

Steven looked sharply at her. "You don't think-" he stopped, unsure of how to finish that sentence.

"Oh I don't know," her hand absentmindedly moved to her belly. "It's just a few days, and it could be a thousand different things. But if I were ..." she paused, "pregnant..." she looked up at him. "It wouldn't be a bad thing, would it?"

"No, of course not," he felt a smile begin to tug at the corners of his mouth. "It would be a great thing."

"Really?" she turned to him, grinning. "I kind of thought so too, but I didn't know how you'd feel. I mean it feels a little like we're betraying Faith – but then I think about it and I think it would be just the *opposite* of betraying Faith. It means we're moving on with our lives – *choosing* life, and that's what she would have wanted. Plus, she was always telling me she wanted a sibling."

"Really?" Steven swallowed a lump in his throat.

"Well, once or twice. Although," Laura paused for effect, "she requested we name it Traugott."

A laugh burst from Steven's mouth, at the same time that tears sprung to his eyes, and he wiped at them quickly. It still felt odd to be talking about Faith this way, as a thing of the past, but it felt good to be talking about her too, remembering her.

"Oh God," he gulped. "You know we're going to *have* to now. No way am I going against one of Faith's last requests."

"Well," Laura had tears in her eyes too, "she also said she'd settle for Sammy."

"Whew," Steven wiped his forehead. "Well then *that's* what we're going with."

Laura laughed. "We still might be jumping the gun a little bit."

Steven shrugged. "Even if we are, it doesn't mean we can't start trying."

Laura looked at him, wide-eyed. "You're ready?"

"Well, yeah," Steven admitted. "I mean, we'd talked about having more kids once I was done with med school – The timing would be right…" he trailed off.

"Unlike last time," she finished, seeming to know exactly what he'd been about to say. "You know what?" she stopped and looked at him. "The day she died, you told me that you thought Faith's life was destined for something miraculous because of the circumstances under which we had her. Before that, I remember at one point saying that Faith was the only reason we were together in the first place," she paused, looking sheepish as she remembered that afternoon. "But you know what – we were both right. Not in the ways we might have meant it at the time, but we were. I'd meant that Faith was the only reason you'd stayed with me and married me – and I was wrong about that. But I *do* believe that you and I met and fell in love for a reason – and that reason was Faith. And what Faith taught us - *that* was the grand miracle you'd been expecting from her life."

"What did she teach us?" Steven asked.

"Well, forgiveness, for one," Laura said. "Love, life..." she spun in a wide circle, gesturing to the land around her. "Every day since I lost her – or at least since I started to climb out of my grief – I've tried to see the world as Faith would have seen it. And it's *refreshing*, Steven. I've started dwelling on all those beautiful little things you learn to skip over as an adult."

"But I promised her I'd do anything for her, and I couldn't," Steven argued.

"How so?" Laura looked at him with compassion.

"I couldn't save her."

"Maybe that's not the *anything* God had in mind," Laura told him. "Maybe *this* is."

"What is?"

"Carrying on," Laura said simply, before squeezing his hand and walking ahead to place one last kiss on Faith's headstone before they headed towards home, and the rest of their lives.

༄

Laura

It wasn't until Laura heard the tiny giggle in front of her in line at the grocery store—and looked down to see a blonde girl grinning up at her—that she realized she hadn't thought about Faith all morning. Or maybe she had, but it had been unconscious.

Grief was a funny thing, Laura thought. Or a strange thing, rather—there was really nothing funny about it.

Grief was a strange thing, the way it snuck up on you like a hunter, intent on ruining your false sense of peace and security. It found her in the most unsuspecting of places—places she usually had no memories of Faith.

It reminded Laura of the time when she was twelve and had gotten her first cavity filled. For days afterward it had been only a dull ache, until she had bitten into something hard, sending a shockwave of chills and pain through her body. She'd cried to her mother, and Anne, in her very matter-of-fact way, had simply responded, *That's the trouble with things like that. Most of the time it's a dull ache you can go days without noticing, but every once in a while you hit it wrong, and then there's no pain on earth as great.*

She wondered now if her mother had been talking simply about cavities or had known even then that someday her daughter would need the strength of those words. It was the thought that she was with Faith now that comforted her. She liked to picture the two of them getting to know each other, pictured Faith growing up under her grandmother's watchful eye. She didn't know what heaven was like, but she figured heaven was what each person made of it—and that was hers. Her daughter growing into a woman and getting the chance to *live*, a chance that she had been robbed of. She'd deal with the anger forever, she knew, but like Steven, who was now working every day toward his new dream of opening a Faith McCord Memorial Children's Trauma Wing, she wanted to make something of *her* life as well. She may never know why Faith was taken and she was alive—but she knew that every day she continued to breathe, she would work to make sure that life wasn't wasted. Faith deserved at least that much.

"Do you remember that quote about God not giving you more than you can handle?" Abby asked her softly, later that afternoon.

Laura nodded silently, eyes focused on the canopy of leaves above where they lay on their backs outside their father's house, staring up at the autumn sky.

"Do you remember Mother Teresa's response to it—about how she wished God didn't trust her so much?"

Again Laura nodded, this time turning her head to look at her sister. Abby said nothing. "What about it?" Laura inquired, curious.

"Nothing, really. Just making conversation."

At that, Laura burst out laughing, the feeling foreign but refreshing. "What happened to the days where we could do this for hours and just be quiet?"

"Those days are long gone." Abby chuckled, and then continued somberly. "We've both changed a lot since then."

"We have," Laura nodded, reaching out to grab her sister's hand. "But despite all of those changes—most of them excruciating, you know what?"

Abby shook her head and waited for Laura to continue.

"You and I are lying on our backs, on an autumn day, and have spent most of the afternoon staring at the leaves and branches above us. Some things never change," she smiled. If she squinted her eyes hard enough, she could almost see Abby as a little girl again, braids hanging straight and long over her shoulders.

"The only thing that's missing is Mom's classical music coming from the house," Abby contested, seemingly intent on finding the negative in this situation.

And Laura, not for the first time in their lives, pointed out what her older sister failed to see. "You're wrong," she told her. "See that leaf?" She pointed to a particularly orange leaf, falling first one way, and then the next, back and forth in a slow and floating descent. "It's falling to the rhythm of Mozart's clarinet concerto. And that one's falling to the bumblebee concerto." She pointed to another leaf, spiraling at warp speed toward them.

Abby smiled and closed her eyes, listening for the sounds of a memory carried in on a breeze, and then pointed toward the branches above them. "That branch twists around the leaves in a way that makes it look like a dog's head," she said, almost in a whisper.

There she is, Laura thought, smiling at Abby's participation in their childhood game.

"That one spells Brad," she said, elbowing her sister playfully in the ribs. "Don't you have a date with him you should be getting ready for?"

Abby made a face. "Ugh, yeah." She rose slowly, wiping off the seat of her jeans before setting off for the house.

"How are things going with him?" Laura asked, curious about the man her sister had met a few weeks before and had been seeing casually since. "What's he like?"

"Good on paper." Abby wrinkled her nose, and Laura laughed.

"Keep me posted."

"I will," Abby called.

Laura listened as her sister drove off, staying on the ground for a few more minutes before standing up and brushing off her jeans. She started for the house, knowing John was waiting for her. The two of them had begun a slow and steady climb back toward normalcy. Today she was driving him to visit Faith's grave, where they'd been going every Sunday since the summer, to sit and talk. Sometimes she told him all the ways she was angry, sometimes she cried, and other times they sat in peace, reminiscing and smiling about the little girl they had both loved so much.

˜

Epilogue

Laura stood on her back porch with her eyes closed, willing the early October sun to feel on her skin the way it had felt when she was a child.

She'd done the same thing a year ago today, the day her daughter had died. On that day, she'd wondered if life was even worth living—if she had anything left to give. Today she took a deep breath, knowing she'd found her answer.

She placed her hand on her belly, felt the baby move. It was a boy, she was sure. And they'd name him Sam, like Faith had wanted. And slowly they'd rebuild their life from the ruins.

The strength of the human spirit is a truly unbelievable thing, she thought now. It perseveres through the direst of circumstances. Everyone in the world has at one time experienced a loss that has shaken him or her to the core, but all it took her was a drive this morning on the Eden's expressway during rush hour traffic to realize just how many people live through it on a daily basis. How many people persevere through the pain. How many people are making a conscious choice to get out of bed and soldier on, even through the bleakest moments of their lives. If they didn't, who would set the example? Who would show the world what it truly means to love someone?

Because what Laura had discovered was this—that the greatest testament to the ones you love is being able to let them go and know that your life will forever be better for their presence in it, however fleeting. Abby had done it for Tom; she had done it for Faith—people did it every day, on every level.

It takes a deep love to consciously choose what is best for the other, even if it means that person can no longer be in your life. It takes an even deeper love, the deepest kind—to take that life and turn it into something that person would have been proud of, to do so as your last gift, a testament to the mark he or she left on your heart.

To do that was to *truly* be able to say, whether looking into that person's eyes while saying it or by simply whispering it to his or her memory, *Anything for you, mi amore.*

Made in the USA
Charleston, SC
29 April 2010